W9-CLL-048

Outstanding praise for Louisa Ermelino and
THE SISTERS MALLONE

"Ermelino writes with perfect pitch and captures the details of life in the old neighborhoods with authenticity. Part *noir* novel, part feminist anthem, this ode to sisterhood is wickedly funny—emphasis on the wicked. Read it as the perfect literary counterweight to *The Sopranos.*"

—*The Record* (Bergen County, New Jersey)

"Louisa Ermelino is in many ways the Fannie Flagg of Italian New York. *The Sisters Mallone* is the blackest of comedies . . . deliciously wicked. . . . As Ermelino so deftly, amusingly, scandalously shows, these women were full-blooded human beings capable of doing anything a man could do."

—*The Sun-Sentinel* (Fort Lauderdale, Florida)

"Enjoyable. . . . The sisters are complex, interesting, likeable characters."

—*The Deseret News* (Salt Lake City, Utah)

"Ermelino weaves a tale of the immigrant dream and the men encountered by three daughters pursuing it."

—*The New York Daily News*

"The action of the novel depends on mutual love among the sisters."

—*The Milwaukee Journal Sentinel*

". . . a breezy narrative and boisterous dialogue . . ."

—*Publishers Weekly*

And praise for Louisa Ermelino's
THE BLACK MADONNA

"Ermelino's frisky, old-fashioned storytelling possesses time-less appeal."

—*Entertainment Weekly*

"*The Black Madonna* is fast-paced and delightful, one of those books you can't put down until you've devoured every last word."

—*The New York Post*

"An Italian version of *The Joy Luck Club*."

—*People*

The Sisters Mallone

Louisa Ermelino

KENSINGTON BOOKS
http://www.kensingtonbooks.com

This book is a work of fiction. Names, characters, places, and incidents either are products of the author's imagination or are used fictitiously. Any resemblance to actual events or locales or persons, living or dead, is entirely coincidental.

KENSINGTON BOOKS are published by

Kensington Publishing Corp.
850 Third Avenue
New York, NY 10022

Copyright © 2002 by Louisa Ermelino
Published in arrangement with Simon & Schuster, Inc.

All rights reserved. No part of this book may be reproduced in any form or by any means without the prior written consent of the Publisher, excepting brief quotes used in reviews.

All Kensington titles, imprints and distributed lines are available at special quantity discounts for bulk purchases for sales promotion, premiums, fund-raising, educational or institutional use.

Special book excerpts or customized printings can also be created to fit specific needs. For details, write or phone the office of the Kensington Special Sales Manager: Kensington Publishing Corp., 850 Third Avenue, New York, NY, 10022. Attn. Special Sales Department. Phone: 1-800-221-2647.

Kensington and the K logo Reg. U.S. Pat. & TM Off.

ISBN 0-7582-0433-7

First Kensington Trade Paperback Printing: June 2003
10 9 8 7 6 5 4 3 2 1

Printed in the United States of America

FOR THE SISTERS CUTOLO
RUBY, LUCY, ARIANE

and of course, for Carlo

Back then a sock in the jaw could set anyone straight.

—"Compulsory Travel," Lucia Perillo

1952–1953

ETHEL AND JULIUS ROSENBERG EXECUTED FOR TRANSMITTING ATOMIC SECRETS TO SOVIET AGENTS

Maria Callas Smash Hit at La Scala
Opening in Milan in Verdi's Sicilian Vespers

WATERFRONT BOSS JOE RYAN INDICTED

President for Life of the Internat'l Longshoreman's Association Charged with Stealing from His Union

Chapter One

That Friday was the first day of Frankie Merelli's wake. He had died on Monday, but what with the police investigation, the state of the corpse, and the undertaker's pride, it was four days before the body was ready for viewing. Frankie Merelli was being waked downtown, laid out in Nucciarone's funeral parlor on Sullivan Street, just the way Gracie wanted. She had pictured the first day of Frankie's wake. She was the widow, after all. She had seen it in her mind like the newsreels that came before the movie at the Loews Sheridan on Greenwich Avenue.

The family would gather in front of the building on Spring Street where Frankie had lived as a son, a husband, and a father. There would be a bouquet of carnations tied with a white ribbon pinned outside the door, a card announcing the funeral information. The family would walk together, slowly, arms linked, in an unofficial procession up Sullivan Street to Nucciarone's. As they passed St. Anthony's Church, the women would bow their heads, make the sign of the cross and kiss the tips of their fingers. The undertaker would be waiting for them outside the funeral parlor. He would escort Frankie's mother into the viewing room and the rest of the family would follow in hierarchical order. It was how it was done in this neighborhood. It was the tradition.

But Anona balked at this ritual, remembering the funerals in Bocca al Lupo, the whole village walking endlessly behind the black death coach pulled by plumed black horses. This American thing, she said, was a poor second, a stroll a few blocks north to sit in what looked like someone's front parlor. Nothing would convince her. She wouldn't do it.

It was the least she could do for Gracie, Mary and Helen told her. The sisters wanted everything to go smoothly. It should all be normal and ordinary, just another wake, just another funeral, even if nothing about Frankie Merelli's death had been ordinary.

But then Gracie said it didn't matter how they got there and Helen had shrugged. If Gracie didn't mind, then . . . and Gracie didn't mind. She was willing to go along with what Anona wanted. Gracie was easy that way. It was her strength and her weakness, and maybe the reason she was burying a husband. Forget the family march up Sullivan Street, she said. She would meet her sisters at Anona's at Thirty-eighth Street and Tenth Avenue and they'd go downtown together.

Helen came early to Anona's, to the apartment in Hell's Kitchen where Anona had raised them. Alone, Anona liked to remind them. She had raised them alone because there was no one else to do it. Mary showed up next and they all sat down at the kitchen table. It was clear of dishes and food. When she wanted to, Anona followed the old ways. They would eat later or not at all. They were in mourning, she said, but she did pour them all shots of the anisette that she made in the cellar. She counted out three coffee beans for each glass and they sat together to wait for Gracie.

"*Peccato* about Frankie," Anona said.

Helen looked over at Mary before she drained her glass. She chewed on one of the coffee beans. It was bitter in her mouth. But Helen liked bitter. Anona used to say it was the most Italian thing about her. "Be honest," Helen said to Anona. "You never liked Frankie."

"I don't like him for Gracie's husband but I don't wish him dead. It's always wrong when a son dies before his mother."

Anona stuck out her bottom lip. She looked around the kitchen. "We have no luck," she finally said. "We're cursed," and she shook a fist at the statue of St. Rita.

"Don't go on about curses," Helen said. "We don't believe in them."

"Ha, Miss Smarty Pants. These bad things, they just happen? It's the *malocchio*. What else?" Anona lowered her voice, looked around as if the evil eye might be skulking, even now, around a corner or under a chair, waiting to pounce. "I rack my brain trying to figure it out. I talk to myself. Who? Why? Look at your father, your . . ."

"What's Frankie Merelli got to do with our father?" Mary said. "It's not the same thing, is it? You know that." Mary looked over at Helen. "We're talking apples and pears here, no?"

"Never mind," Anona said. "Did I finish? You always gotta interrupt. That's why you don't learn nothing."

Helen laughed but Mary felt bad then and reached across the table, touched Anona's hand. "Tell the story. Go on. I want to hear it."

Anona pulled her hand away and moved it into her lap. "What's to tell? You know the story," she said. She paused, but not for long. She leaned forward. "Your father, he comes home one night with a headache, next day he's dead. Whatta you think? Then your grandfather, Nonno, same thing, and right after that, the baby . . . your little brother, that sweet little boy." Anona sat back in her chair. "Right after Gracie he was born, so close Mrs. McGuire downstairs called them Irish twins. That's what they call them when babies come one right after the other, Irish twins, because the Irish, they have babies like that, one on top of the other."

Anona knew about the Irish, they all did, living with them all these years. Hell's Kitchen belonged to the Irish. They controlled the piers. They controlled everything. When Anona's husband came to this country, to New York, you had to be Irish to work. The signs said NO WOPS. But he fooled them, Anona said. He didn't look Italian. He had white skin and blue eyes and black hair. He was a merchant seaman who spoke Gaelic; his name was Malloni and he made it "Mallone" and he got a job on the piers. He brought Anona over when he'd saved up the money and they had lived here, Italians in an Irish neighborhood, Italians on an Irish block.

Anona closed her eyes, slumped in her chair. "How your mamma loved that little boy . . ." Like always when Anona told the story, she lost her queenly bearing, her terrifying presence. Anona was always so fierce, even now, even old. When they made the decision about Frankie, she hadn't even blinked, but when she told the story about their mother, she shrank. It made Mary sad to see Anona so small in her chair and she put a hand on her shoulder to comfort her.

"When they came to take his body," Anona was saying, "they had to pull it out of her arms. Poor Emma. She went screaming through the halls, banging on all the doors, asking them, begging them, the Irish, to pray for her, to tell God to give her back her baby boy. God listened to the Irish, she said. They were always in church, weren't they? I remember," Anona said, "how they closed their doors and stood behind them calling her crazy."

Anona opened her eyes. "And the next week, she was dead, my Emma, *figlia mia,* the same as the others, just like that," and Anona snapped her fingers, as she always did at this part of the story. "My only child, my daughter. I could only have the one. I only ever had the one."

Mary was thinking of Gracie. She put her hand to her forehead, pressed her temples, remembering how Gracie as a child would always start to cry when Anona snapped her fingers and how Anona would stop to wipe Gracie's snotty nose with the handkerchief she kept under her sleeve. Gracie was always crying, Mary remembered. She was, after all, the baby sister.

Anona went on. "The Spanish influenza . . . 1918 it started . . . you were all just babies . . . lucky ones." Anona made an arc over them with her hand. "They took the bodies away on carts. So many bodies, piled up like logs. In just this building, almost a hundred. Emma was so glad when your father didn't go to the war, and look . . . look at how it ended up, worse . . . They buried the dead so fast half the time they weren't even dead, but just passed-out and they'd come to and sit right up in the grave."

"Well, Frankie's not sitting up anytime soon, that's for sure," Helen said. She had less patience with Anona than Mary did. Helen had no interest in the past. Frankie was a case in point. Once something was done, it was over.

"Never mind Frankie," Anona said, as if she had read Helen's mind. "How's Gracie? She was crazy for him, that one. How's she making up?"

"You mean holding up?" Helen said.

Anona didn't answer but got out of her chair and went over to the shrine she kept for St. Rita. "Maybe I light a candle for Frankie," she said.

"That's nice, Anona," Mary said, but Anona didn't light the candle. Instead she walked to the window and looked out, hoping to see Gracie.

"You should've found yourself another husband," Helen teased.

"One man was enough for me," Anona said, wiping away the fog her breath made on the windowpane. She turned back to Helen. "Not like some people I know."

Gracie was at the door. She had turned the knob and walked in without knocking, knowing that Anona never locked her door except at night, and then only because too many times one of her neighbors had stumbled in, having lost his way after one too many beers downstairs at Mike Hanley's Bar.

Gracie was their baby and they all came over to her, and one by one they held her in their arms. She cried and Anona took a folded handkerchief from inside her pocket, shook it open and put it in Gracie's hand. Helen took one arm and Mary the other and they walked her to the table. Anona pulled out a chair and after Gracie sat down, she went to get her a glass.

"No, thanks, Anona," Gracie said. "I can't." Anona waved the bottle of anisette that was shaped like the Vatican, the stopper topped with a cross. *"Uffa,"* she said, rubbing Gracie's shoulder with her free hand. "Have a drop. It's good for you."

Mary half-smiled. "You've been out of the Kitchen too long," she said to Gracie, putting the glass in front of her. "Don't you know it's medicine for what ails you?"

Gracie took the glass and held it up while Anona poured. Gracie wasn't used to drinking and she squinted her eyes when she swallowed. Anona was satisfied and went into the bedroom to get dressed. She had washed at the sink in the kitchen before they came. "Where's Charlie?" Anona called from the bedroom.

"With Frankie's mother," Gracie said. "They'll walk together to the funeral parlor."

"How'd she take that? You not walking with them, not following the rules?" Mary said.

Gracie shrugged. "I told her I needed my sisters. I needed my grandmother." Gracie shouted to be sure that Anona heard. "I told her I needed my family."

Signora Merelli had been furious with Gracie, but Gracie

didn't tell this to her sisters. "We're your family," she had said to Gracie. "Me and your son, Charlie. We're all you have left now that our Frankie is gone." And she had broken down into great choking sobs, clutching Charlie, wrapping her arms around his head.

Gracie hadn't answered. She didn't expect Signora Merelli to understand what it was like to grow up Italian in Hell's Kitchen, three girls and an old woman, with no men to protect them, to support them, or as Anona said when they were sad, to tell them what to do.

Gracie had loved Frankie. She loved her son, Charlie. He was her breath, her treasure. But . . . it was different. And she wasn't going to explain.

Gracie looked at her sisters, one on either side of her. As kids, the three of them would sleep together in the big bed in the little room off the kitchen. She remembered what it was like, the feeling that it was good to be alive.

"I'm glad we're Italian," Gracie would say in bed at night, lying between her sisters on the lumpy mattress filled with cotton that Anona would empty out every spring and wash in the laundry tub.

"Why?" Mary said.

"Because Anona says it's better."

"All I can see different is we eat good," Helen said. "The Irish eat shit. Potatoes. Oatmeal. They eat like crap." She turned, pulling the blanket.

"What a mouth on you," Mary yelped, tugging back. "You got no class, Helen, just like Anona says." Mary was the eldest and liked to play big shot. But it was Helen who was the boss. The boss of the *baccausa,* Anona would call her. The toilet, she meant, the outhouse, three flights down in the back yard.

". . . and they're always drunk," Gracie went on. It was hard to breathe, lying between her sisters, but at least she had the blanket. Anona always put her in the middle because Helen and Mary fought, threw punches at each other with their small tight fists. Gracie would never do that and so always she slept in the middle, to separate them.

"Yeah," Helen said. "But they have a good time, don't they? Believe me, when I grow up, I'm gonna have some good times."

"You gonna smoke?" Gracie said.

"Why not?"

"Girls don't smoke."

"I will. Lucky Strikes."

"Maybe I will, too," Mary said. Anona was not far off when she called Helen the boss.

"And I'm gonna drink," Helen said.

Gracie turned over flat on her back. "Girls don't drink."

Helen put her lips against Gracie's ear. "Don't kid yourself," she whispered.

Anona came out from the bedroom, elegant in a black silk dress and the hat Helen had bought for her on Division Street only a few weeks before. Anona had wondered out loud what she would do with such a big black hat. She didn't go to Mass and figured the next funeral was hers, so why did she need such a fancy hat?

"You never know," Helen had said, and then Frankie was dead and Helen showed up at Anona's with a new black dress for Anona to wear to the wake and as Anona stood in front of the mirror, Helen had hugged her from behind. "It looks beautiful," she said. Then she whispered into Anona's good ear, ". . . and . . . you can wear the hat."

• • •

They were all dressed in black, they all wore hats with veils, but Gracie's was so dark, so heavy, that it completely obscured her face. Helen and Mary had made sure their eyes showed through their veils, and Helen paid close attention to her lips, which she had painted very red.

"This veil," Helen said, folding it up over Gracie's face as they stood by the door ready to leave. "Frankie's dead, not you."

Mary pinched Helen's arm. "Let her be," she said, making a face that Gracie couldn't see.

Helen raised an eyebrow but finished arranging the veil. "Leave it like this for now," she said, and kissed her sister's cheek. Helen and Mary had lost husbands, with a minimum of grief and fanfare. But Frankie Merelli, they both knew, had been the love of Gracie's life.

Chapter Two

Frankie Merelli should have been a beautiful corpse. He was young and handsome and his wife had brought an exquisite set of clothes to the undertaker's back door. But Frankie Merelli had had an unkind death.

It was unfortunate, the neighborhood said, what had happened to Frankie Merelli. He had everything to live for. *Mala fortuna.* What bad luck.

Poor soul, the always compassionate neighborhood women, led by Teresa Gigante, head of the St. Ann Society of Mothers, were saying about his widow. Their heads shook as they sat with knees apart, hands resting in the black trampoline of their laps, the deep hems of their dresses stretched taut from knee to knee. They sat on wooden folding chairs, arranged in neat rows on the ground floor of Nucciarone's funeral parlor on Sullivan Street, gesticulating, their voices a deep hum that rose louder and louder, until they realized again that they were with the dead and tried to whisper. Always sensitive in the face of someone else's pain, they hid the sullen contentment of knowing that the *malocchio* had found a place to rest away from them and theirs. Tragedy was their entertainment. If they weren't mourning its presence, they were awaiting its arrival.

Gracie sat in the front row facing the coffin, Mary to her right, Helen to her left. They sat, the sisters, like a trinity of black birds, pale skin and pale lips veiled, except for Helen, whose mouth was a slash of red behind the black net.

Anona was in the back, against the wall, dwarfed by the great round brim of the hat with the black ostrich plume. Anona was a woman who never told her age. Her mouth was lined and pinched, her cheeks smooth. She had insisted on sitting against the wall at the funeral parlor when Old Man Nucciarone in his silk top hat tried to lead her to the big upholstered armchair up front where Frankie's mother sat with eyes red and scorched from crying. Anona didn't want to hear all that screaming and carrying on, and besides, she always liked to cover her back. Sullivan Street was a long way from Hell's Kitchen. She told this to Gracie when she married Frankie and moved down here. But she had told important things to all of them and not one of them had listened. Sighing, Anona shifted her bulk. Too bad the wake wasn't in Houlihan's. She didn't much like the Irish, but she had to admit they knew how to send a soul off to the next world. Sometimes even the corpse got to dance.

"Where's Charlie?" Gracie said to her sisters, looking around. "I can't see him. Can you see him?"

Mary touched Gracie's shoulder. "He's over there, by the coatrack. Anona's got him. Don't worry. We're all here with you. We'll always be here. You know that." Gracie almost smiled. Her wadded handkerchief was a white ball in her lap, the lint collecting on her dress. She was, the neighborhood women thought, remarkably self-controlled, or was she, they wondered, numb with the shock of her young husband laid out, stiff and powdered, in front of her?

Gina Gidari had poked Teresa Cerubbi not minutes after they had paid their respects. "Maybe she's not so unhappy. Who can tell? He wasn't no bargain from what I hear." Anna Albano nodded and was about to speak when Jeannie Popeye leaned over from the row behind. "I live across the hall from them," she said. "He was out plenty, lemme tell you. Gracie's a good soul. But him? He couldn't shine her shoes."

Jeannie stopped talking when she saw Dibby and Lena Santulli come in. They lived in the building on Spring Street, too. Dibby had been Frankie's friend, the closest he had to a friend on Spring Street. Frankie had preferred to spend his time on the East Side; he didn't like anyone knowing his business, but Dibby, he told Gracie, was different. He was a good skate. They had worked together down the docks, shaped up together on Pier 13. Dibby was supposed to be Frankie's *goombah* at his wedding to Gracie, and then Charlie's godfather. But the Mallone sisters did things their own way, and Dibby had understood when he was left out.

Jeannie Popeye knew how close they were and she didn't want Dibby to hear her talking about Frankie. She shushed the others and kept her eyes facing straight ahead until Dibby and Lena passed.

• • •

In the front row, Helen stood up. She was the tallest of the sisters at five feet four inches and she hennaed her hair so red that Anona would light candles in penance. "I need some air," Helen whispered, motioning to Mary. She made the gesture of puffing on an imaginary cigarette, then leaned close to Gracie and reached out a hand in a black-satin glove and patted her sister's knee. "Mary and I are going outside You'll be okay?"

Gracie nodded and Helen raised her eyebrows at Mary to say, "Let's go," when Frankie's mother appeared in front of them. She semi-swooned and fell forward into Gracie's arms. With this, Helen and Mary made their getaway, as mother and wife embraced in their seemingly unbearable grief.

Outside in the street, Helen and Mary stood with the men, who stared at them and then looked away. Both Helen and Mary were something to stare at: Helen, her hair hennaed, her dress slim and long, fitted all the way down, so narrow at the bottom that Anona never stopped wondering how she walked, and Mary, smaller, with peroxided blond hair, spit curls visible through her veil. Her dress was full, but pulled in at the waist with a wide belt that ended up under her bosom, two black cones that stuck out in invitation.

The men watched them slyly, their eyes shifting. They were not used to such elegance on Sullivan Street. They had to go off the block to see the likes of the Mallone sisters. Mary recognized Sam and his partner Al from the candy store on Spring Street but when she smiled at them, they pretended as though she hadn't caught their eye.

Helen lifted her black veil and set it on the brim of her hat, waited for Mary to do the same, then took out a pack of French cigarettes. She tore off the gold paper and held the pack out to Mary who shook her head, no. Helen took out two cigarettes and put them both in her mouth. She struck a match, cupped the flame in her hands, and inhaled, lighting them both. The smoke coiled from her lips to her nose and she blew it out in rings as she handed one of the cigarettes to Mary, who took it this time, and put it to her lips. The men watched, shifting from foot to foot. They knew Helen and Mary were Gracie's sisters, Frankie Merelli's sisters-in-law from outside the neighborhood. Everybody knew them. They came down to Spring Street all the time to pick up Gracie and take her out. They drove cars. They smoked cigarettes. They stuck out like sore thumbs and they didn't seem to care. Someone snickered, "Whatta you expect? They grew up with the Irish."

"Yeah," Joey Gugliano said. "You live with them, you act like them."

Mary leaned against the wrought-iron banister and inhaled. "Anona's right," she said. "You are always leading me astray."

"Anona never said that. And if she did, she didn't mean it. I'm her favorite. I've always been her favorite." Mary didn't answer. It was true and she didn't answer because this truth didn't hurt. Helen was right. Anona had a soft spot for Helen. They all did. Helen had always been wild. A spitfire, Anona called her. When Helen was little, she was more like a boy than a girl, as though that baby Emma had loved so much, that little baby boy, Gracie's Irish twin, were still with them.

"Besides," Helen said, "wasn't Nick Andersen the one who turned you bad?"

"Please, don't start with Nick. I never did anything I didn't want to do. If Anona didn't believe that, she would have killed Nick when he first walked in the door. Whattya think?"

"C'mon. I love the old pain-in-the-ass. You know that. But enough about Nick. Tell me the truth, big sister . . ." And Helen moved closer. "You don't feel bad at all?"

Mary looked around again at the tight circles of men standing nearby. "No," she said. She changed the subject. "Look at them," she told Helen, "watching us from under their eyelashes. You know what's going on in their minds? They're thinking that if they had a chance, if we'd give them half a chance, they could show us what it's all about, and then they realize they don't have a chance in hell, and then they hate us and tell themselves they wouldn't want us anyway, but if they did, if they really did . . ." She crushed her cigarette under her very high heel. "Give me the Irish any day."

"I don't know. I liked Frankie," Helen said. And she had. Some nights she would come over to Gracie's and they would play cards, the three of them. Gracie couldn't keep the cards straight in her mind. She'd get bored and not pay attention but Helen was good with cards and she and Frankie would play at the kitchen table long after Gracie went to bed. They would drink and they would smoke, but they never talked. She liked that he treated her like one of the boys. She felt like she could relax with Frankie. She could be herself.

"I liked him too," Mary said. "He was a charmer, that Frankie . . . and a looker. A regular George Raft. I'll give him that. But when all's said and done, he was a rat bastard. Come to think of it, George Raft was no bargain neither, always playing the big shot. Nick told me he was nothing but a gofer."

"But . . ."

"Don't say nothing. I don't wanna hear it. Frankie was a rat bastard. We did the best we could."

1937–1939

LINCOLN TUNNEL OPENS, LINKING NEW YORK AND NEW JERSEY

LOUIS LEPKE SURRENDERS

COLUMNIST WALTER WINCHELL HANDS OVER CRIME BOSS TO FBI DIRECTOR J. EDGAR HOOVER

AMELIA EARHART DISAPPEARS IN THE SOUTH PACIFIC

Chapter Three

Gracie Mallone met Frankie Merelli at a roof dance on Sullivan Street three days shy of her nineteenth birthday, the year the *Hindenburg* blimp blew up over New Jersey. From the first moment she saw him, she was done for. He was dark and slim and clean as a whistle, she told her sisters. She found him exciting, but she kept that part to herself.

Her sisters would have been surprised. They thought of her as backward when it came to men. On the one hand, they blamed Anona for keeping Gracie so close, so tied to home, and on the other, they figured Gracie was just that way because, despite Anona, they had both done just as they pleased. When it came to men, Helen and Mary were bold and flirtatious and got what they wanted. Mary was thirteen when she brought home Nick Andersen. And Helen? As a little girl she was always with the boys. She was what the neighborhood called a tough, and when she grew up, she went through men like playing cards. Helen and Mary thought they knew everything; Gracie could have told them a thing or two. But what she felt with Frankie Merelli, she didn't want to share. They could think what they wanted. This feeling, this man, was hers, and all bets, as they say, were off.

The funny thing was, she hadn't wanted to go to that dance on Sullivan Street. She was shy and her grandmother was unrelenting. With Gracie, Anona said, she wasn't taking any chances. One out of three was better than none. By then, only Gracie was left at home with Anona.

Mary was long married to Nick, and Helen had already buried

a husband, Mick Mullen, who died under a beer truck. Helen's heart was soothed by a large insurance payout that made her a great fan of beer companies and a loyal drinker of Schlitz.

"Wait for my pension before you do anything crazy like get married," Anona told Gracie. "There's plenty of time. If you can't find a good man, you're better off without one."

"You had a good man?"

"Of course. Do I look like a dope to you?"

Helen said it was easy for Anona to say whatever she wanted because she was so old, there was no one to contradict her. And then, who really knew anything about Anona but what she told you herself? According to Helen, Anona was older than the history books. Mary said the pension was another of Anona's schemes, that between the two of them, she and Helen, Anona never had to worry about the rent.

Anona saw it different. Alone in the apartment with Gracie, Anona swore she'd drink bleach if Gracie left her dependent on charity. She made Gracie promise to wait for the money from the government to come through before she would leave, before she would even think of leaving. In only a few more years, Anona said, the government was going to give money every month to widows and orphans. Social Security . . . she'd heard all about it. That Mr. Roosevelt . . .

"It's a good country, America," she told Gracie. "I'm glad I came."

Gracie felt obligated. She'd had it easy compared to her sisters; they'd always looked out for her. The least she could do was look out for Anona, even though Helen and Mary insisted that Anona could take care of herself and the whole of Hell's Kitchen.

So Gracie promised. Anona made her swear with one hand on her heart, the other on St. Rita's head, and then Anona put a holy card in Gracie's cupped hands and she set fire to it with a wooden kitchen match. Gracie dropped the burning card on the floor, and Anona got mad, saying it didn't count, but Gracie wouldn't do it again. She knew she had to draw the line somewhere.

Frankie walked Gracie uptown after the dance but she made him leave her off two blocks away, afraid Anona would be out the window smoking her homemade pipe and throwing curses. The next time they went out, Gracie let him kiss her and not so much after, his hands were up under her skirt and down inside her blouse and she was meeting him every night. He would hold her up against the brick walls near the Hudson River piers and press against her until he was almost out of his mind and talking marriage. Gracie told Anona she was at the Children's Aid Society on Sullivan Street learning how to knit.

Frankie wanted to get married quick. There were rumors of war in Europe, he said. Suppose he had to go? She could keep him home. He loved her so much; she was so different from the girls he knew in the neighborhood. She was so delicate and white with those big blue eyes. He would kiss her shoulder, luminescent in the moonlight that shone off the river and he would beg her to tell him the truth about who she was and where she came from.

"Four Thirty-five West Thirty-eighth Street," she'd tell him, her hands in his hair. His would move under her dress, touching the soft skin high up on her leg. "Germany," she'd say. The tips of his fingers followed silk, marking the way, and now she'd answer, "Norway," then "Denmark," shout "Sweden," as he touched her there. She had gotten the geography medal in fifth grade.

He said the merchant seamen in the Kiwi bar on Houston Street, so blond their eyebrows and beards were almost invisible, had brought her to him from across the sea. "Say yes. Say now,"

Frankie begged. So she did and not long after she brought him home to meet Anona.

Gracie thought Frankie had made a good impression on the reluctant Anona, but she was wrong. Anona had been unconvinced.

"I smell a rat," she told Gracie.

"Why? What's wrong with him?"

"Too good-looking . . . like a girl. No good . . . and how'd he pay for that suit? He don't even have a job."

"How do you know?"

She pointed to the clock. "It's three in the afternoon. What's he doing over here if he's got a job?" Anona checked the candles in front of St. Rita, thought about putting oilcloth on the countertop under the saint. She made the sign of the cross with the crucifix at the end of her rosary beads and kissed the Christ figure before she put the beads back in her apron pocket.

"But you're never satisfied," Gracie told her. "Nick's crude. Mick Mullen's a drunk."

"Mullen? He's dead, no? The beer truck, no?"

"Oh, stop it. And Frankie's not any of those things. What's wrong with Frankie?"

Anona didn't answer right away. "Is he cheap?"

"No."

"He throws his money around?"

"He likes nice things."

"Ha, a broken suitcase who spends money like water. A *spiccone*. I knew it."

"Money isn't everything. You say that yourself."

"Yeah, easy to say, but it's nice, no? Your sister Mary, she lives good, no? That takes money."

"So you want me to find a guy like Nick?"

"God forbid, that hoodlum."

"So what's the matter with Frankie?"

Anona held up her hands and counted on her left with the index finger from her right. "Number one, he's too clean. Number two, he's got no job. Number three, he's the only son of a widowed mother. Number four. . . ."

"Enough. You're not being fair."

Anona put down her hands. "And he loves you so much. All the time, he wants you. And I bet he's jealous, right?"

"So?"

"The sure signs, *cara mia,* of a cheater."

"Anona. . . ."

"And don't forget the pension. You promised to wait for the pension."

It would be almost three years before Anona got her pension. And then there was the matter of Mamma Merelli, as Helen called her, the woman for whom any other woman was a threat and a curse. Every girl in a four-block radius wanted Frankie Merelli, according to Signora Merelli. She prayed Frankie would use his God-given gifts to advance them both: his face, his smile, his voice. If he'd had the breaks, she was convinced, he could have been a movie star. For her money, he was better-looking than most of those *judruls* in Hollywood, but never mind. Signora Merelli was happy to settle for a good match. She had her eye on Rosanna Treculo, whose father owned the fish store on Bleecker Street. She had no brothers. One crippled sister, poor thing . . . a botched abortion, so they said, but who's to judge? Rosanna was perfect. And there was Gina Lorenzo, of the Thompson Street *lattecini freschi* Lorenzos. Signora Merelli's corseted chest heaved just thinking about all the girls suited for her Frankie. She could go on and on.

"I'm not wearing no rubber apron and stinking of fish," Frankie told his mother when she brought up Rosanna Treculo.

"Gina, then. Cheese. Cheese don't smell so bad."

"The apron, Mamma. What about the apron? Anyway, stop it. I got a girl."

But she wouldn't stop. And for sure Frankie Merelli was a catch—handsome in a neighborhood where good looks might take you anywhere. They called him "Good-Looking Frankie" from the time he was sixteen and Lorraine Caifano had said it out loud at the San Gennaro feast on Mulberry Street.

There were so many girls that would have warmed Signora Merelli's heart to call *figlia*. She hadn't figured on an orphan, from Hell's Kitchen no less, without a pot to piss in or a window to throw it out of.

Gracie hadn't worried. She knew that Frankie was hers no matter what his mother did or said. His mother didn't hear him sing "My Funny Valentine" in her ear or hear his heartbeat when Gracie rubbed against the swell in his pants. And Gracie was no dope, as Anona would say. She would never go, had never been, anywhere "inside" with Frankie alone, not even in a car. The best he could hope for was a dark hallway. It didn't take long before he was desperate to have her.

Of course, Gracie never knew about the other women, like Gianni Esposito's wife, Carla, who would leave the sign lit over the hardware store on the nights her husband went to the Knights of Columbus on MacDougal Street. When the neon hammer and thumb flickered, Frankie knew the coast was clear. Frankie was always welcome. There were women in the jazz clubs on Fifty-

second Street and at the bars on Eighth Street and the whore-
houses in Pennsylvania, but despite all these distractions, Frankie
Merelli wanted Gracie Mallone.

"Blue eyes. Big deal," his mother said. "So what? Your grandfather had blue eyes."

"I don't wanna marry my grandfather, Ma. For Chrissakes, get
off my back. I'm gonna marry Gracie and that's that."

Signora Merelli rethought her strategy. She called for a sit-
down. When the Mallones met her, she reasoned, when they saw
just what kind of background Frankie came from, she knew it
would be as clear to them as it was to her why the match would be
a *sbaglio,* a terrible mistake.

So a confident Signora Merelli went to Anona's house. She
had not, however, figured on the Mallone sisters: Helen with her
flaming hair, Mary in a dress cut so low in front Signora Merelli
thought they would pop out any minute. Trying hard to keep her
dignity, Signora Merelli explained that Frankie was her soul, her
heart, her one and only. She told them that the Merellis were pure
Napoletani . . . going back to the seventeenth century, to
Masaniello, the fisherman who led the revolt against the Spanish.

"What? Who?" Mary interrupted.

"The fisherman, you know, in the seventeenth century," Helen
said, rolling her eyes. She watched for Anona's reaction to this
astounding news.

Anona was rocking hard in her chair. Mary went to hold the
back of it, afraid she would tip over. But Anona suddenly brought
the chair to a halt, stood up, and put up her hand, palm out, like
a traffic cop. *"Aspetto,"* she said. "Us, too, we're Naples people.
Frankie don't tell you? Whatta you saying here?"

Signora Merelli squinted. "Of course," she said. "My Frankie,
he tells me everything. There's no secrets between me and my
Frankie. But your name . . . is Irish . . ."

"Ha!" Anona said. "It's a long story . . . none of your business."

Signora Merelli bit her bottom lip until just before the moment she would have drawn blood. She ignored Anona's palm so near her face. Signora Merelli was a small woman. "You have three granddaughters," she said. "I have only this one son. When I lost my husband, I was still a young woman. I need my Frankie." She sniffed. "Me and my Frankie we're together, just the two of us since . . ."

"Wait. I know . . . the seventeenth century?" Helen offered. Gracie thought Helen was being rude. Mary did, too, and resisted the urge to pinch her.

The room went silent. Signora Merelli's head itched under her hat. She would have liked to take it off but a lady always wore a hat. Instead, she opened her pocketbook and rustled around for a handkerchief. The one she withdrew was trimmed in pink and white cotton edging she had crocheted herself and had her initials embroidered in one corner along with the outline of a yellow butterfly. Signora Merelli dabbed delicately at her nose. She had a large nose, which she referred to as Roman, a nose Anona would have called a pepper. Signora Merelli closed her pocketbook with a defiant snap and opened her mouth to speak when Anona took a step closer and wagged her finger violently in Signora Merelli's face. "You don't like Gracie for your son? Well, I don't like your son nohow. You take your son and you stick him up your ass."

All hell broke loose. Signora Merelli lost all pretense at decorum. She shouted until the cords in her neck almost tore open the white starched collar of her dress, pinned with, Helen noted later, a very beautiful cameo made with coral from the Bay of Naples. Anona raved in the long-forgotten dialect of Bocca al Lupo that none of them understood.

Gracie sat down quietly in the chair Anona kept by the window that looked over the street while Mary tried to calm the old women down. Helen stayed on the sidelines, smoking a cigarette, thinking that she would like to have met Mamma Merelli under different circumstances, in a Tenth Avenue saloon on a Saturday night, for instance, and slammed her one in the kisser.

When it quieted, Signora Merelli's hat sat sideways on her head and Anona's voice sounded like a scratched phonograph record. Helen gave Gracie a drag from her cigarette and whispered in her ear that it was time for her to stand up for herself. Gracie didn't need much convincing. One poke from Helen, an index finger in her side, and she was ready.

This was it, Gracie told Anona. She had waited long enough. She was marrying Frankie. They were going for their blood tests first thing and they were getting the license. Then she turned to her future mother-in-law. "And don't think for a minute that we're living anywhere near you," she said.

Mary was impressed. Helen was more of a skeptic, especially after Gracie did end up living on Spring Street. Frankie had begged, swore it was the last thing he'd ever ask her to do for him. Signora Merelli had taken to her bed, a bread knife clutched between her breasts. She wept until her eyes closed up and then she screamed that she had gone blind. She cried so hard and so long that the super came to say that everyone in the building was complaining. The noise had made Mrs. Conti's twins colic. The super promised Frankie the apartment on the floor above for $22 a month and threw in a paint job if he could just get his mother to shut up. The news of the apartment, the idea of her only son nearby, seemed to console Signora Merelli. She agreed to see Dr. Pecorarra, who came to the house and gave her an injection that put her to sleep for a week.

Gracie and Frankie were married downtown at City Hall on

October 20, 1939, the month after the war started in Europe. In all the confusion and hysteria, the fact of Frankie not having a steady job, or any job, had fallen by the wayside. Gracie wanted a real life, a husband with a steady paycheck, but she also believed that everything would work out. And here she was in a white crepe dress with a corsage on her shoulder marrying the love of her life. Helen and Mary were the witnesses in matching hats that had been made to order on Division Street. Frankie had wanted Dibby Santulli to be his witness. Who ever heard of this? he told Gracie. There was supposed to be a girl for her and a guy for him. Didn't she know anything? She knew what she wanted, Gracie told Frankie, right there in Anona's kitchen when they made the wedding plans, Anona pretending that they weren't planning a wedding, making believe it was a day like any other.

Mary and Helen were impressed. "I think baby sister's really coming into her own," Mary told Helen, with a maternal pride. Helen agreed. Maybe Gracie wasn't such a piece of cake. Frankie should have paid attention, but he was blinded by lust.

To make her position clear, Anona stayed home on the big day. "Sure he's got clean fingernails," she told Gracie, when Mary tried to coax her into coming to the wedding, having bought her a navy blue dress with white stitching and a pleated bodice, which Anona ignored even though it was being held in front of her face. "You don't get dirty playing cards."

St. Rita, who had failed to answer Anona's prayers, spent two weeks in the cupboard with the doors nailed shut. Anona was disgruntled with St. Rita for more reasons than one. It had started two years ago, when she'd failed to find Amelia Earhart.

1952–1953

Rocky Marciano Knocks Out Jersey Joe Walcott for Heavyweight Championship

KING GEORGE VI DIES
Elizabeth to Ascend Throne

GENEROSO POPE JR. TAKES OVER THE NATIONAL ENQUIRER

Chapter Four

Anona always said that after the honeymoon, a man is either boring, crazy, or just looking for a good time. Frankie Merelli, she told Gracie, was the last kind: he was just looking for a good time.

It was around seven o'clock on a Friday night when Frankie came home and said he wasn't hungry. Gracie shrugged without looking up. She was married thirteen years; this was nothing new. She behaved like she always did, acted like it hardly mattered. "We waited until six-thirty, but Charlie wanted to eat," she said. The apartment door opened up into the kitchen and as soon as Frankie came in the door, he could see she was clearing the table.

"Where is Charlie?"

"He's doing his homework."

Frankie sat down, got up, went into the living room and came back out. Gracie was putting the dishes in the sink. "Can you wait for that? I want to wash up."

She looked at him. "When I'm finished. What's the rush?"

"I need to wash up. I'm going out."

"Out? You just got home."

"I'm going out. What's the big deal?"

"Nothing. But you're just gonna have to wait." Gracie took her time with the dishes. Out, she thought. He was always going out. Sometimes it felt like he only came home to sleep. Wouldn't he like it if she asked him where he was going? But she wouldn't. She'd bust, she'd decided long ago, before she'd ever give him the satisfaction of asking. She'd choke first.

Frankie went into the bedroom. She could hear him hanging

31

up his jacket on the back of the bedroom door. Nobody was neater than Frankie. He came into the kitchen in his undershirt and sat at the table waiting for her to finish. He took a pack of Camels, tapped out a cigarette and lit it. "The ashtray's dirty," he said.

She took it off the table and emptied it into the garbage under the sink. She washed it carefully, taking her time. Then she dried it carefully, taking her time, facing him, watching the ash on his cigarette end grow.

"Gracie . . ."

She put the ashtray down in front of him, hard, loud. He crushed the butt in it and got up and went over to the kitchen sink wedged in the corner next to the window that looked out over the alley. On the wall facing the sink was a medicine cabinet with a mirrored door. Gracie watched Frankie wash his face and hands and arms up to his elbows and under his armpits. He lathered his shaving brush and turned to look in the medicine cabinet mirror behind him. She watched him shave the shadow of beard that darkened his face, and then she handed him a towel, a clean undershirt. She stood next to him with his toothbrush, spread the paste along the bristles. There was a hand-washed, hand-pressed shirt, collars and cuffs lightly starched, just the way he liked them, hanging on the kitchen doorknob. She took it off the hanger, held it out for him. He slipped into the arms, fastened his cuff links, looked in the mirror again to do his tie, smoothed his hair down with his two palms.

Charlie came through the front door running. Gracie pulled him by the shirt collar and she smacked him, not hard, but hard enough. "What's that for?" he wailed.

"You're supposed to be doing homework."

"I finished, Ma. Jeez . . . Give me a break."

Gracie bent down, kissed the top of his head. "How was I supposed to know?" She pinched his cheek, then patted the red spot she'd raised with her affection. "Look, Daddy's home."

Charlie ran to Frankie, grabbed him around the waist and hugged him hard. Frankie raised his arms. Gracie noticed his long graceful fingers, the nails buffed. Gracie pushed aside a vision of Frankie on Mulberry Street at the Golden Dragon Restaurant with another woman, his long, graceful fingers around one of those porcelain spoons they give you with the wonton soup.

"Charlie, sweetheart, whatta you doing?" Frankie yelled. "Gracie, please. I'm trying to get dressed here."

She grabbed Charlie but wished she hadn't. She wished she'd waited for Charlie to rub his nose on Frankie's shirtfront, leave a smear of snot on Frankie's silk tie that came from Sulka on Fifth Avenue. Frankie was so handsome, she thought, looking at him, even while she wished him ill. She couldn't help how she felt about him.

Helen had tried to teach her not to go for looks. Helen would come home to Anona's flashing bracelets and rings and fur wraps of stone martens biting each other's tails, and once with a Pomeranian dog that she named Buster who disappeared down an alley a day later, all gifts from men with mugs like the underside of a truck. Helen liked men but she could take them or leave them. She never understood women who waited, like Maureen Halloran, whose Billy went away for ten years to Sing Sing, or Eileen Grady, who worked six days a week in a laundry and handed over her money to Johnny Blue, who got blind drunk in Hanley's Bar night after night. Helen liked men for what they could provide and for their raw energy, which she admired. And if truth be told, Helen liked women, too, but only sometimes. For Helen, love was casual. It never kept her awake.

Gracie, Helen said, had been a sucker for good looks, and Gracie had to admit Helen knew what she was talking about, because looking at Frankie, even now, her breath still stuck in her throat.

She looked away, called Charlie over, put her arm around his shoulders and held his head while she wiped his nose with her handkerchief. "Can't he do that himself?" Frankie asked her.

"You should talk."

Charlie squirmed free and was off, out the door, into the hall.

"Where's he going?"

"Out," she said, "just like you. He's going out."

"What's that supposed to mean? Something smart?"

She held out his jacket for him and he shrugged into it, adjusting the shoulders, pulling the sleeves down over the lightly starched cuffs of his shirt. She fixed the back of his collar, then backed away and sat down.

"Don't wait up," he said, coming over to her, bending from the waist, one hand on her shoulder, the other holding his jacket against himself. His lips touched her cheek. She smelled cologne. She hadn't seen him put it on. He straightened up, shook his shoulders again to set his jacket just right, checked his cuffs. "And look out for that kid. I don't like him in the street all the time."

He was gone. She listened at the door for the sound of his footsteps on the worn slate stairs, the slam of first one hallway door and then the next. She imagined him turning down the street, disappearing around the corner. She made herself a pot of espresso and took the tin of pignoli cookies down from the shelf over the stove and sat at the kitchen table stirring sugar into her coffee. She ate one, two, five cookies and scraped the sugar from the bottom of the tiny gold-rimmed coffee cup with the small silver spoon from the set Mary and Nick had given her when she married Frankie.

Gracie thought about how long she had been married and how many nights she had sat here alone and how maybe it was time to teach Frankie Merelli a lesson. Not for the first time, she packed a suitcase with mostly Charlie's things. She threw some comic books in the bag. If she let Charlie pack himself, he'd take the whole house and she just wanted to get out. She had the weekend before she had to worry about school, not that Charlie was much for school anyway, but she didn't want him to miss if she could help it. Sister St. Bernard had it in for him as it was.

Gracie remembered how when she was a little girl the nuns at St. Michael's would taunt her for being Italian. Sister Marie Clare would sit Gracie in the back, then call her up to the front and poke a pencil through her hair looking for nits. She would do this in front of the whole class because, and this she would say out loud to Gracie as she stood there, facing the class, "one of you can infect the lot, and I can't trust that your house is clean. You people are not known to be clean." Then she would make Gracie hold out her hands, palms up and palms down, and she would inspect her fingernails for dirt. If there was a bad smell, she would go over to Gracie's seat and ask if she was wearing "some vile amulet against God and his saints." Anona had tried to do the best for them. At least up here, in Hell's Kitchen, Gracie could go to the Catholic school. Downtown, at St. Alphonsus, it would be years before they would accept Italian children. Gracie kept quiet and endured the humiliation, but when Sister Marie Clare accused of her stealing, Anona got called in, and that was the end of that. She wouldn't even let Gracie go back for her sweater, which was hanging on a hook in the back of the classroom. One of the Murphy kids could bring it, she told Gracie, in front of the sister, unless they sold it on the street before they got it home. And here was Gracie now, in an Italian parish, and still the school was filled with Irish nuns. Poor Charlie.

She took four five-dollar bills from her underwear drawer and put them in her purse. She grabbed her coat, shut the light and went out. Her mother-in-law's door was closed tight and it was too cold for the *pittacuse* to be gossiping on the stoop. She whistled for Charlie, found him in Sam & Al's candy store and pulled him out by his arm when he wanted a Pepsi.

"Where we going?" he asked her.

"It's a surprise," she said. He was a good kid and she loved him.

Chapter Five

Helen and Mary were at Anona's when Gracie arrived. They came to visit the old lady often and always on Friday nights. So it was the three of them and Anona, like the prayer . . . "as it was in the beginning, is now, and ever shall be, world without end, amen."

Anona said nothing when any of them came back to her. She didn't care how they showed up, with or without husbands, flush or broke, happy or sad. She welcomed them with her scowling silence and covered the porcelain-and-wood table with food. When they were all together with her on Tenth Avenue, she felt sixty again.

Gracie had pushed open the door with her foot, her suitcase in one hand, Charlie hanging on to the other. Helen took the suitcase and Mary gave Charlie a quarter to go downstairs and make friends (the Irish were easily bought, she told him, even now) but Gracie said it was too late and so he got sent to sleep in Anona's bed even though he complained it was only nine o'clock. Helen upped the ante to fifty cents that he could have tomorrow and

Gracie washed his ears and neck with a washrag and after that he was glad to get away.

"So what is it? What's going on?" Helen said, when they were all settled around Anona's table. She lit a black gold-tipped cigarette, and exhaled, her mouth a perfect O. The tip of her tongue poked a hole in the puff of smoke to make a perfect ring.

Anona leaned over and poked Helen in the ribs. "When you gonna stop smoking? I got asthma. I'm old. Any minute chances are good I stop breathing. You think smoke in my *faccia* helps?" Anona coughed into the man's handkerchief that had been sticking out of her apron pocket.

Helen got up and put an arm around Anona. She kissed her cheek, then turned to take another drag on the cigarette. She blew the smoke into the air above Anona's head. "Okay? Happy? Now I'm not blowing smoke in your face."

"Emma never smoked. She had class, your mother."

"How did Emma get in the conversation?"

"Forget Emma and pay attention to Gracie," Mary said. "She didn't come here to listen to this crap."

Anona screwed her hand into the air in a rude gesture. "I never forget Emma. And she didn't have no sewer mouth like some people. She was a real lady."

Helen sat back down. Anona said something about how tight Helen's dress was. Helen ignored her and turned toward Gracie, who was pouring herself a glass of wine. "Tell us," she said. "We're all ears."

". . . a sausage skin," Anona muttered.

"Would you stop now?" Mary said. She wet her finger and flattened down the curl on her right temple, then adjusted the front of her dress. She was the shortest of the sisters but she had the largest bust, and she was always, according to Anona, exposing herself. Mary claimed it was more like making the best of what she had. And Nick liked the way she dressed, she said. It made him remember when she was fifteen and they'd go to the Cotton Club in Harlem to see Duke Ellington. Mary patted her bosom now, as if to reassure herself that it was just as alluring as it was when she was fifteen at the Cotton Club on Nick Andersen's arm.

"Go ahead," she told Gracie, who was taking a strip of roasted pepper from one of the oval dishes that filled the table and laying it across a heel of bread.

"Nothing. There's nothing to tell. I just needed a break. Hmmm, Anona, this is so good."

"C'mon. You don't pack a suitcase for nothing," Helen said, irritated. She put out her cigarette in the crystal ashtray Anona called a candy dish.

"What can I tell you? It's Frankie. He comes home late, doesn't eat, goes out again all dressed up like Paddy's pig . . . and here I am, pressing two shirts a day, cooking for nobody, stretching forty-five dollars a week. For what? What am I? Some kind of dope?"

Anona bristled. "I didn't raise no dopes. The hell with him. Leave him. Stay here with me."

"But what about Charlie? He needs a father," Gracie said. She cut the flower top from the mozzarella.

"You didn't have no father. We did all right. You go to work. I raise Charlie. Finish. *Basta!* You only got the one. Now's the time to leave. Your husband, he stinks!" Anona spat into her handkerchief. "Pthew! That's what I think for your husband."

"Don't listen to her, Gracie," Mary said. "Anona hates men. Nobody's any good, according to her."

"Pthew! I spit on your husband, too, that other *judrul.*"

"I don't believe you said that. Nick's so good to you." Mary reached over for a gaeta olive. It was difficult to get a rise out of Mary.

Anona raised her chin. "I never forget."

"I know. You're an elephant. What is it now? Twenty years?" Mary took the olive pit out of her mouth with two fingers, her pinkie arched, and placed the pit on the side of her plate.

"You were thirteen. You should've been in school."

"Nick's still here, ain't he?" Mary sucked the oil from the olive off her fingers.

"Where's he gonna go? He's an old fart. He's even too old for me," Anona said.

Mary refused to take offense. "Yeah, too bad. Twenty years ago Nick could have straightened Frankie out like that," she said, snapping her fingers. She cut a slice of bread, dipped it in a saucer of olive oil and sprinkled it with salt. She turned to Gracie. "Listen, sweetie, I don't know what Frankie's up to but he's crazy for you. He'll get it out of his system and he'll get old and fat and before you know it, he'll be carrying your grocery bags. Watch and see."

Anona reached over and tugged at the seam of Helen's dress, as though she could alter the dress by pulling at it, make the dress not cling so closely to the curve of Helen's hip. It was how Anona expressed her disapproval. Helen grabbed Anona's hand without looking down and squeezed it until Anona let go. It was their private war. There was nothing Anona could do about the way Helen lived, and she didn't know the half of it.

Gracie and Mary had husbands . . . not bargains, but husbands. They were respectable; they were married women. Helen was on her own, known from the Copa and the Stork Club uptown, to Trudi Hellers and the gay bars in Greenwich Village, to the gambling cellars in Chinatown where they played fan-tan all night and laid their heads on wooden pillows to smoke opium in pipes brought from China a hundred years ago. Anona couldn't tell Helen what to do but she could complain about Helen's dresses, and she did. A touch here, a poke there. She made her point.

"Mary's right," Helen said. "Nobody's perfect. They all got something wrong. Irishmen drink. Look at my poor husband Mickey, under that truck." She held up her glass. "A toast to Mickey. God rest his soul."

"To Mickey," Mary said, and drained her glass. She leaned back, thoughtful, then sat up. "Italian men cheat," she said.

"But Frankie, he gambles, too," Anona added. "Don't forget the bum gambles."

"Good, Anona, I'm glad you mentioned that. Gracie feels much better now." Helen went over to the window and lit another cigarette.

"You think he's got a girl?" Gracie said. "That son of a bitch. You think that's what he's doing? How could he do that, the bastard? Who the hell does he think he is?"

"He's got a girl, we should cut off his *cazzo*. That's what we should do," Anona said.

Mary shook her head, loosening the curl she had so carefully flattened down with saliva. "We have to look at all the angles and remember one important thing about Italian men. They may cheat, but they never leave. Why? Because they're lazy. And let's face it, who's lazier than Frankie?"

"Lazy bum," Anona mumbled.

"And Charlie. Frankie loves Charlie," Helen added.

"How about his mother? Frankie would never leave Mamma Merelli!"

"And me? Where do I fit in?" Gracie sliced into the provolone. She held out her glass for more wine.

Helen reached for a toothpick. "Hey, Gracie, we're just talking facts here."

"So what are you telling me? That Frankie's cheating? That he's got somebody else?" Gracie suddenly put her elbows on the table and cradled her head in her arms. She started to cry. "If he ever left me, I'd kill myself. I swear. He tries to leave me, I'll drink iodine." Her voice was muffled, her mouth pressed against her arms.

Mary came over. She stroked Gracie's head, combed through her sister's hair with her fingertips. "Don't you worry about nothing" she crooned. "In the meantime, Helen'll ask around, see what she can find out. But I know men. Frankie's full of shit. He's got it too good. You're the one should get out more."

"Yeah," Anona said. "Always home, taking care of him. You were made to order for him."

Gracie lifted her head. "That's what his mother always says. 'You were made to order for my Frankie.' What a nerve!"

"I wouldn't live two minutes with your husband," Anona said. "Not for all the tea in California."

"China, Anona, all the tea in China."

"Not all that tea, either."

Mary took Gracie by the shoulders and made her look up. She didn't want to just baby Gracie. She wanted to make her feel strong and protected and confident. "Now forget everything," she told her. "You got nothing to worry about. We're all here. And I don't want to hear you talk crazy. Kill yourself? Over that horse's ass? You got better things to do. You got Charlie."

Helen lit a cigarette and put it between Gracie's lips. "And you got us," she said. Mary got the rock glasses and a bottle of twenty-five-year-old scotch from the case Nick had brought over last week. And Anona shuffled the cards. But Gracie knew she couldn't just keep coming here, running home to Anona, waiting for Frankie to come crying for her and bring her back to Spring Street.

She thought about how he'd carry her suitcase up the stairs and tell her how sorry he was and how he couldn't live without her. He'd reduce her to that girl all those years ago at the rooftop dance, the girl pressed against the wall in the dark by the river. But then he'd be off, to work, or to God knows where and she'd be back to the reality that Frankie was all the things Anona and her sisters said he was.

And if she waited him out? He'd calm down, like Mary said. She knew he would. But Gracie didn't know if she wanted to wait thirty years to have her husband by her side, shadowing her every move. She wanted some good times now. The women downtown, her neighbors in the building on Spring Street, they were ready to sit out their lives on park benches and kitchen chairs. Their men came home at night eventually and that was good enough for them. They reveled in their virtue, even if it was false and the most important thing was appearances. If no one knew about it, you could do anything. You couldn't sit in a bar, but you could hide your wine in the piano like Rubina Micaletti, the clink of the keys alerting the whole fourth floor of 196 Spring Street in the afternoons when the doors were open. But this hidden life of women was news to Gracie, and try as she might, the ways of Hell's Kitchen were the ways she was used to. The life wasn't any easier for the Irish, but they knew how to have a good time with and without their men. Sometimes she thought of her marriage to Frankie as a moment of madness that had put her into a long sleep. Things were going to change, she decided. She didn't know when, or how, but she wasn't going to twiddle her thumbs waiting for him to get old and fat.

1929

HERBERT HOOVER BECOMES 31st PRESIDENT OF THE UNITED STATES

STALIN UNDISPUTED DICTATOR OF THE SOVIET UNION

NIKOLAI BUKHARIN EXPELLED FROM THE COMMUNIST PARTY

Two Dead in a Hail of Bullets at Broadway's Hotsy Totsy Club

Jack "Legs" Diamond Sought for Questioning

Chapter Six

Helen was twelve when she started hanging around Buck O'Brian's clubhouse. She was a scrawny thing, hair tied up in a knot under a pea cap, a "tough," always with the boys, even dressed like a boy in knickers and argyle knee socks, so Buck O'Brian himself didn't know she was a girl. Mulligan knew because he had seen her in church those Sundays his wife made him go despite what he did for a living. Some of the other guys knew, too, and they figured Buck knew because common knowledge was that Buck knew everything.

Helen went to the club and asked to be a lookout. The country was deep in Prohibition, it being 1929, and the West Side belonged to Owney Madden and Dutch Schultz, and Buck O'Brian serving booze like he did was against the law and so was the crap game that went on in the back. When Buck didn't boot Helen's ass right out the swinging doors, Buck's crew figured he was just having fun, playing her like a fiddle, so to speak, until they heard him tell her to come back the next day for a tryout, which was when they figured that Buck didn't know that this kid he was hiring to be lookout was a she. No one said a word.

Except Johnny McGuire, who jumped up and started hollering his lungs out that he wasn't working lookout with no girl. It got quiet again, dead quiet. Everybody watched Buck, until Helen knocked Johnny McGuire down, ripped the shirt half off his skinny back and sank her teeth deep into his shoulder. Then everybody watched Helen.

Buck got off the bar stool and he put his big hands, the fingers like pork sausages, around Helen's waist and lifted her right up and sat her on the bar, where she dangled her legs, her hands on the rim of the bar, shreds of Johnny McGuire caught under her nails. Buck's lip was pulled up, one incisor showing, sharp and pointed, and he looked around at his gang and snarled down at Johnny McGuire, who was only twelve himself and trying not to cry, sawdust stuck in his eyelashes where Helen had pushed his face into the floor, the imprint of Helen's teeth a perfect bloody red circle on his bone-white skin.

"Can't you see she ain't no ordinary girl?" Buck O'Brian said. "How you gonna get anywheres in this world if you can't tell one thing from the other?" And he boxed Johnny McGuire's ears with those big hands of his, caught Johnny McGuire's head right between his hands, one hand for each ear, so that it seemed Johnny would fall over when Buck took his hands away. But Johnny didn't. He just took off his cap and wiped his hand across his forehead, marking it with a smear of dirt, and then he slunk off mumbling.

Buck didn't care what people said under their breath. If he couldn't hear it, it wasn't meant for him. It was a good policy or else he'd have been killing people all week long instead of only when he had to.

So Buck asked Helen what he could do for her and she told him how she lived with her granny and her sisters, Mary and Gracie, their father coming home from the docks one night with a headache and dead the next morning and their mother the same. Helen wiped her eye like there was a tear there and Buck O'Brian did, too, and she told him she wanted to work for him to help out the family and she'd been watching for a while now, and them boys? She told him lotsa times they weren't really paying attention like they should. Buck wouldn't be sorry if he gave her a chance; she'd show him just how good a lookout a girl could be.

Buck O'Brian must have got a kick out of her because when she left the bar she was in his employ and he told her to bring her sisters along if they were anything like her.

So when the cops almost got her and Mary, too, it shouldn't have been a big surprise, except that Anona didn't know any of it was going on.

That time the cops came, Gracie was sitting near the window writing in a notebook, the pencil straight up, tearing into the blue-lined paper, when Helen smashed through the door, Mary right behind her. The two of them ran into the narrow bedroom off the kitchen and before either Anona or Gracie could move, before they had time to go in that bedroom and ask what was going on, there were shouts in the hallway and heavy footsteps on the stairs, and Anona slammed closed the door and stood there, her back against it, holding it shut with her weight.

The cops were outside, hollering and banging on the door, but Anona just leaned against that door until she could feel them pushing hard from the other side and then she stepped back and told them to move away so she could open up and she did, because she said later, God knew how long it would take to get another door if they broke this one down.

The first in was O'Leary. His big flushed face was a fixture in the neighborhood. It was almost purple now, like an eggplant, from running up all those steps. He was breathing too hard to say anything, but took a step sideways to let in his partner, Reilly. Tom O'Leary and Dick Reilly, big pink Irish cops, who could break open your head with a billy club if they told you to move on and you didn't.

Anona offered them something to drink but Reilly said for her to quit fiddling, they wanted those little pissers that had run in here not a minute ago.

Anona folded her arms. "Where? Who?" she said. "I don't see nobody."

O'Leary poked Reilly. He took a step closer to Anona. "Listen, lady, with all due respect, two boys just run in here, street rats, they was, hanging outside Buck O'Brian's. They was up to no good and we're taking them in."

Anona shrugged. She pulled her gray knit shawl tight around her shoulders. She reached in her pocket, took out a lace handkerchief with her initials embroidered in dark blue thread and blew her nose.

"Well, we'll just take a look around anyway," O'Leary said. "If them buggers is here, we'll find 'em." He nodded toward Reilly. "Let's move it. They'll be out the window while we stand here shooting the bull."

Reilly tousled Gracie's hair as he moved past, following O'Leary into the bedroom. Helen and Mary were in the bed, covers pulled up to their chins, and when they saw the cops, they started screaming, shrill little-girl screams like knives drawn across dinner plates. O'Leary fell back, one heavy black shoe digging into Reilly's instep, which made Reilly punch him in the shoulder because it must have hurt.

Anona shook her head. "Huh," she said and sat down heavy in her rocker. Helen and Mary screamed some more from inside the bedroom. Gracie got up and rushed inside to join them, to get into the big bed with them and scream, too. All three of them would scream together all the time just for fun, even though Anona would get mad. She said they'd break her eardrums and ruin their voices and besides, she'd tell them, in a variation on her favorite theme: "It's not ladylike unless you're getting killed."

The three of them came out of the bedroom holding hands. Mary had put Gracie in the middle. "My granddaughters," Anona said. "They look like boys to you? *Poverine* . . . scared almost dead."

Helen stared straight at O'Leary. "We ain't scared," she said. She and Mary stood there, angelic in the long gowns that Anona had made for them from scraps of bedsheets.

"Yeah, it'd take more than them to scare us."

"You shut up," Anona said.

O'Leary went back into the bedroom, poked at the blankets rumpled in the middle of the bed with his nightstick and picked up the bedclothes that hung over the edge so he could look underneath the bed. If he had pulled back the blankets, he would have found the pea caps but he hadn't, so he came back outside defeated. "Devils must of got away," he said to Reilly. "I could of swore they come in here. Must have jumped right out the window."

There was no window in that bedroom, which was hardly even a room, and Helen gave each of her sisters a furious look in case they thought they would be smart and mention it.

The cops walked out, Reilly mumbling to O'Leary. "Demons, they are," they could hear him saying. "One minute they're there, the next . . ."

"Little bastards. I know they was in there. Next time I'll hold on so tight, I'll break the little bugger's arm off before he gets away." Reilly clutched at his hand, which was starting to swell where Helen had bit almost completely through the web of skin between his thumb and forefinger, which is how they got away in the first place.

"You'd better get that looked at," O'Leary said. "Make sure you ain't got no rabies."

• • •

When the cops' voices and footsteps had faded, Anona came after Helen and Mary. She lunged, pulling an ear, twisting a curl. She spat out a deluge of curses in her mysterious southern dialect from a town so small it was never on a map. A place she said, where people didn't go, they only left.

"Jackals should eat you, you should die like a dog."

Mary kept her head down but Helen spun around the room until finally, taking hold of Mary's arm, she pulled her out the door and yelled, her feet already on the stairs, "I love you, Anona. You did real good."

Anona went to the window and Gracie came over to stand beside her. They watched Helen and Mary run down the street peeling off their long white gowns. They ran so fast, they blurred.

Anona dug her fingers into Gracie's shoulder. "You're the one," she said. "Quiet. Good in school." Anona yanked Gracie's hair when she didn't look up.

"I'm not so good in school," Gracie said. She wanted to be like her sisters. She wished she'd run out the door with them, that they had pulled her along.

"It's enough you're in there."

Gracie dropped her pencil. The cat jumped down from the shelf over the stove and batted the pencil across the room. It disappeared in the space between the baseboard and the wall where the mice left droppings the size of beans. "Get it out," Anona said. "Money don't grow on trees."

Gracie kicked off a shoe. "The teachers give them to us. We don't have to pay," she told Anona, who grabbed her hair, pulling her halfway off the chair. "We always pay," she said. "Don't forget it." Gracie picked up the notebook that had fallen on the floor. She got down on her hands and knees and retrieved the pencil.

"You're a good girl, Gracie," Anona said, smoothing her hair, "not like those other two."

It made Gracie think of what Helen always said. "Who cares about good. I'm not waiting for heaven to get my crown." Like in the summer, when Hell's Kitchen would blister. Kids would fight for a place to sleep on the fire escapes because it was hard to breathe inside. The Irish families were the size of platoons, with every kid that could walk carrying another. You could die from lack of air in those tenements in summer.

Anona complained that it wasn't ladylike to sleep outside like that but Helen would stand up to her and hand out the pillows and the sheets to her sisters through the window. "It's hot like hell," she'd tell Anona. "What's ladylike got to do with it?" and Anona would give in because she knew when it wasn't worth the fight and maybe she was glad of the big bed to herself, not having to open up the *brande* in the kitchen. Helen told Mary and Gracie that Anona'd be right out on the fire escape with them if she could get through the window.

Then they'd get themselves settled and be off to dreamland until Hanley's closed. There was a bar on every corner in Hell's Kitchen and during Prohibition every bar became a speakeasy. Hanley's was the one under their building. It was the one where their neighbors went to drink. The easiest one to crawl home from, Anona said.

Sometimes they'd wake to singing, more often to thuds and shouts. The worst was when Ed Brady on the floor above would forget and pee out the front window instead of the back. "Just what you deserve," Anona would shout out to them, "for sleeping outside like bums with no bed." And then they would listen to Anona talking to St. Rita about what a lady Emma had been and how she didn't know where these girls had come from and they'd watch her spit on her fingers and rub the head of St. Rita's statue until it glistened.

In the mornings, there might be a body or two passed out on the stoop and the sisters would scramble over them on the way to school. Mickey Finn was glad when one was his dad so he could go through his pockets and maybe pick up some loose change.

In the winter, they would all huddle together and Anona would tell them stories, teach them wisdoms while they sat at the end of the bed in their nightgowns holding on to her feet. Anona was everything they had. She would hold them tight in the circle of her arms, all three of them, and tell them how she was one woman who never longed for sons. She had dreamed them, she said, had made promises to her saint to send Emma girls. To her mind, men were horses. "Get yourself a good one and hope he don't die too young," she always told them.

No matter, they were a house without men. Anona would whisper to them as they fell asleep. You're strong, she would say, and there's three of you. And she would kiss each of their fingers and each of their toes, sixty kisses. By the time she was finished they would be asleep.

Anona never said it straight out, about how she had loved Emma, but they knew from the way Anona talked about her all the time. But Emma wasn't real to them. She was a fairy princess, alive in Anona's imagination. There weren't stories that put her in the world and no sign of her anywhere, not a picture, only Anona's admonitions. "Too good for this world," she would say. They were always hearing how beautiful their mother had been, how refined, and how they were nothing like her. "She would have wanted you to be *signorine*," Anona would tell them, "and look at you." Anona would tug Helen's hair, wipe Gracie's nose, chase Mary with a pot.

"Ladies," Helen would sneer. "It's bad enough we're girls."

Helen, especially, made Anona crazy. Mary was tough but Helen was flint. She'd swim naked off the pier with the boys and hitch rides on the sides of the trains that tore down Eleventh Avenue from Sixtieth Street to the Thirtieth Street yards, where so many kids lost limbs and lives they called it Death Avenue. Helen even talked about joining the Tenth Avenue Cowboys, affectionately known as the "dummy boys," whose job was to gallop on horseback down the train tracks waving a lantern at night and a flag in the day to warn people walking that a train was close behind. All the kids loved the dummy boys; they were the neighborhood heroes. Every girl wanted to date one; only Helen wanted to be one. "As soon as I grow enough so's my feet reach the stirrups," she told Anona, who would either pray or curse, but always under her breath.

Tough was not all bad, no? Anona would ask the statue of St. Rita. Spunk could get you through rough times, she would explain to the saint. Later Anona would take it all back and shout that she should have kept them in the house, away from the windows, like the Sicilians did, their chairs facing inside, away from the street.

But this was a new country and this was an Irish neighborhood. The Irish girls weren't locked away. They didn't sit home and do homework around the kitchen table. They worked outside in steam laundries and factories making candy and gum and twine and soap and who could blame them for taking a drink or hanging out in a dark hallway with some boyfriend talking soft in their ear? Anona said they were all fast. Tomatoes, she called them, nothing like the Italian girls who lived with their families on Thirty-ninth Street and went straight home after work and never got near a boy without the father's say-so. "In Sicily," Anona said, "a girl could only see her *fidanzato* from a balcony. He'd get a stiff neck looking up at her so many hours."

"You're not from Sicily," Mary would say.

"I hear things," Anona explained, raising her eyebrows and blinking once.

There hadn't been any men in the Mallone house for as long as the girls could remember, and Anona had learned to enjoy a drink or two in Hanley's Bar under the house, rather than alone in her kitchen, and when Prohibition came, they knew to let her in when they saw her face through the slit in the door. And the Mallones didn't live on Thirty-ninth Street, and besides, Anona never stopped telling them that they always had a place to come home to, man or no man. They should never forget that they could always come right back to her. She was never going anyplace. She'd always be right here, waiting in the woods, like a wolf, like the Mother of Rome.

Anona would tell them about Nonno, who was four times her size and how, right after she came over on the boat, he raised his hand to her. The nerve, she'd say, remembering, and she'd lift up her arm high with her hand open to show them just how he had done it.

They'd move closer to her when she told the story. "And then what? What'd you do? What?" they'd ask her.

"I waited for him to fall asleep."

"And?"

"I took the broom handle . . . Pow! Right on the head." The sisters loved to hear the story. Anona would tell it to them over and over, like she told all her stories. Helen would clap. Mary would jump up and down, and Gracie? Gracie would feel a little bad for Nonno, not knowing what hit him like that. "Pow!" Anona would say again. "Right here." And she'd poke between her eyes with a finger. She'd pause then, take a breath. "When he opened his eyes, I was sitting in this chair. The next time," I told him, "I put a stake through your heart."

"Just like that? You told him just like that?"

"What'd I say? You got potatoes in your ears?"

"How come," Helen said, "Mrs. MacLaughlin don't do that when her husband gives her them smacks?"

Anona made a face. Her upper lip curled in disgust. "A stupid," she'd said. "Not like me. Not like you." And then she'd pull them close, smothering them, until they cried out that they couldn't breathe, their mouths open like fish, buried in the softness of her. "Nonno learned his lesson," she'd say, releasing them, tumbling them into the sheets she had washed in the sink and hung to dry on the roof. "You gotta make them know what they can do and what they can't. You gotta let them know right from the start."

The Mallone sisters never knew their grandfather. The fever took him, the one that had taken their father and Emma and the baby boy, but Mary said it could be Anona had knocked him off, realizing early on that she didn't need a man.

Helen agreed. "We're born man-killers," she liked to say. "We get it from the old lady."

The night Helen didn't come home was a night so cold the mop in the kitchen froze solid and Mary and Gracie wet the bed because it was just too cold to get up and pee in the pot.

"Where is she?" Anona kept saying, slicing the bread, banging the plates. "She was in school today?" she asked Gracie.

Gracie shrugged. "We're not in the same class. I don't see her all the time." Mary said nothing, stringing tags, the homework they all did for a few extra pennies, ten cents a hundred.

"Where could she be?" Anona kept saying. She wouldn't stop until Mary said maybe she had gone with the boys to Twenty-third Street, to where the coal barges were tied up, where Helen would climb up on the barges with the most daring of the boys when the watchman wasn't looking and throw down chunks of coal that broke apart and all the kids waiting on the pier would scramble to pick up the pieces and run away.

But Mary knew that Helen was at Buck O'Brian's clubhouse. It hadn't worked out for Mary. She didn't like standing around, hiding her hair under a greasy borrowed pea cap, looking like a boy. She'd gotten herself a factory job and that was that. And the two of them had not even considered bringing Gracie, who was so far under Anona's skirts that she might have given the game away. But Helen? Helen officially stayed in school and played hooky and worked lookout and ice-skated on the river when she couldn't swim in it. If a truant officer spotted her, she'd head for the roofs, where no one could get her. She knew her way around up there and she loved a chase.

Anona said they wouldn't eat until Helen was home. It got later and later and finally Anona sent Mary downstairs to Hanley's to see what she could find out. Mary was gone for what seemed like forever and when she came back, Anona was pacing and the apartment was dark and smelled funny. There was a pot of something evil brewing on the stove and a line of candles lit in front of St. Rita.

"What? What?" Anona said, when she saw Mary at the door.

"They pinched her," Mary said. "They raided Buck O'Brian's and the cops got her, took her away." Gracie started to cry. She was sitting with the cat in her lap and it jumped down when she started to shriek. "Shush," Mary said. "It's no big deal."

"Whatta you talking about, no big deal? Why her?" Anona stood still in the middle of the floor.

Mary shrugged. "They picked up everybody."

"They took Helen? She's a little girl . . . a baby!"

"They don't think she's no baby," Mary said.

"Whatta you mean? Whatta we gonna do?"

"She's okay, Anona. I saw her. I stood on the rail outside the police station and I could see her in there. Helen was fine. They was feeding her candy."

"You saw her? You sure?"

"I told you I did. That red hair of hers was sticking up all over."

"And then what?"

"I went inside to find out what was going on and the sergeant started asking me questions and I got scared and then he called out to them in the back. 'I got another one out here,' and I turned around and ran away."

"Who scared you? Who?" Anona wanted to know.

"The cop at the front desk. He said we was neglected and belonged in a home or maybe better yet a reformatory, and when I ran away, I fell down the steps. Look at my hand."

"*Porca miseria,*" Anona said, and she broke an egg and separated the yolk from the white. She beat the white in a dish and dipped twine in it and wound it around Mary's wrist to make a cast and then she beat the yolk with sugar and gave it to Mary to drink.

They ate that night without talking except for Anona, who mumbled and groaned and cursed under her breath. Mary and Gracie cleaned the table around her. She sent them to bed and she sat at the table with a glass of espresso, sugar crusted around the rim, and a jug of homemade wine, talking, praying to St. Rita, the plaster saint she had carried with her from Bocca al Lupo.

Chiunque mi ha dato il mal'occhio!
Me lo porta via!

Whoever gave me the evil eye!
Carry it away!

She whispered these words in the dark.

Anona sat at the table all night and with the first sign of light she shook Mary and Gracie to tell them Helen wasn't home and then she made them get dressed. "Get going," she told them. Gracie sat up, rubbed her eyes with her fists.

"Where?" she said.

"Spoustade," Anona said, banging the heel of her hand against her head. "Your sister . . . you forgot your sister?" Mary climbed over Gracie and got out of bed. The floor was cold and she sat back down on the edge of the bed, pulling her legs under her, rubbing her toes with her hands. Anona turned away. "Hurry up," she said, and went to get her shawl off the back of the chair. She didn't have a coat, just a wool shawl, sometimes two, and layers of skirts. Gracie always thought about this, years later, when Frankie took her to buy a coat, a gift for her birthday, a beautiful coat with a fur collar and cuffs, how when they had gone to find Helen, Anona had only been wearing a shawl, a gray knitted shawl with silver threads. How Anona had never had a coat.

Gracie was scared now. Anona didn't go anywhere unless it was serious, like the time she went to the principal's office at St. Michael's when Sister Marie Clare had branded her a thief, but Mary told her to button her lip because it was better than going to school and sure as hell better than the factory. Anona pushed them both out the door as soon as they had pulled on their clothes and they were halfway down the stairs before it slammed shut behind them.

• • •

Mary, always the mother, took Gracie's hand when they went up the steps of the West Thirtieth Street station house and held it the whole time they were inside. "We're here to get our sister, Helen Mallone," Mary told the cop behind the desk. "This here's our granny." Anona stood behind them, arms folded, forehead wrinkled. She wasn't afraid but she was unsure about her English. What did she send her granddaughters to school for if not for moments like this? For when they had to stand up for themselves and speak good English?

The desk sergeant's name was Connors. His eyes were tiny and blue, buried in the flesh of his face. He looked in his ledger, following his thumb down the page of names. Mary leaned over the desk, watching the sergeant search his book.

"Mallone? Redheaded kid? Coulda fooled us when all that hair came falling outta that hat. We never took her for a girl."

"That's her, yeah, Mallone. Where is she? Why didn't they send her home. She's just a kid."

"Ha! Vincent Coll was just a kid, too, but lemme check. Hang on." He went into the back of the station house, heaving himself from his chair. Gracie wanted to go sit down on the bench against the wall but Anona glared and Mary yanked her arm and told her to stand up straight. They wanted to get the information and get out, she told Gracie. There were sounds and smells in this place they didn't want to know about. She put her mouth next to Gracie's ear. They call it "the slaughterhouse," she said. "Why d'you think they call it that?"

Sergeant Connors came back and stood behind the desk. "Social Services took her," he said. "They brought her over to the old precinct house, on West Thirty-seventh. It's where they take care of the welfare cases."

"But she's got *us*," Mary told him. "She don't need no Social Services. We live with our granny here," and Mary pointed to Anona. "She takes good care of us. She raised us since we're babies."

Another cop came up to the desk. He was bigger than Sergeant Connors. They all looked like mountains to Gracie, who wondered if more and more of them would come out of the back rooms, each one bigger than the one before. "These are the kids, Mike, asking about Helen Mallone. And this here's the grandmother. They don't seem to have nobody else."

Officer Mike Malachy took his time looking them over. "The kid we had here last night wouldn't say nothing to us about nothing. Then when she wouldn't tell the lady from Social Services nothing neither, they took her. We couldn't put her out in the street, a little girl like that, now could we? Even if that's where she belongs."

"Not for nothin', girlies," Sergeant Connors said to Mary and Gracie, "but what's your sister doing hangin' around a joint like Buck O'Brian's anyway? We nearly fell over when we saw she was a girl."

"I don't know," Mary told him. "She was probably just taking a walk."

Officer Malachy shook his head, bit off a piece of fingernail he'd been worrying while Connors was talking.

"Well, we gotta get her," Mary said. "Our granny here's half-crazy. She's been calling out the window all night. We've got to get our sister and take her home."

Connors looked up. "She don't seem crazy to me. Don't she talk?"

"Sometimes."

Anona unfolded her arms and crossed them over her chest. She held on to herself, her hands clutching her shoulders, and she closed her eyes and started moaning. It was a high-pitched wail, a sound that she had brought with her from the other side, a legacy of her origins, reserved for death and times of terror. She rocked on her feet. Gracie ran over to her and held on to her skirt. "Do something," she said to the policemen. "You gotta find our sister, I'm telling you." Connors came from behind the desk to get Anona a chair. His eyes were wide, more white than blue. Anona's voice pitched higher. Connors had the chair behind her but was frozen in place. Anona swayed.

"Listen, kids," Malachy said. "She can't come to no harm with Social Services. Tell your granny that. You come back in a few days. We'll find out where she is."

"*No.*" Mary stood with her feet apart, her arms flailing. "We've got to get her back now. And we're not leaving until you tell us where she is."

Connors was losing patience. He'd been here all night. The last thing he needed was some nutty old woman and two urchins ending his shift. Malachy was scared, he could tell. He believed in the fairies and he didn't like this old woman making sounds like the souls burning in purgatory. Connors could feel the hairs on the back of his neck standing up.

"Get out of here," he said, "and take your granny with you. Get out. That's all I'm gonna say. One more minute, I'm calling the truant officer and you'll be up the river same as your sister!"

"She don't go to school," Gracie said, pointing at Mary, who turned on her heel, took hold of Gracie's arm and pulled her and Anona out of there. Anona's eyes had been closed; she had transported herself with her litany and finding herself on the precinct steps confused her. "*Che fa . . . ?*" she said aloud, standing her ground, but Mary kept going, dragging Gracie all the way down the steps until Gracie thought her arm was out of its socket.

"C'mon, Anona," Mary said. "They ain't gonna help us here. We're in hot water and we're gonna get ourselves out. And you, Gracie, for Chrissakes . . . Don't you know enough to shut your trap? Did that cop ask you about school?"

"No."

"Then you shoulda shut up."

"*Appunto* . . ." Anona said out loud but to herself. She was still somewhere else, somewhere on the other side. "Never tell nothing. Listen to your sister." She nodded her head.

"But you don't have to go to school. I wanted him to know you ain't no kid so maybe he'd listen to us."

"Who knows if I'm supposed to be in school? I ain't taking no chances." Mary'd been picked up once for truancy and she told Gracie that you didn't ever want to go to them places where they sent you. They mixed everybody together, orphans and truants with murderers and thieves and they treated everybody bad.

"So now what?" Gracie asked.

"Let me think," Mary said.

"We're never gonna find Helen, and I'm hungry."

"Let's get Anona home, and see what we can come up with."

Mary took Gracie around to the factory on the corner and bought her a whole bag of candy broke in pieces, all different colors, and they sat down on a stoop, Gracie eating and Mary thinking. Gracie's dress pulled up in back and she could feel the cement cold against the backs of her legs where her woolen stockings were torn. "You ready to go?" Mary asked her. "I got an idea."

And Mary took Gracie's arm and they walked over to Buck O'Brian's and right through the swinging doors. It was dark inside and it stank of beer and tobacco and sweat and Gracie put a handful of candy in her mouth, so she would be sure to keep her mouth shut like Mary said.

"I'm looking for Buck O'Brian," Mary told a guy sitting on the bar stool nearest the door.

"Scram, kid."

"I'll call the cops," Mary said. "We got friends in the precinct house, me and my sisters. Sergeant Connors and Officer Malachy, Mike we call him. I'll tell him how you dragged us in here off the street on our way to school. I'll tell them all kinds of things you done and we seen."

The guy slid off the bar stool and Gracie started to wet her pants. "What's going on?" somebody called out. It was Buck O'Brian and he called Mary over and Gracie followed, still holding her sister's arm, and Buck O'Brian listened to Mary's story because he had a soft spot for cheeky girls but when she told him he had to help them get Helen, he said they were out of luck.

"But she was working for you."

"Listen, sweetheart, I'm sorry about your sister. I liked her, but them's the breaks. And hey," he laughed, "she ain't sitting in no jail cell. They probably got her somewheres with three squares a day, which ain't bad."

The other men in the bar laughed with Buck. If Buck laughed, something must be funny.

"She's only twelve," Mary said.

Buck O'Brian raised his eyebrows. "My old lady was twelve when she had me."

Mary spat on the floor at Buck's feet. One of his stooges came toward her but Buck held out his arm and smiled. He moved the matchstick in his mouth from one side to the other. Gracie stood there, frozen, until Mary pulled at her. Mary yanked her so hard that Gracie dropped the bag of candy, and when she tried to reach down to get it, Mary stepped up and kicked it so the pieces went flying everywhere.

"Forget it," Mary said. "If it's been in here, you don't wanna touch it no more," and she dragged Gracie through the swinging doors and out into the sunlight.

"Those bastards!" Mary said when they got outside. Her heart was pounding, her whole body shivering with rage. She only calmed down when she saw how afraid Gracie was. She put an arm around her shoulder and pulled her close. There was no sense the both of them being afraid. "How you supposed to tell the good guys from the bad when they're all the same?" she said to Gracie.

"Anona says all men are bad until you teach them different."

"Yeah, hit them on the head when they're sleeping."

"Well, it worked, didn't it?"

Mary made a face and called Gracie a dumb cluck but Gracie was too cold and still hungry and had to take a piss so she was in no mood to pick a fight. "Now what are we gonna do?"

"Shhh . . ." Mary took out a half-smoked cigarette, straightened it as best she could, and lit it with a wooden match she scraped against the concrete.

"You smoke?"

"Oh, Gracie. A girl's got to have some fun." Mary put her face right next to her sister's. "When you work in a goddamn factory twelve hours and your back hurts and your feet hurt and your head's filled up with the stinking smell of that filthy candy boiling in those goddamn vats, you got to have some fun or life just ain't worth living."

Gracie took the cigarette end from between Mary's lips and puffed. She swallowed the smoke and forced herself not to cough.

Mary and Gracie had left Anona on the stoop and she had

gone upstairs to rock in her chair and brew a tea over which she said an ancient incantation willing away the evil eye.

> *In nome del cielo!*
> *Delle stelle e della Luna!*
> *Mi Levo questo mal'occhio*
> *Per mia maggior fortuna!*
>
> *In the name of the sky!*
> *And of the stars and moon!*
> *May this evil eye change*
> *to good fortune!*

She was out the window waiting and when she saw Mary and Gracie coming up the street and when she didn't see Helen, she leaned out so far and yelled so loud, there was a head in every window on the block. Mary told her what had happened and Anona went off by herself to speak to her saint. She told St. Rita this would be the end of her. How much more could she take? "Send her back," she told her saint, "or things will never be the same between us." Anona said there was a time to beg and a time to threaten. With the saints it was a fine line.

Anona lit three extra candles, then wiped her face and set the table. The three of them ate bread with oil and salt for supper and didn't talk at all. Mary got up to clear the dishes and said she was going out.

Then Anona started and didn't stop. *Puttane* went out alone at night, not her granddaughter. She kept shouting while Mary got dressed. But when she knew she had lost the fight, when Mary was putting the final finger waves into her hair, Anona pointed a finger at Gracie. "You . . . you do your schoolwork so you don't end up like the other two."

And Gracie knew she meant Helen, who was gone, and Mary, who was going out into the dead of night to God knew where.

Mary bent over to kiss Anona but the old lady pulled away, rocking in her chair, mumbling under her breath.

"Uh, oh," Mary said to Gracie. "Take a good look. If those curses work, you'll never see me again." Mary blew her sister a kiss and was out the door, leaving the room filled with the scent of cheap perfume that made Anona cough.

Gracie started to cry. It was night and she was alone with Anona, who was wheezing in the corner and she imagined the rest of her life in this miserable dank apartment with the porcelain piss pot under the bed, she and Anona sleeping together until that morning Gracie would find her dead and be lying next to her, too scared to move.

"Be quiet," Anona said. "You, too, you make me crazy."

Gracie could never forget that night. She thought of her two sisters: Helen, brazen and fierce, coiled tight as a bedspring, her idol, and Mary, tough and protective, yet soft, like a mother to her. Her sisters, who kept her safe, whom she always imagined next to her, one on either side, were gone.

Chapter Seven

The days dawned. Helen was gone, Mary missing since that night she left smelling like sin. If Gracie had learned one thing in her short life, it was that the world moved you forward no matter what you did. The good and the bad things that happened might slow you down but they didn't stop you unless you died.

Anona kept Gracie home. Suddenly Anona didn't care about her going to school, only that she was inside the apartment, safe, near. When Gracie complained, Anona threatened to tie her to a chair if she even went by the door. She sat Gracie by the window and gave her boxes of tags and pieces of string to pull through them to keep her busy while she prayed to the statue of St. Rita, whose hands were rubbed clean of color from where Anona held them when she asked for things. Anona's arrogance with the saint after Helen had disappeared softened once Mary was gone. They were best friends again. And while she prayed for the return of her girls, she asked for plagues to rain down upon the powers that held them.

"How can you do that?" Gracie asked her.

"Do what?"

"Ask the saint to do those terrible things. How can you ask a saint to do that?"

"Saints can do anything."

"Hurt people?"

"Why not? If it's your saint, and you ask her, she should do it, no? If you're good to the saint and you want a little favor, you should get it, no?"

"But Anona, you're asking the saint to do bad things."

"Who says they're bad?"

"Tying people's intestines in knots? Scooping out their eyes?"

"I only ask her to do that to my enemies. What am I supposed to do? Wish them good luck?"

"Never mind."

"What do those nuns teach you anyway?"

"I told you to let me quit and go work with Mary. She said she could get me a job in the candy factory."

Anona coughed, hard enough to bring up blood, and then she spat into her handkerchief with a very loud noise. "Who?" she said. "Where?" She took hold of Gracie's arm and pinched it until her skin was pink and mottled.

"Mary . . . the candy factory," Gracie said. She rubbed her arm, which was beginning to welt. "Mary said she'd get me a job with her in the candy factory."

"You're more *stunade* than you look. You don't have the brains God gave you. Go to sleep. Leave me alone."

Gracie got undressed in the corner near the stove and snuggled down far into the bed that they all had shared. Anona had her own bed, a fold-up one covered with a fabric case that stood in a corner of the kitchen, but now she slept in the bed with Gracie, who covered her head with the blanket and talked and talked even though Anona told her to shut up because Gracie didn't want to think about Anona dying and waking up next to her dead. Gracie never closed her eyes anymore but lay in bed until she was so tired that she fell asleep despite herself, and every morning, she breathed a sigh of relief when she saw that Anona was already out of bed and another night had passed.

Breakfast was bread and coffee with hot milk and Anona would beat an egg yolk into Gracie's bowl and the two of them would sit and wait for Mary and Helen to come home, Anona with her arms out the window, smoking her pipe while the women sat talking on the stoops below, their conversation drifting up to her. She would pay very close attention to their gossip while all the while pretending not to pay any attention at all, just puffing on the hand-carved pipe that had been Nonno's before he died. Anona always said later that hell froze over the night Mary left, the night she met Nick Andersen.

The night Mary came looking for someone to help, someone who could get things done, who could find Helen and bring her back, Nick Andersen was in the back room of the Silver Dot Club, drinking imported scotch whiskey from a crystal glass. Mary knocked on the door. She opened it before anyone said "come in."

The glass and ice splintered on the floor; scotch spilled everywhere. Nick was on his feet, his gun out and cocked before he saw it was a woman. He relaxed but held the gun steady. Nick Andersen was a cautious man.

Mary took a step closer, ignoring the gun in his hand. He could have been holding a flower out to her for how concerned she seemed. Nick took his stance, nervous now, puzzled, and he squinted at her in the dim light. She was just a girl, small and delicate and beautiful.

She stared into his face; she didn't look at his gun. Nick Andersen took a step backward. He started to sweat in great beads along his forehead and tried to loosen his collar before he crashed to the floor like a felled tree. It was the way Mary always told the story.

Nick would always think it was the beginnings of a fever, one that would have killed an ordinary man, that had taken the breath out of his diaphragm and knocked his knees out from under him, but Mary always said it was the sight of her standing there, perfect as a doll, her lips a red cupid's bow, her hair curled over her ears. Mary knew what got to young boys, she told Gracie later, and she figured grown men weren't much different.

Nick took up a lot of room on the floor. His skull had missed a table leg by not much and when he opened his eyes, Mary was over him, running her small cool hand across his brow and down over his flushed cheek.

"You okay, mister?" she said, pulling her hand away when he opened his eyes, suddenly being demure, and then standing back up straight on her legs, smoothing down her dress, running her hands from her bosom down to her waist as though she stood in front of a mirror, as though she were standing all alone watching herself.

For another moment, Nick closed his eyes. He wanted to call out, to open his mouth and fill his lungs with air and shout at her. Who was she? . . . and how could she . . . just walk in here?

Benny Squint was outside, pounding on the door. "Boss! Boss! You okay? What's goin' on in there?" If Benny Squint had been where he was supposed to be, outside Nick's door the way he was now, things would have turned out differently. Nick didn't answer right away. The door rattled on its hinges. Nick looked at Mary, saw her chest heave, her breath shallow. He wanted to see if she was afraid and what she would do. She stood there, watching him, her eyes half-closed, willing her breathing back to normal.

"It's nothin'," Nick shouted through the door. "Get lost." He looked at Mary again. She should be home, asleep, he thought, a blanket over her, pulled up, caught under her chin. He imagined her under a soft pink blanket, her flesh pink like the blanket, soft like the blanket, and he moaned and rolled over halfway on his side. He reached out a hand and caught her ankle, his palm covering her instep, the buttons of her boots cutting into his skin.

She didn't pull back the way he expected her to, the way he wanted her to. He wanted to scare her, to convince himself that it had been chance, not courage, that made her stand there unflinching, in the back room of the Silver Dot Club. His hand still holding her ankle, she leaned in very close. "Leggo," she said. She pushed at the side of Nick's head with one small hand and stood up. The fake gold ring with the cut-glass stone that she wore on her third finger left a thin bloody scratch on his temple. She shook his hand off her ankle.

Nick got up from the floor, conscious of his size. The bulk he had always been admired for suddenly made him uncomfortable. He sat down in the red velvet chair and poured himself a drink. He left her standing there and lifted the glass to his lips, watched her through the amber of twenty-five-year-old scotch.

"I ain't got all night," she finally said to him. "I'm looking for Owney Madden. This here's his club, ain't it? I need to talk to him. I need help."

"Well, I'm here, is all. You'll have to settle for me," and he drained his glass, set it down on the teakwood table whose leg had almost cracked open his skull and folded his arms across his chest.

She thought she would turn and leave and she wondered what he would do when she did that. Would he follow behind her, get up quick and catch her arm and pull her back into the room?

He thought about keeping her somewhere, like a songbird, closed in a room with silk wallpaper. He could see how smooth her skin was, how very young she was, too young. His head ached. He rubbed a hand over his face and when he looked up she was standing in front of him, legs apart, her hands hidden behind her back. He wondered what she was holding until he realized it was just a pose. "So, just what kind of a guy are you anyhow?" she said. She was thirteen years old. She didn't have a lot of patience for the game he was playing. "Listen, you gonna help me or what?"

"That depends on what you want. Come over here and tell me."

She sat down on a footstool next to his chair, told him to keep his hands to himself, and then gave him the story, all about her sisters and Anona and Helen gone missing, how she had to leave school and work in the candy factory because she was an orphan and even with all that it didn't hardly matter because a girl couldn't make a decent wage.

He touched her hair with one of his big hands and held her hand with the other and she let him. Outside were noises, scuffling, glass breaking, a bloody drunken brawl going on for sure, but he ignored it.

Mary was at some sad part of her story. It was all sad parts now and she started to cry. "So I gotta find Helen," she told him. "I gotta get her back." She smelled of cheap perfume, dime-store lavender. He thought about getting her some good stuff, French, the next time a boat docked, and he imagined her taking the opaque glass stopper from the crystal bottle and dabbing behind her ears and the pulse at her wrists, the soft creases of her arms and legs.

"Stop," he said. "We'll get your sister back in no time. Don't you cry." He knew it would be an easy enough thing for him to do, find some kid who had been taken out of Hell's Kitchen by the charities. A few questions to the right people was all it would take, and Nick knew all the right people.

He said he would take her home but Mary said no, she wasn't going back, not until she could walk back into Anona's holding Helen's hand, so he brought her to the suite of rooms he kept in the Broadway Central and left her there. It was still early for him, he told her. He had a long night in front of him.

For Mary, the suite in the Broadway Central was her dream come true. When Nick left, she stretched out to her full five feet in the porcelain tub that was big enough for her and both her sisters, wishing they were there with her. Mary soaked in that tub and thought about Helen and hoped Nick was right about getting her back. She didn't know if she could trust him, but she could take care of herself. If all she got out of this night was this bath, she'd still be ahead.

She fell asleep worrying about Helen even though Nick had

promised to get her back. Even though he had told her she could forget it, that it was as good as done.

In the early morning, she felt a weight in the bed next to her. She felt a hand up under the men's dress shirt she had worn to bed. It was a big hand, but it was slow and careful and she smelled liquor. Lips were at her ear, whispering, cajoling, kissing, licking. Nick was very drunk and she pulled herself out from under him and when he reached for her again, she pushed with both her arms and both her legs until he rolled off the bed and passed out on the floor where he fell.

Mary found Nick's money roll, and she peeled off five of the hundreds that folded in half, had made a magnificent bulge in his side pocket. She cut a small slit in the lining of her coat and slipped the bills inside. Freedom, she thought: a lot of rent, a lot of food and a lot of peace of mind. She figured her name was gone but she knew what that was worth. She preferred the worn bills and the greasy stain they left on her fingers. She took a pillow off the bed and curled up next to Big Nick Andersen on the floor.

Chapter Eight

Gracie didn't think any of them were ever coming back. Those two weeks felt longer than any time she could remember and the big kitchen with the coal stove and the wall of wooden and glass closets, where they kept their clothes and dishes, didn't feel safe anymore. The shrine of St. Rita took up almost all of the countertop with its burning candles, the *brande* folded in the corner, upholstery cover permanently fitted over the iron edges, stood like a New World shrine to the missing sisters.

Gracie begged Anona to let her go back to school, telling her the truant officer was gonna get her and then all of them would be gone. Anona put a broomstick near the door and said nobody was getting past; she'd beat the life out of them and throw the body in the alley. Gracie liked the idea of the truant officer dead in the alley but didn't know how they would get it there. Dead bodies were heavy, she told Anona. It took four men to carry out Kevin Nolan's father when he fell in the house and cracked his skull open. Kevin had told Gracie how he had tried to pick his father up, but he couldn't even move him. He was like a block of stone, just lying there in all that wet blood. Anona didn't want to hear about the weight of dead bodies. She just wanted to sit in the window and watch the street for her girls to come home.

When Mary did come home it was in a long black car. Anona called Gracie to the window to see this car and they were both hanging out the window, looking at it, the kids in the street climbing all over it, around it, rubbing their hands on it. Then this big man, taller than the Irish cop who stood on the corner and dressed in a suit and tie and coat and hat got out on the driver's side. He didn't even yell at the boys swarming around the car but gave them all nickels before he walked over and opened the other door and Mary stepped out. She was dressed in a fitted suit with a tight skirt and a fur collar and Anona started waving her arms, taking up the whole window, shoving Gracie behind her and leaning out so far that Gracie held on to the ties of Anona's apron, worried about her pitching out the window. Gracie saw her losing her balance and flying down past everybody's front windows, landing in the street, hitting with a great big thud, like the piano Anona'd bought one Christmas and paid all kinds of money to have hoisted up into the apartment.

Yelling curses and names, Anona banged her head on the window frame and fell back. Gracie took her chance and moved to the window and right away saw it was Mary and watched her go up the stoop and into the building before she turned and pulled her shirt up out of the waistband of her skirt and started fanning Anona.

Gracie was kneeling by Anona crying when Mary knocked on the door. "Christ," Mary said. "You call this a homecoming?" Gracie looked at her and Mary wrapped her arms around her sister and hugged and kissed her and rubbed her face in the fox collar that was dyed black and went all around Mary's neck and down the front of her suit.

"Anona's dead!" Gracie shouted into the fur, but Mary held her away.

"No, look," she said, pointing. "She's batting her eyes." Mary laughed and poked Gracie in the side. "You can't kill Anona; she's the devil," Mary said.

Mary got down on the floor and patted Anona's face and gave Gracie a handkerchief to wet but Gracie stood there staring instead. Anona's eyes did open and she sat up and started hitting Mary and screaming at her like she had out the window. Mary put her arms around Anona and hugged her tight and put her face against Anona's cheek and told her to be quiet, that she had Helen.

And over in the doorway, there was Helen, standing in front of the big man who had opened the car door. She walked in and Gracie threw herself at her and they circled in a mad dance, tripping around the room, falling on top of Anona, and then they were all crying and drooling and kissing and rubbing until Anona sat up and started hitting Mary and Gracie and even Helen, until Mary got back far enough out of Anona's reach and pulled her sisters with her. Anona lay spent in a heap on the floor and then she sat up.

Mary and Helen and Gracie knew that she couldn't get up by herself so they waited until the tall man went over to her and lifted her up in his arms, picked her up off the floor in a bear hug and left her standing on her feet, before he left through the open door.

"Who was that goon?" Anona said. She was shaking her head, her face flushed, and Mary came over and put an arm around her shoulder and made her sit in a chair.

"That's Nick Andersen." Mary's voice was hushed, like she was introducing Calvin Coolidge, the President of the United States. "He's the one got Helen back, and look, that's not all, look . . ." And she pulled her old coat out of the bag she had dropped on the floor and tore at the lining with her red fingernails, long and shaped into ovals. She dug inside and came out with hundred-dollar bills and held them under Anona's nose, let the bills drop into Anona's lap. "We got nothing to worry about for a long time."

Anona took the money and crumpled it with her fingers. "It's real?"

"It's real all right."

"So where'd you get it? From that *gagootz* you came in here with? He looks like a big dope to me." Anona's face was still flushed from when Nick lifted her up and swung her around like a girl.

Mary always said that he had swept Anona off her feet and it was true. They had all seen him do it.

"Yeah, that big dope runs Hell's Kitchen," Mary said. "Well, him and a coupla other mugs."

"He gave you the money?"

"Not exactly gave it to me, but he's got so much, Anona, he never even missed it. It's like candy wrappers, I swear."

"And what's he want with you?"

"He likes me."

"Huh."

"He got Helen back, didn't he?"

Helen and Gracie had been sitting on the edge of the rocking chair, holding each other. Gracie didn't want to let Helen go, even when Anona called out to her, her arms open. Anona never put down her arms until Helen went to her. "Where were you?" Anona said. "What happened to you?"

But Helen didn't answer, her head crushed against Anona's huge bosom, and when Anona let go and asked her again, Helen shrugged those skinny shoulders of hers and said she had been "somewheres uptown, the Bronx, maybe," with the nuns.

"Oh, Gesù, nuns . . . "You're sure nuns? Nobody else?"

Helen shook her head. "Nuns," she said, "the Sisters of the Bleeding Palms."

"And nobody hurt you? Nobody touched you?"

Helen pulled away. "I told you I'm okay look, I even got fat," and she pushed out her belly until it made a little round ball against Anona's palm. "The food was crappy but there was a lot of it."

"Crappy? What kind of word is crappy? That's English? Nuns taught you that?"

"Leave her alone, Anona. She's back. Who cares what happened? It's over."

"For once," Anona said to Mary, "you're right," and she petted Helen and sat her down and combed her hair with her fingers and made her rice pudding that she fed to her with a demitasse spoon as if she were an infant. Anona kept asking Helen questions and touching her everywhere with her free hand, the one that wasn't holding the spoon, until Mary came over and held both Anona's hands and told her to stop worrying. "We're all back together, Anona, just like always. And since when couldn't our Helen take care of herself?"

"So tell us," Gracie said to Mary, "about this big dope that took you home."

"Shut up, Gracie. He ain't no dope. Did you see that car? That's a Cadillac, a 1929 Cadillac and he gets a new one every year. That's what he told me. And them bills I brought? That's just spillover. I told you. He don't even know they're missing, that's how much he's got."

Anona rocked in her chair. "You're ruined," she said to Mary. "That's the end of you and a decent man."

"Whatta you talking about?"

"He's gotta be a gangster, a hood. He ain't no Rockefeller. Where you gonna go with him? And he's old . . . as old as the hills . . . as old as me . . ."

"Nobody's as old as you, Anona," Mary said. "But fine, I'll get rid of him. If he shows up again I'll tell him to get lost."

Anona stopped rocking. "You're not getting rid of him so easy. He'll be back. Where's he gonna find a girl nice like you, young like you, beautiful like you?"

"He was awfully good to me. Look at this suit." Mary pulled at the collar. "Real fox . . . feel it! And I got lace underthings and silk stockings and, wait." She went back into the bag and came out with a blue velvet box. "This is for you, Anona. 'For your granny,'" he said. "He never had no family of his own he can remember."

Anona flipped open the box. Inside was a pearl brooch. She scraped the center pearl against her front teeth, chipped at it with a fingernail to see if it would peel.

Mary made a face. "So you think he's way too old?"

Anona closed the box and slipped it in the pocket of her sweater. "Don't think about it. They get old fast anyway. You be surprised."

They slept all together in the big bed, even Anona, but Mary got up sometime in the night and opened the *brande*. Gracie heard her sighing. She got up to see. Mary'd wrapped her suit jacket around her fist for a pillow and was sleeping with her face in the fur collar.

Gracie went back to school but not Helen. She wouldn't go back. She said she had learned everything that she needed to know. She said enough was enough. Anona was mad but Mary was right there defending Helen, soothing Anona. "We don't got to do nothing we don't want," she told Anona, "now that we got Nick."

Nick Andersen came every day and he always came with presents: dresses and linen towels and baskets of food, rashers of bacon and big round loaves of bread. He brought special things for Anona, pails of beer and bottles of real scotch whiskey that had been smuggled over the Canadian border, and he took them all out in the car to Coney Island and Long Island and sometimes into New Jersey. Anona was afraid of the car but she came because she said she couldn't trust him and would wish under her breath for Emma to have been here because she was getting too old to manage three girls. If she had known what was in the trunk, what he was doing when he'd stop at a big house and leave them in the car for twenty minutes, that he was delivering the scotch that had been smuggled over the Canadian border, she might have complained out loud.

"What are you saying?" Mary would shout from the front seat, knowing Anona was praying under her breath, her hands folded tight together in her lap entwined around the rosary beads of dried olive pits. Helen and Gracie would be on either side of her, their heads stuck out of the car, feeling the wind on their faces, watching the side of the road go past.

Like always, they were all together, except better, because they had food and clothes and Mary didn't have to work in the candy factory or anywhere else for that matter and the rent was paid six months in advance.

People in the neighborhood talked. They gossiped behind their hands about the Mallones, but Anona pushed past them in the hallways, sneered at their faces peering from the half-open doors and if they tried, which they did, to invite themselves into her confidence, or into the apartment, Anona would close and bolt the door. The first to point the finger, Anona said, finding Mrs. Kelly outside the door, ear pressed to the keyhole, Mrs. Kelly, whose daughters carried her home drunk on Saturday nights. Mary and Helen and Gracie giggled and ate fried eggplant and hunks of cheese cut from the wheel Nick Andersen had brought. The statue of St. Rita wore robes of silk and a cape trimmed in mink that Anona had sewn with small careful stitches.

Nineteen twenty-nine was a year the Mallones would remember. They had lost Helen and they had found Nick Andersen. The Bugs Moran gang was massacred in Chicago on St. Valentine's Day. Nick took Anona and Mary and Helen and Gracie to the opening of the Pierre Hotel on Fifth Avenue and

Sixty-first Street. They were guests of Owney Madden. And even after the stock market crashed on October 29 and men jumped from their office windows, life stayed sweet for the Mallones. If Nick Andersen had money in the stock market, it didn't matter. What he had to offer the inhabitants of the West Side was still in demand.

1952–1953

Playwright Lillian Hellman Defies the Dies Committee

Testifies She's Not a "Red"
But Won't Reveal If She Was
Three or Four Years Ago

CUBAN MILITARY COUP

General Fulgencio Batista Becomes
Dictator of Cuba For the Second Time

*New York Yankees Defeat Brooklyn
Dodgers to Win the World Series*

Chapter Nine

After Frankie left Gracie sitting at the kitchen table, he came down the steps two at a time like he used to as a kid. On the second floor, Dibby Santulli was closing his door, his back to Frankie, but when he heard footsteps, he turned to see who it was. They looked at each other. "Hey, Dib," Frankie said, and stopped to put a hand on Dibby's shoulder, but he didn't ask him where he was going and Dibby returned the favor. Dibby, too, was getting away from his wife, in the time-honored tradition of hardworking men, but Dibby was going out to sit in the back of Sam & Al's candy store with some of the guys to bullshit about the docks, about the neighborhood and maybe send one of the kids playing outside for a piece of cake up on Bleecker Street or to Sutters Bakery on Greenwich Avenue.

Frankie, on the other hand, was looking for trouble, and by the time he hit Sixth Avenue and grabbed a cab going west, Dibby and Spring Street were a memory. All Frankie could think about was Doreen. He sat back and closed his eyes. Doreen. He loved that name. He loved the way it felt in his mouth. Dor . . . een . . . It was so . . . so . . . *American*. . . . She was so American, from out West, one of those *O* states . . . Ohio . . . Iowa . . . Wyoming . . . one of those. She'd been a cheerleader, had shown him a picture of herself in a red pleated skirt, black-and-white shoes with laces, and a fuzzy sweater with a big letter across the front. He had wanted to reach into that picture and cup those fuzzy breasts, find her nipples with his teeth, taste mohair on his tongue.

She'd come to New York to be a dancer. Sometimes she did

little steps for him. There's a broken heart for every bulb on Broadway, Frankie'd told her (he'd heard that somewhere) and when that made her sad, he put his arms around her and said he knew a few people. Maybe, he said, he could help her. She was impressed and grateful. Who could ask for more in a woman?

He'd taken a big step setting her up in an apartment on Horatio Street. A horse that was a long shot at Belmont had paid the first three months' rent with enough left over for his secret stash. With every score Frankie made, he remembered to take something off the top for the pot.

His mother had put him wise on his wedding day. "Always hold something back," she had whispered into his ear. Her wedding gift had come in two envelopes. One was handed to the bride, a gift for them both, the other was slipped into Frankie's pocket. Inside was $200, meant only for him.

The cab stopped and Frankie threw the driver a deuce and told him to keep the change. He gave one quick look around and went into the building. He could feel the sweat start under his arms, not sure if it was nerves or excitement. The apartment was five flights up, in the back. Doreen hadn't been so thrilled with it at first. She said it was dreary. She complained that the air from the alley was dank, and told him she hated the flapping clothes, the long underwear, giant cotton bloomers and lines and lines of bleached white sheets.

Frankie told her apartments were hard to come by in this neighborhood. He didn't tell her that he had staked the super for something in the back. He had wanted it dark, secret. The idea of a place where a woman waited only for him made his heart beat double time.

And Doreen didn't tell Frankie that she was desperate for a place to live. She was uptown with three other girls and was two months back on the rent. What she did tell him was how she'd never met a man like him, a man who knew his way around like he did, a man who was nothing like the boys back home. Frankie could see the boys back home behind his eyes. Big sweaty farm boys in overalls, hanks of yellow hair, oversized teeth. He would groan aloud when he thought about them touching her, their baseball-mitt hands all over her, their big thumbs hooking under the elastic of her underpants, mounting her from behind in a farmyard. It was torture for him. He loved it.

Now, standing outside the apartment door, Frankie waited, just to imagine Doreen on the other side. He took out his key and was about to knock. He reminded himself that he paid the rent; he didn't have to knock. He loved it.

She was on the couch reading. She was always reading, so Frankie figured she was smart. There was a row of drugstore paperbacks with lurid covers on the windowsill. Frankie'd never seen so many books. His mother had almost bought him an encyclopedia once when he was a kid, but his father had come home from work and thrown the salesman out the door. In truth, Frankie didn't like Doreen's books. He thought they ruined the decor and attracted roaches (roaches liked paper, his mother said—that's why she never saved the grocery bags) but Frankie kept his opinion about the books to himself. Doreen did have a lot of time to kill when he wasn't around.

He could smell her perfume from where he stood. She looked up at him, big blue eyes, big red lips. "Hi, honey," was all she said.

The streets were quiet when Frankie came home to Spring Street. It was past 3 A.M. The Napoli Bar was closed. He stood across the street and smoked a cigarette. He looked up at his mother's window just to make sure that she wasn't hanging out, her elbows resting on a pillow, waiting for him. He wasn't surprised her windows were dark. Gracie never let on to his mother when he went out. Gracie never even let on to him how she felt, if she missed him when he wasn't around.

She used to be crazy for him. He knew the Irish were cold fish. That's what he'd call her when she sat there, saying nothing: a coldhearted *Mick.* And if she wasn't Irish, she might as well be. That building on West Thirty-eighth where she grew up was all Irish. His friend Paddy Bailey told him an Italian family could never make it on that street, and if they did, they were one tough bunch of guineas.

And how did Gracie even know what she was? She and her sisters only knew what Anona wanted them to know. And who could trust Anona? Who could trust those sisters, for that matter. When Frankie first met Gracie and found out she was from Hell's Kitchen, he got a little nervous. When he found out she was Italian and not Irish, he relaxed, but then when he got the story, he was nervous all over again. The Mallones weren't like any Italians he knew. The grandmother fooled you. But her, too. Whoever heard of an Italian woman drinking in bars, unless you counted the Amerusos. They drank together, husband and wife, in Milady's on Thompson Street. They'd close down the bar and hold each other up walking home, trying not to fall. But they were the only ones.

Italian girls were raised strict no matter where they came from, but not the Mallones. They ran wild from what he had heard. Mary was with that hoodlum from Owney Madden's gang since she was a teenager and Helen was in the streets like a boy from ten years old. Frankie remembered the way she blew smoke rings in his face, puffing on those French cigarettes the first time he met her. And Gracie didn't tell him much. She was close-mouthed when it came to her family. "Don't tell nothing," Anona had warned her. "The first fight, they throw it all back in your face."

But the Irish kept dirty houses. He'd been in their houses. There were so many roaches on Danny Brennen's mother's kitchen clock, you couldn't tell the time. Gracie was neat as a pin. You could eat off her floors.

Still, those sisters! The whole neighborhood buzzed when Gracie's sisters came around. Frankie had to admit, though, that he liked them. They were live wires, especially Helen. Not that he would have wanted to be married to either one of them. He'd have to kill Gracie if she went around the way Helen and Mary did. Not that he'd last long if he ever touched Gracie. The first time he'd met Mary and Helen, they had pulled him aside and warned him. He'd heard of brothers doing that, fathers, but sisters?

He couldn't figure them out. Mary's husband, Nick, was old enough to be her father and Helen already had one husband in the grave. Maybe it was two, he wasn't sure. Gracie aways fought with him when he brought it up. No, compared to her sisters, Gracie was quiet, but then, standing there alone on Spring Street, looking up at the building, Frankie went hot, flushed, and remembered what she could be like when they were alone.

Mornings he didn't feel like shaping up at the docks, he'd stay under the covers and after Charlie went to school, he'd call to her and she'd come to bed with him for the whole day until his mother banged on the door asking if they were dead in there.

Frankie's mouth was dry. He ditched his cigarette butt between two parked cars and crossed the street, walked into the hallway of 196 Spring Street, and held the door so it didn't bang. He went up the stairs easy. On the fourth landing, he fumbled for his key. He kept the Spring Street key next to the St. Anthony medal on his key chain. The key to the Horatio Street apartment was at the other end. He didn't think Doreen should be next to St. Anthony. It didn't seem right.

He worked the key into the lock slowly, gently. He felt it slip in, and just before he turned the doorknob, he reached down with his left hand and touched himself. He hated guys that did that, but this was different, a quick admiring stroke. He wondered if Gracie would be sleeping. He wondered if she would be mad at him and if he could convince her not to be.

Frankie stepped into the kitchen, closed the door behind him. If he had looked, he would have seen that Charlie was not asleep in the kitchen, that his *brande* was not set up, but Frankie didn't look. It was dark and he was blind with desire. He stepped through the living room and into the open door of the bedroom. He took the wooden hanger off the hook on the back of the door and hung up his jacket. Then his pants. Nothing, no one, not Marilyn Monroe, could make Frankie take off his clothes and not hang them up.

He was unbuttoning his shirt, overcome with passion and love, calling out, whispering in the blackness. "Gracie . . . Gracie . . . sweetheart." He put one knee on the bed, reached out a hand. He touched the chenille spread. He felt around. More chenille. He stood back up and turned on the light. The bed was untouched except for the dent his knee had made, the pillows folded over at the top into neat rolls under the bedspread. He couldn't believe it. He was very close to tears.

He took his pants and jacket off the wooden hanger and put them back on and went downstairs and started walking uptown to Tenth Avenue and Thirty-eighth Street.

The Village was closing up but there were still sailors on the streets. If they had asked, Frankie could have steered them to an after-hours joint or two, but it wasn't his business where they went.

It was a long walk to Gracie's old neighborhood. He took Sixth Avenue and cut over west at Thirty-fourth Street, where he started cursing the blocks, one by one. He should have stuck with the girls downtown. He needed to come up here? Why? he asked himself. Why didn't he listen to his mother?

By the time he got to Anona's, he was furious that Gracie had left him, just like that, and taken his son, just like that, and that Anona, that crazy old lady, had taken them in, because he was sure she had. She was always ready to take them in, always ready to give him wrong. He hadn't forgotten the time Anona had told him right to his face that they would all be better off if he just took gas.

He stopped in front of Anona's building and looked up. They'd knocked down almost a hundred tenements in Hell's Kitchen, he thought. They had to leave this dump standing?

Frankie walked into the hallway and stomped up the stairs like an elephant on parade. He could see light underneath Anona's door. No one answered when he knocked. He knocked again. "Go away," someone inside said.

"Let me in. It's Frankie."

No answer.

"I want to talk to my wife. Let me in!"

"Shut up," someone yelled from downstairs. "Keep your trap shut," from upstairs.

The door opened. He couldn't see in because Anona blocked the way. She didn't give him a chance to speak. "You get outta here," she said. "Don't make my neighbors mad. It's Friday night. Payday. They like to punch people on Friday night. Go away. And don't come back." She slammed the door. Other doors opened and slammed shut on floors above and below. Frankie heard shouts and growls.

The door opened again and this time it was Helen who stood there. She had a highball glass in her hand, the ice cubes fresh.

"Can I come in?" he said.

"No," she said, and stepped outside. "I just wanted to give you a chance to plead your case." Helen leaned into the door frame. "So? You got something to say for yourself?"

"I'm looking for my wife and kid," Frankie said.

"Why? You lost them?"

"Ma'nudge," Anona said, opening the door. "You gotta put on a show?" she said to Helen.

"Please, Anona, compared to what this building's seen and heard, Frankie's small potatoes."

"Ba!" Anona said and closed the door again.

"Can I have a drink?" Frankie said.

Helen shook her head and took a sip from her glass. "No drink, you've had enough to drink."

"What is this," Frankie said, "a Jap prison camp? You're gonna crucify me now?"

"Frankie, Frankie," Helen said. "When are you gonna grow up? You got a nice wife. She's crazy about you. You got a kid. Why you always doing the wrong thing?"

"You're nuts," he said. "What did I do? You tell me. I did something?"

"Gracie feels like you're doing something. 'Something's not right.' That's what she's telling us. 'Frankie's always going out, always all dressed up.' And look at you," Helen said, leaning over and fingering his lapel. "Where *are* you going all the time?"

Frankie was getting mad. "I'm supposed to look like a bum?" he said. He put his hand over Helen's and squeezed her fingers. He was careful when he did this. He didn't want to hurt her, just make his point. "I think this is between me and my wife. I don't understand why everybody's gotta get involved. Just because Gracie don't like me to go out at night's no reason to think I'm killing somebody."

"C'mon, Frankie," Helen said. "And let go of my hand."

He did but never took his eyes off her. "Listen, I love my wife and I love my kid. I go out once in a while. I don't do nothing. I like the East Side and I like to look good. I eat some Chinks, maybe I play a game of cards. I can't hang out on a wooden chair in the back of a store on Spring Street in a wrinkled pair of pants. Give me credit for having some class." He held his hands out in front of him. "Whatta you say? Gimme a break here."

"Whatta you want me to do?" Helen said.

"Let me take Gracie and Charlie home."

"That's up to Gracie."

"Well, where is she? Lemme talk to her."

Helen shrugged. She drained her glass. "I think you should leave and maybe come back tomorrow. Things look different in daylight. You know what I mean?"

"You want me to go all the way downtown . . ."

"I don't care where you go, Frankie, as long as you get out of here. Tomorrow's another day."

The door opened and Anona pulled Helen inside. She had been listening the whole time, her ear red from where she had pressed it against the door. "Here's your hat, what's your hurry," she said to Frankie, before, once again, she slammed the door in his face.

Frankie went downstairs into the street and yelled up at the window. Bottles rained down and a few brown paper bags of wet garbage. Something splattered on Frankie's sleeve and he took out his handkerchief and wiped it off. He sat down on the stoop. The sun was coming up. An old whiskered bum came and sat next to him and offered him a slug of rotgut. Frankie said no but gave him a buck. "You think this is bad?" he told Frankie. "Owney Madden's beer was half ether." The old man finished off the pint and curled up inside the doorway. "But that's before your time," he told Frankie just before he fell asleep. Some guys, Frankie thought, have it easy.

Chapter Ten

Anona boiled milk in the morning for coffee. Gracie had a headache and a dry mouth. She wasn't used to late hours, and apricot sours were her idea of booze. Helen was scrambling eggs for Charlie, whose nose was in a comic book at the table.

Nick had shown up in his black Cadillac sometime around midnight looking for Mary and they had left after a few hands of pinochle. Anona said she loved to take his money. Helen and Gracie had slept with Anona in the big bed they had shared when they were kids. They made a bed for Charlie in the kitchen. In all his ten years, Charlie had never slept anywhere but in a kitchen, except as a nursing infant when he lay in a bassinet on his mother's side of the bed.

Sometimes, when Frankie was out late, Gracie would let Charlie come into bed with her, but she would always carry him back into the kitchen after he had fallen asleep. When he got too big to carry, she would walk him into the kitchen, half asleep. He never remembered moving from her bed to his *brande*. Only that in the morning when he opened his eyes and saw where he was, he was disappointed. Gracie knew that Charlie would have liked to get into the big bed with her and Helen and Anona. Gracie could read him like a book, but she knew he was too afraid of Anona to say anything and Gracie was secretly relieved.

Helen put a dish mounded with eggs in front of Charlie. He asked for the ketchup bottle. "Ugh," Anona said, looking at him. "I don't know how anybody eats in the morning." She poured scotch into her coffee. "Just a drop," she explained to Helen, who came and took the bottle away. "Ha, it's empty anyways," Anona said, "a dead soldier." Anona liked that . . . *dead soldier, another dead soldier.* Nick had taught her to say that. He said he had learned to say that in France in the First World War.

Mary had a picture of Nick in an army officer's uniform on her bedroom dresser but it was a fake, and, Anona said, a disgrace to the heroes of Father Duffy's Fighting 69th. Nick even got a pension from the Great War. He had finagled the records and was collecting some poor dead veteran's money. It was the reason there were two names on his mailbox.

Anona sat in her chair by the window and leaned out to see what was going on in the street below. "That *moltedevane*'s still down there," she said.

"Who?" Charlie went over to the window to look. "It's Daddy!" He turned to his mother. "How come he came to get us so soon? It's only Saturday. I don't want to go home yet." Charlie loved Anona's house. Uncle Nick had had it fixed up so the walls were smooth and the floors were covered with carpets in patterns and colors. Aunt Mary called them "oriental" and once was telling him the story of how Uncle Nick got them but his mother had shushed Aunt Mary and he never found out where the carpets came from or how Uncle Nick had managed to get them.

Anona wouldn't move from here. She was afraid that if she left, Emma would think she had forgotten, and then, Anona said, something terrible would happen. She had to stay here with Emma and the ghosts.

Gracie came by the window and wiped Charlie's mouth with her napkin. "Daddy misses you," she told him.

Anona pulled Charlie's sleeve. "Sonny boy, get Anona some more coffee. Two sugars. Stir it good, like a nice boy."

"Then I can go down?"

"Wait. Can't you wait until you finish eating?" Gracie said.

"What about Daddy?"

"What about him?"

"Is he coming up?"

"What are you going to do?" Helen asked Gracie.

Gracie shrugged. "Let's see what he has to say."

"*Madonna* . . ." Anona said. "Always he says the same thing. He cries . . . he begs . . . like a woman . . ."

"Anona, stop . . . the kid," Helen said. "It is his father."

"So? Everybody's got a cross." Charlie stood in front of Anona with the coffee.

"Anona, you don't like my father?"

"I don't like anybody, sonny boy. When you get old you'll see what I mean."

Gracie went to stand by the window. Frankie was looking up and saw her. He started waving his arms. Then she couldn't see him anymore, and moments later, he was banging on the door, calling her name. She could hear he was out of breath from running up the stairs.

"I'm gonna let him in, Anona, okay?"

"No. I wanna get dressed in peace. He's gotta wait."

"You're a real *strega*," Helen said. "The poor dope's been out there all night."

"*Appunto*. He's a dope."

Charlie was by the door. He put his mouth to the keyhole. "You gotta wait, Daddy. Anona says you gotta wait."

"And you tell him, sonny boy, that he's gotta be quiet. I don't bother nobody around here. I don't want him making it bad for me."

"Daddy," Charlie said through the keyhole, "Anona says . . ."

Gracie pulled him away from the door and cracked it open. Frankie was there, eyes bloodshot, suit wrinkled.

"Anona's getting dressed," she said, not giving him a chance to say anything. "If you want to wait, you can come in when she's done." And then Gracie closed the door in his face. Anona went by the sink to wash. Then into the bedroom, where she took off her nightgown and put on a clean pressed silk slip trimmed in lace and over that a housedress. Handkerchiefs folded into triangles went into both front pockets, along with a handful of hairpins she took from a cut-glass covered dish that anchored the starched doily on the top of the dresser. Then she sat in the chair by the window and undid the long thin gray braid that went down her back. She combed her hair, working it into a coil at the back of her head. When she finished, when the last stray hair had been caught with the last hairpin, she settled into her chair and raised her right hand like a papal blessing as a signal to Gracie, who was waiting by the door to let Frankie in.

He was still furious but he was worn down. He just wanted to get Gracie and Charlie and go back home, but he wasn't getting off the hook so easy. Gracie stood with her arms folded in front of her. When he looked at Helen, she raised her eyes and turned her palms up as if to tell him he was on his own. Anona glared like Sitting Bull. Charlie smiled at him, but even Charlie stood where he was. Helen had promised him fifty cents after breakfast and he wanted to go downstairs.

Mary appeared. "I thought you might need me," she said. "But I left Nick downstairs." She smiled at Frankie. "I wouldn't want to stack the deck," she said. Charlie ran over to her and put his arms around her waist. She kissed the top of his head. "So, let's hear it," Mary said to Frankie.

"Yeah, let's hear it," Gracie said.

"What? Hear what? I come to take you and Charlie home."

"Christ, Frankie. Why do you think I left?"

"You think we could do this in private, Gracie? You think maybe we could talk about this without an audience?"

Charlie saw his chance to take the money and run. He'd seen it all before. He couldn't count how many times his mother had packed a suitcase and brought him to Anona's. He left Mary and shuffled over to Helen and whispered in her ear. She petted him and handed over two quarters. "I'm goin' down," he said, to no one in particular. "I'll be downstairs," and he was out the door, shirttails flapping.

"What? What'd I do?" Frankie was saying. "I work. I give you money every week. I try to take care of myself, not like all those other guys downtown. They get married and let themselves go. I do everything for you, Gracie. All I care about is you and the kid." His eyes filled with tears. In the background, Anona coughed and spat into one of her handkerchiefs. It sounded forced.

Frankie was pleading now. "Let me take you home. Please. Whatever you want, I promise. We'll go to the Automat for lunch. Charlie will love that. Look, I've got a pocketful of nickels." He put his hand in his pocket and jangled the loose change. The sound startled Gracie. As a rule, Frankie hated change. It made a bulge and ruined the drape of his pants.

"The kid can get anything he wants. You too!" Frankie said. Now he was crying. He took out a handkerchief, one of many that Gracie had boiled and pressed and folded into a neat square with his initials showing and placed in the top drawer of the dresser. There was one dresser in their bedroom. Frankie had the first four drawers. Gracie had the one on the bottom. It was with one of these handkerchiefs from the top drawer that Frankie wiped his face and blew his nose. He came closer to Gracie. He touched her arm. "Please," he said. "If you don't come home, I'll kill myself. I'll come back with a gun and shoot myself in the head."

The thought of Frankie with his head blown off made Gracie's eyes water. "*S'fachime*," Anona said. "Don't come here with no gun. Go shoot yourself in your own house."

"Please, baby . . ." Frankie's voice was sincerely low.

"Here we go," Mary said. "But when are you going to toughen up with this guy? What do you think is going to change?"

Gracie hesitated. "I don't know, Frankie. Mary's right. It's always the same." But she was falling for it, couldn't resist him, his black eyes, the straight line of his nose, his beautiful hands clutched in supplication. Helen said later that if Gracie was an ice cube, Frankie was an oven.

"Not this time! I swear. I should get cancer in my mouth if I'm lying! . . . On my tongue . . . my tongue, Gracie. Look at me." He stuck out his tongue, pointed to it, begged her some more, his speech garbled, and then he started to bawl like a child, or as Anona put it . . . like a woman.

Gracie crumbled like the sides of the hills in Lucania when the rains came. "Okay, Frankie. One more chance."

Frankie looked up at her. He stepped forward, took her hands in his, and kissed her palms. His eyes were rimmed in red. The sweet smell of his aftershave that had made Doreen murmur was gone; he smelled like the bum downstairs with whom he'd shared the stoop. "You won't be sorry, Gracie. I promise."

It was settled. Helen sighed and traced her eyebrows with her fingers as though she had a headache. Gracie kissed Anona and Helen and Mary goodbye before she left. "You come here any-time, you hear?" Anona said. Inside her apron pocket, she gave Frankie the horns, her thumb holding down her two middle fingers, the second finger and the pinkie pointing at him.

Frankie and Gracie left together. He carried the suitcase. They picked Charlie up downstairs, which was just as well. Jimmy Mulligan had taken his fifty cents and had him on the sidewalk in a choke hold.

After they were gone, Anona put up another pot of espresso. And Helen broke out another bottle of scotch. Mary poured. "They could play on Broadway," she said, shaking her head. "If I caught Nick . . . just once . . ."

"*Uffa!* You couldn't lose him in a crap game," Anona said. She shuffled the cards for a game of rummy.

"Forget it," Mary said. "Let's not talk about it."

"Speaking of, isn't Nick downstairs?" Helen asked her.

"I told him not to wait if he saw Gracie leaving with Frankie." Mary shook her head as she cut the deck. "Even though I thought this time was it. I thought she really meant business," Mary said. "I guess I was wrong."

"She's not ready," Anona said. "Maybe next time, maybe never."

"Listen, she didn't catch him dead to rights. You can't hang a guy for going out looking good," Helen said.

"I don't wanna talk about that *shambayone* no more," Anona said. "If he's cheating, he'll get what's coming to him."

"He will?" Helen teased. "How? You gonna put a curse on him?"

"Don't make fun, you," Anona said. "You should know better."

"Well, you know what I think?" Helen said. And she looked from Anona to Mary. "I think we should keep an eye out. Frankie makes a wrong move, I think we should do something about it, before he gets too out of hand. He's a shit-the-pants. It wouldn't take much to scare him."

Anona grunted her assent and dealt the cards. "I think you're right," Mary said, and left it at that. But if it were up to her, they'd do more than scare him. He'd be no good to anybody if she had her way. Nick was so good to her, had always been, that she couldn't stand the idea of a man not treating a woman right. Gracie deserved better but life was long. It would all work out in the end. They would make sure of it. They sat together at the table without talking and played rummy with two decks until it was dark.

On Spring Street that night, Gracie turned away in bed. "Are we still fighting?" Frankie said to her back. He hid his nose under her arm. He groped for a nipple through the cotton of her nightgown and felt it go hard. He licked the fine lines in the crease of her arm until she turned around.

Chapter Eleven

It was early Saturday afternoon. Gracie was pressing shirts. Frankie was at the kitchen table, reading the *Daily Mirror*, a toothpick in his mouth. She had just served him lunch, minestrone soup, *finnochio* salad with black olives, and focaccia with onions from DiFiore's on Sullivan Street across from the church. Frankie stretched, wishing there were sun. Their apartment was always dark, being in the back. The back apartment on Spring Street, unlike his love nest on Horatio, was a sore point with Frankie.

Gracie didn't mind. She liked the cool breeze that came into the small kitchen window from the alley where the sun never reached. It took the clothes on the line a long time to dry, but when she stood over the stove in the summer, it was a blessing.

But Frankie always wanted to face the front, to feel the sun through the window and to be able to look out over Spring Street and see what was going on: his bookmaker coming out of Sam & Al's, the shylock going into the Napoli Bar, the Petillo sisters walking back and forth to work in the Butterick Building on Varick Street. He liked the one who always walked in the middle, Josie, the one with the big ass.

From the back apartment, he could almost reach into the window of the apartment next door. Facing the back, he was subject to private conversations, brutish lovemaking and the sight and smell of vile things thrown into the yard below.

He had asked his mother to approach the Widow Verducci, who lived alone in five front rooms on the second floor. "She don't need five rooms," Frankie told his mother. "Tell her I'm doing her a favor. The front is noisy. Old ladies hate noise. That's why they're always banging on the ceiling with their brooms."

Signora Merelli, who hated to ask for anything, said she would try. She went to call on the Widow Verducci, bringing pound cake and cookies from Sutters Bakery, where it was so busy and crowded you had to take a number and wait to get served.

Frankie was standing in the hallway when his mother came out. "It's a nice apartment?" he asked her.

"Eh . . ."

"You told her?"

"Frankie, she don't wanna move."

"But what'd she say?"

"She said you don't pluck a chicken until it's dead."

Frankie cursed the Widow Verducci and all the Verduccis in America and Italy, past and future generations. His mother told him to calm down, that curses come back, and that the Widow would die like everybody else, but Frankie told Gracie later that with his luck, the hag'd outlive Charlie.

Frankie stretched again and folded the newspaper in half. "She should drop dead," he said, remembering.

"What? Who?" Gracie looked up from ironing her fourth dress shirt. She was just finishing the front, the iron clicking as she moved it around the buttons.

"The witch . . . that old crone, Verducci. I was thinking how friggin' dark this apartment is." He stood up. "I gotta take some air."

Gracie said nothing. Mary and Nick were coming over later. Better Frankie goes, she thought. Who wanted to hear him? Nick was taking Charlie for shoes. He had promised him a pair of wing tips from Siegel Brothers.

Out of Frankie's earshot, Gracie had held Charlie by the throat and told him not to say a word until he had the shoe box under his arm. Frankie never wanted anything from Gracie's side. Only his side. She had to smile, remembering the diamond ring Signora Merelli's brother had given Charlie for First Holy Communion that had turned out to be paste. Frankie had thrown it in the street. It was one of Gracie's weapons in the arsenal she kept on reserve for family fights.

Gracie watched Frankie move around the apartment, getting dressed. She was hanging up shirt number six when he walked out the door.

Downstairs, Frankie hailed a cab to take him over to the East Side. It was a beautiful day. He thought about walking but he might sweat, and he hated that. It would ruin his whole afternoon.

Frankie never hung around the neighborhood with the *judruls* who sat backward on chairs in front of the building. He liked his business to be his own, and besides, he had friends on the East Side, important people. He was partners with the Ciminelli brothers when they bought their first garbage truck. He had lost his share in a crap game a couple of months later, but he'd been there at the beginning and no one could take that away from him. You never knew when your luck was gonna turn.

The card game was in the back room of the Café Roma on Mulberry Street. Frankie hung his jacket over the back of his chair and rolled his shirtsleeves to just below the elbow. He put his cuff links, gold with a center pearl, on the table next to his chips and touched the St. Anthony medal on the key chain in his pocket for good luck. At four o'clock he was down six hundred and excused himself to make a phone call.

Gracie was serving coffee and cake to Nick and Mary when somebody yelled up in the hallway that there was a call for her on the pay phone in the candy store. Gracie told Charlie to go down and see who it was. Charlie wanted to wear his new wing tips. Gracie told him just for today, that they were only for church and anything that happened in church, like a wedding or a funeral, and it had to be somebody they knew getting married or buried, not just anybody, before he could wear them.

"He's a good kid," Mary said.

"And you're good to him."

"Hey, he's all we have. We're nuts about him," Mary said, "he reminds us of our Sonny, right, Poppa?" she said, touching Nick's hand. She pushed the sadness away, the loss of their son, their only child, and turned to Gracie. "So how's Frankie?"

"Since that last time, he's perfect. He's just spoiled. His mother spoiled him."

"But everything's good between you and him?"

"Yeah, why?"

"Nothing. I'm just asking. I'm glad for you." She checked her spit curls with a wet finger, she had four today, one at each temple and one on each cheek. "When you're happy, we're happy."

Gracie imagined what Frankie would say if he could hear Mary. "The Three Musketeers," Frankie called the Mallone sisters. And when he saw Charlie's shoes he would blow a gasket. She might have to bring up the fake diamond ring.

Frankie was glad it was Charlie who came to the phone and not Gracie. He told him to tell Gracie not to wait for him to eat, that he was stuck on the East Side and wouldn't make it home in time, and that Charlie should get a Pepsi from the ice chest in the back of Sam & Al's and tell Sam to put it on his tab. Charlie got the Pepsi and a package of Yankee Doodles and watched while Sam entered it in the black-and-white notebook he kept on a string near the cash register. The pencil he used was a stub. Frankie told Charlie that Sam was a crumb who pinched pennies but Sam said that he used a stub because the nice pencils were forever disappearing into some cheapskate's pocket.

Charlie ran upstairs. "He's not coming home," he yelled and he flopped on the couch with his stash.

"Who? What are you talking about?"

"That was Daddy. He's stuck on the East Side. He said to eat without him."

Gracie got up and went into the living room. Mary pleated her lips together and frowned. "That's all he said?" Gracie asked Charlie.

"Yeah," Charlie said, stuffing two Yankee Doodles in his mouth at once.

Gracie picked up the one remaining cupcake. "And who said you could buy these?"

"Daddy. Daddy told me I could." She raised an eyebrow but Charlie didn't budge. "He did."

"Okay, we'll eat without him." Gracie came back into the kitchen.

"Come out with us," Nick said. "We'll go to Peter Luger's for a steak."

"Na, thanks," Gracie said. "I already made eggplant. Why don't you stay?"

Mary stood up. "Forget the eggplant. You're always sweatin' in this kitchen. We're taking you out. Get dressed. We'll take Charlie and go get the car and pick you up downstairs."

"I don't know . . ."

"C'mon. Live a little. You'll be home early, guaranteed."

"Eggplant? I love eggplant," Nick said. Mary never cooked. He looked at her, eyes wide.

Mary shook him by the shoulder. "Get up, Poppa," she said, and because he was old and had surrendered his will, Nick got up and waited by the door. Gracie called Charlie into the kitchen to say that Aunt Mary and Uncle Nick were taking them for steak. She wiped his hands and mouth with the dishrag before she would let him leave. She heard Nick telling Charlie he could stay over if he wanted, and holding on to Nick's big hand, Charlie twisted around, and before he could ask, Gracie nodded her head yes.

Left alone, Gracie looked in the mirror opposite the kitchen sink, where Frankie shaved twice a day. In the medicine cabinet behind the mirror she found a tube of lipstick and carefully followed the line of her lips, filling in the color, startled at the sight of her bright red mouth. She took off her housedress, found a blue dress with pearl buttons down the front that Helen had given her for Christmas and pulled it over her head. She finger-combed her hair. It was still a beautiful brown-gold color and stood out around her face. Checking herself in the medicine cabinet mirror again before she closed the light, Gracie liked the way she looked. She looked good and it felt good to be going out. She was going to ask one of the Bruno brothers in the hardware store on Prince Street to come up next week and put a full-length mirror on the back of the door.

Meanwhile, Frankie was up five hundred bucks at seven o' clock, and when he left the East Side at nine, he was holding eight hundred. First thing, he peeled off three hundred for his personal stash and put it in his wallet behind his driver's license. The rest went in his money clip and into his right pocket. It was a beautiful night. He didn't want to go home. He put his hand in his pocket to feel the wad of bills and his fingers brushed against his key chain with the two keys. The one to the apartment on Horatio Street felt hot against his fingers. He suddenly wanted to see Doreen real bad. Poor thing probably thought he was dead. It had been three weeks. He had been laying low since Gracie came back from Anona's.

But he couldn't show up empty-handed. For sure, she'd be mad at him. He debated back and forth with himself until he looked up and saw that he was on Canal Street, in front of Maurizio's jewelry store. The store was closed but he knew Maurizio lived in the back and bought and sold swag any hour of the day or night.

Frankie rang the bell and Maurizio came to the door. He brought Frankie inside and emptied a felt bag of jewelry on the table between them. Frankie fingered an emerald-and-diamond bracelet, got him to knock fifty bucks off the price and handed over the money. He slipped the bracelet into his pocket where the money had been and kept his hand on it all the way over to Horatio Street, trying to count the stones, always losing track. He avoided Sullivan Street and Spring Street and walked up Hudson.

He stopped at Frenchie's, the lesbian club where his friend Ernie tended bar and where, after three drinks, he could have sworn he saw his sister-in-law Helen in a Borsalino at a table near the jukebox. But the light was bad, and he thought maybe he was seeing things, maybe he was just nervous about seeing Doreen again. There were rumors about Helen. But it was hard to know anything for sure. Helen would be in the San Remo with poets and the Minetta Tavern with wiseguys. She had husbands, boyfriends, girlfriends. She would go to the Laurels on Van Dam Street dressed in a man's suit and hat.

Gracie had laughed at him when he'd told her where he'd seen Helen and what she'd been wearing. "She's been dressing up since she was a kid hustling nickels," Gracie had told him. "She always said it was easier not being a girl."

Frankie forgot about Helen and instead thought about the bracelet, how he would tease Doreen with it, hold it between his thumb and forefinger, let it dangle, catch the light. He could see her now, all quivery, the line of sweat that beaded her upper lip when she got excited.

Doreen was getting dressed when he walked in. She just looked at him, mascara brush in one hand. "Well, look what the cat dragged in," she said, turning her back and going into the bedroom. He followed her and sat on the bed, slipping on the pink satin coverlet, while she finished her makeup at the vanity table like a movie star.

"C'mon, Doreen, I got tied up. The business I'm in, I don't

know one day to the next where I'm gonna be. Let's go out, hear some music, get something to eat." He stood behind her, moved his hand down the front of her slip, held her lace-covered breast. "You look like Lana Turner," he said, his hands resting on her shoulder. "I really missed you." He felt her relax. Lana Turner was her favorite movie star.

She took a tissue and blotted her lips. Frankie let go of her and reached into his pocket. He held the bracelet in front of her eyes and she turned around, smiling. Frankie smiled back. They were all the fucking same, he thought.

He didn't want to go out. Not now. There was nothing outside that he wanted. It was all right here, he thought, a cigarette in one hand, the other on Doreen's bare leg, but Doreen got up and finished getting dressed. She said she was going out, with him or without him. Frankie was getting tired of paying his dues but she had him by the balls; he *had* disappeared for three weeks.

They went down the block to Fedora's and they sat side by side in a dark corner of the restaurant. He felt for her knee under the table, pulled the nylon of her stocking away from her leg and rubbed it between his fingers. He ordered her steak and shoe-string potatoes. Doreen liked meat. She was a 100 percent red-blooded American girl, after all. The waiter brought a bottle of champagne. Doreen squealed when he held the bottle out for her to see. Frankie held her hand. He told her that someday there'd be a big diamond glittering just there and ran his tongue along the finger where that diamond would sit. "Close your eyes. See it?" he told her. "Can you feel it?" he said, his hand up between her legs, past the tops of her stockings.

By the time he was feeding her cheesecake, he was counting the steps back to Horatio Street. Outside, he had a moment of panic when Doreen slipped her arm through his. This was crazy, he thought, he was too close to home, but he looked around at all the different faces in the street and he felt better. He was miles away from Spring Street, miles and miles away from Spring Street.

Frankie adjusted the collar of Doreen's coat, camel's hair, with a little bit of cashmere. He should know, he had paid for it. That horse again. She ran her hands down his lapels. He nuzzled her neck and whispered something dirty in her ear. She giggled, moved back and balled her hand into a fist, made to hit him. A stray thread snagged the button on her glove. She pulled. The glove slipped off and fell on the sidewalk between them. Frankie bent to pick up the glove, his eyes on her face. He held the glove in his hand, touched it to his cheek, brought it to his lips, closed his eyes, and kissed it.

Something hit the back of his head . . . hard. His knees buckled. An arm swung him around and a fist whacked into his mouth. Another punch closed his eye. He tasted blood and thought he heard a woman screaming. He thought it sounded like Doreen, and then he went down.

Chapter Twelve

Two cops picked Frankie off the sidewalk and threatened to book him for vagrancy. He told them he'd fallen down on his way home and made them feel his coat: vicuña. Did derelicts wear vicuña? They let him go but told him to keep moving.

He looked around, realized Doreen was gone and caught his reflection in a store window. He was filthy, covered with blood.

His coat was ruined, his tie cut off at the knot. He could only see out of one eye and that was puffing up. He felt his nose and held back tears of dread, trying to decide whether or not it was broken. Frankie loved his nose. His Roman nose, his mother called it. Who had a nose like this on Spring Street? she'd ask him. Only you, *carissimo,* only you, she'd say, holding his face in her two hands. And she was right. Frankie Merelli had the only Roman nose for blocks around.

He felt along the bridge of his nose one more time. His head hurt. He had to get home and get cleaned up before anybody he knew saw him looking like this, like a stumblebum. He started walking fast with his head down and he didn't look back, not once. He held his breath until he got to the corner of Houston Street and Sullivan, where he slipped down the cellar of the *lattecini freschi* store, where they smoked the mozzarella with newspaper, and made his way through the connecting alleys to Spring Street, until he was standing in his own back yard. He barely had the strength to jump up and pull down the ladder to the fire escape. His heart was pumping so fast, he worried about dying right there. Hadn't Joe Mosca keeled over dead when he was running with that stolen TV set? What had he been, thirty?

Frankie stopped to catch his breath before he climbed the last flight of iron steps. Then he'd be on the third floor, outside his mother's kitchen. He saw her inside at the sink and banged on the window. She turned her head to look. She screamed and grabbed a soapy pot and shook it at him. "Get off there, you. Get away! I kill you, you hear?"

"Ma, it's Frankie! Frankie, your son, Ma . . ."

She came nearer and squinted. "Oh, *Madonna.* It's Frankie?" she backed away and dropped the pot. "Can't be," she said, looking again. My Frankie's always clean. Get away, you bum you!"

"Ma . . . open the window. For Chrissakes, can't you see the shape I'm in?" He pressed his face against the glass. "Look! It's me!"

"Gesù . . ." she said. "What happened? Who did this to you?" She started to cry.

"Ma, just *let me in!*"

She opened the window and helped him in, being careful of her "little laundry," nylon stockings, dishtowels that hung on the clothesline. "Watch," she said, "my clean clothes . . ."

He fell over the radiator and onto the kitchen floor. She leaned over to crumple a brassiere in her hand. "Still damp," she muttered before she closed the window. Frankie had gotten to his feet and was sitting in a kitchen chair, his head in his hands. Blood crusted on his lip. He cried like a little boy. Signora Merelli wrapped her arms around him and for a while they cried together.

She knew he was a bad egg, but he was her love, her prize. When she saw him dressed up, he was so handsome, she had to squeeze her legs tight together not to pee with excitement. She had never told a soul, but one Easter Sunday she *had* actually peed her pants watching him walk down the street and had missed Mass because she had to go back upstairs and change her bloomers.

Frankie had been a long time in coming to her. She had made a pilgrimage to the cloistered nuns in Bedford-Stuyvesant in Brooklyn, to the convent behind barbed wire and broken shards of glass. She whispered her request for a child through a grate and a small door opened and a circular tray rolled out. On this Signora Merelli put her offerings: fruit, vegetables, flowers. The rules were strict. No meat or anything made by man's hand. Transgressions were not forgiven. When she came back after a week, she found a rice paper package tied with silk thread on the tray. Her offerings had been accepted. Inside the package were hosts, their surfaces embossed with prayers. These she ate, one a day for a month, before returning to the convent grate. She did this for two years and . . . *miracolo!* Frankie was conceived. She named him for St. Francis of Assisi in honor of the parish priests, the Franciscans, and every May Day parade, Frankie sat on the float dressed like a miniature friar. She was convinced he would be a priest until she caught him at twelve naked in bed with Tessie Marscarpone, a sixteen-year-old girl who lived on the first floor. Signora Merelli had paid Tessie fifty cents to sit with Frankie on Tuesday nights while she made the novena for the missions in Africa.

Now she wiped his face with the edge of her apron. *"Poverino,"* she moaned. "Who did this to you?"

"I don't know. I didn't see. I was minding my own business when all of a sudden, the lights went out."

"Nothing, Frankie? You was doing nothing?"

"Jesus . . . my own mother don't believe me. I swear, on Poppa's grave."

Signora Merelli crossed herself, pulled an aurora borealis rosary from the front pocket of her apron and wrapped it around her hand. Bishop Sheen had blessed this rosary when he came to speak at the Mothers for Mary Communion Breakfast. It was the rosary she wanted to be holding when she was laid out in Nucciarone's. The dress she planned to wear was pressed and folded in tissue paper in a satin-lined box she kept under her bed.

"Frankie, don't make me nervous. You know how many years I'm praying to get your father out of purgatory, how many novenas I make. You could push him right back down in those flames."

"Forget it . . . just forget it. Who knows? I probably caught somebody else's beating."

"An enemy did this. People are jealous. Never mind. Mussolini always said, 'Judge a man by his enemies.'"

"Ma, you got something to eat?"

"Of course. I got baked ziti, veal parmigiana, roasted peppers, stuffed artichokes. But you should go upstairs. Gracie's gonna be worried about you."

"I can't, Ma. If she sees me like this, she'll drop dead. What am I gonna tell her? Look at me ! I gotta wait awhile. I gotta clean up."

"I don't understand you, Frankie. You gotta go up. You got no choice. You made your bed. You shoulda listened when I told you. Now you're stuck. You got a kid, a nice big boy. It's too late. I told you to stay with your own kind."

"Whatta you talking about? Gracie is our kind."

"Pffft . . . Your father was right. You don't have the brains you were born with. She's Irish! And don't give me that crap she's Italian. I don't care if she's Italian or not. She's like Irish. Look where she grew up. And those sisters of hers . . . Italian girls? Never. *Puttane* . . . that bleached blond, the one with the gangster? And the other one, the redhead, always with the cigarette in her mouth, hangs out in those village clubs where women look like men."

"Ma, where you'd get that? Who told you that?"

"You, *caro*. You told me about her sisters."

Frankie put his head in his hands. "Ma, maybe I mentioned something. . . ."

"You told me. I heard it with my own ears."

"Forget them, Ma. Gracie's a good wife. She's a good mother . . . You can't blame her for her sisters."

Signora Merelli crossed herself with her rosary. She kissed the crucifix, holding it to her pursed lips longer than usual. "You're the one don't wanna go home. I got nothing against Gracie. But I told you, you don't just marry a girl, you marry the whole family."

"You're right. You're right. Can I eat something? Can I get an aspirin? I'm dying here."

"Okay. Don't get excited." She washed his face and put perox-ide on his cuts. The steak she had bought for her dinner, she had him hold over his closed eye and she wrapped a white linen hand-kerchief soaked in alcohol around his head. She made him lie down on the couch. "Close your eyes," she said. "When it's time to eat, I'll call you."

He lay there and tried to figure things out. He owed Smash Nose Pete a few bucks but he had until at least next week. He couldn't think. Doreen? Maybe she was screwing some wiseguy on the sly of him? Frankie sank down farther into the couch. No, he decided. If that was the case, he'd be dead by now, or in a lot worse shape than he was. When Vito fell in love with Anna, her husband went flying off the roof on Sullivan Street. Those guys didn't fool around.

It had to be a mistake, Frankie told himself, and he fell asleep to the sounds of his mother singing *"Mala Femmina"* in the kitchen, like when he was a kid.

Chapter Thirteen

They threw Doreen into the back seat of Nick's Cadillac, a potato sack over her head, knotted at the neck. They told her to be quiet or they'd toss her in the East River. She was so quiet Mary wor-ried if she wasn't already dead. Helen lit a cigarette and told Mary to drive. With Helen on one side and Mary on the other, they dragged Doreen up the stairs to Anona's. She was a big girl and it wasn't easy. Inside the apartment, they set her in a kitchen chair, tied her to the back of it and told Anona not to take the sack off until they were gone.

"Where you going?" Anona said.

"We got something to do. We won't be gone long. You just make sure she doesn't go anywhere."

Helen took a breath. It had all happened so fast. She'd called Mary from the pay phone on the corner of Horatio and Washington Streets but there was no answer. She tried twice more and then gave up. Maybe it was better, she decided. She still had nothing concrete on Frankie. He'd gone into a building on Horatio Street. That's all she had and there could have been a hundred reasons for that: a card game, a numbers parlor . . . She wasn't going to jump to conclusions; she'd give him the benefit of the doubt.

She was ready to quit and go about her usual Saturday night when she saw him. She hated to admit it, she told Mary afterward, but she wasn't disappointed. The girl was a beauty, and she was lying on Frankie like a mortgage. Helen followed them to Fedora's and called Mary again. This time Mary answered. "Where were you?" Helen shouted into the phone. "I've been calling since ten o'clock."

"We took Gracie and the kid to Peter Luger's for a steak. Why? What's going on?"

"I got the bastard."

"Who?"

"Frankie . . . and some broad who could be in pictures. She's beautiful . . . wait till you see."

Mary sighed. "So now what?"

"Come get me. We got some time to figure it out. They just went in for dinner."

• • •

Under the sack, Doreen was whimpering and Helen mentioned rapping her once lightly on the back of the head. "Put that thing away," Anona said.

Mary backed her up. "Someday you're gonna hurt somebody bad with that thing. You're not fifteen anymore. Things are different now."

Helen fondled the leather-jacketed blackjack. She flicked it once before she put it back in her pocket. It had the perfect spring. Billy McGivern had made it for her years ago and he had taught her how to use it. "You're a wee bit of a thing," he had said. "You're gonna be needing something to p'tect yourself with and I'm gonna be giving it to you."

Billy McGivern was her first boyfriend. He had been a dummy boy and a lot of girls had been after him but she was the one he wanted. She might have married him if he hadn't disappeared without a trace before his eighteenth birthday. "He was a wild one, that Billy McGivern," they still said in Hanley's Bar.

"I wouldn't really hurt her," Helen said. "I'm a respectable, grown woman. I wouldn't be doing any of this if it weren't for Gracie."

"If it weren't for Gracie, none of us would be getting involved. I don't know . . . maybe we should have gotten somebody to take care of it for us," Mary said. "Nick still knows people."

"Nick . . . Nick . . ." Anona said. "Who does he know? He's an old man. He's lucky he knows where he is." Mary and Helen both threw her looks but neither answered.

Helen rubbed her palms together and looked at her palms. "Yeah, but you can't depend on a stranger to do it right. They got no investment. They don't feel it in their gut. It's not their sister. It's just money . . . and then they're stupid. You could start out with a broken leg and end up with a massacre."

"Like that time in the Cotton Club when they came in shooting and Nick threw over the table and . . ."

"Mary, spare me the war stories . . . that was a long time ago. There ain't been running boards on cars since I was in knickers."

"Kidnapping . . . this is a kidnapping." Anona made the sign of the cross. "It's twenty years they kidnapped that baby, Lindaberger. That guy went to the electric chair."

"Lindbergh? Charles Lindbergh? Is that who she's talking about?" Helen said to Mary.

Mary nodded. "But they killed that baby. We're not killing anybody."

"Ah," Anona said as Helen and Mary got ready to leave. "I don't know if I like this."

"Well, it's too late now," Helen said. "Besides, we're not doing it for money. It's for Gracie. And what's the big deal? We're just gonna straighten things out."

As soon as Mary and Helen were gone, Anona took the sack off Doreen's head. "Hmmm . . . *bella* . . . Frankie's not so stupid like he looks." She poked Doreen in the ribs. ". . . a little skinny . . . like my Emma. I tell her all the time, 'Eat,' but she was so tired, poor thing, working all the time."

"Where am I?" Tears streamed down Doreen's face. "Who are you?"

"Me? Who'm I? Hey, you're in my house. I'll ask the questions, no? But since it's my house, I should ask you maybe you want something. Tell me. *Espresso? Amaretto?* A couple *biscotti?*"

"I don't believe this." Doreen cried harder. "They told me not to come to New York. Back home, they warned me." Her face was streaked with black from the pencil line that had rimmed her eyes.

Anona tightened her lips, shook her head. "Don't blame New York. They got married men all over."

"Married? Is that what this is about? Frankie? I didn't know he was married. I swear I didn't. He never said anything . . . not once."

Anona rolled her eyes. "Of course, he don't tell you. You're supposed to figure these things out for yourself. He's got a son, too. Nice boy."

"That skunk. He lied to me."

"Skunk? More like a snake . . . So, you hungry or what?"

"Please, please, let me go. I'll never see Frankie again. I promise. Please, before they come back."

"You don't want nothing? You sure? I got nice . . ."

Helen and Mary came back to find Anona at the table, smearing olive paste on bread and feeding it to Doreen. "Ooo . . . Nonna, de-lish . . . What do you call this?" Doreen was saying.

"Anona!"

"What the hell?" Mary came over and pulled Doreen's hair. Chairs shuffled. Helen grabbed the bread out of Doreen's mouth, threw it onto the plate and pushed it out of her reach. They all spoke at once until Anona stamped her foot.

"Shut up you mouths," Anona said. "This is a nice girl. She don't know Frankie's married. You think he's only a snake to Gracie? A snake don't change spots."

"A leopard . . . a leopard don't change its spots," Mary said.

"Who's talking about leopards? He's a snake."

"I didn't know . . . I swear . . . Frankie lied to me, too." Doreen was crying again.

"Listen," Helen said. She paused to light a cigarette. "Maybe you didn't know Frankie was married, but you know now. He's married to our sister, and if you know what's good for you, you'll stay far away. If he even mentions your name in his sleep, we'll find you and cut out your heart."

Mary took the cigarette from Helen's hand and took a drag. "Yeah, and we'll send it to your mother in Ohio."

"Iowa," Doreen said. "My mother's in Iowa."

"Be quiet," Helen said. "They both start with a O, no? Same thing."

"I won't see Frankie again. Ever. I promise."

"Forget it," Helen said. "You gotta go."

"Go where?"

"Send her someplace nice," Anona said. She cut a piece of bread and a triangle of provolone. "How about California? She's so pretty, she could be in the pictures."

Doreen sniffed. "I dance, too," she said.

Anona banged the flat of her hand on the table. *"Perfetto!"*

She pointed at Mary and then Helen. "You send her to California. *Basta!* Finish. I pack something for the trip."

"I don't believe this," Helen said. Mary laughed. She toyed with a spit curl. Today she had only two. They were murder to keep stuck down.

"You sure now, Anona? You sure you don't want to adopt her or nothing?" Anona waved off Mary's words with the back of her hand. She spoke to Doreen. "You gonna like California. Lotsa people go there from here and make it big. You know George Raft?"

"Let's go," Helen said. "We haven't got all night."

"Where are we going?" Doreen asked, hanging on to the wax paper package Anona had handed her as Helen pulled her to her feet.

"We're gonna take you to get a few things and then we're putting you on a bus."

Outside on the steps, Doreen stopped. "Can I ask you something?"

"Maybe," Mary said.

"Who were those little men?"

"What men?" Helen said, opening the car door.

Chapter Fourteen

Waking up to the aroma of peppers roasting, Frankie almost forgot his troubles. He knew his mother was holding the red peppers with a fork over the top of the stove. She would peel off the blackened skin and tear the peppers into strips, marinate them in olive oil, garlic, and oregano, add Sicilian olives cured with red pepper. The artichokes would be steaming in a pot, stuffed with raisins and egg, bread crumbs, parsley, and Romano cheese. He rolled over, covered his eyes with his forearm. He wondered what had happened to Doreen, and thought about how she must have run for her life and how she had left him like a dog.

The rent on the Horatio Street apartment was paid up for another month. He could find her later. He had plenty of time to get over there. He just worried that someone was on to him, that someone was watching.

He ate while his mother talked. She talked until his headache came back. She went on and on about his dead father, about Gracie's *puttane* sisters, about Charlie playing in the street too much,

about how she was alone last Sunday . . . He didn't answer, but
kept his head down, nodding between bites. It took him a long
time to eat, what with the pain in his jaw and his split lip, but Signora Merelli had made everything soft. She had always tried to
make everything soft for Frankie. He was, after all, her one and
only.

While she cleaned up the dishes and put them in the sink, he
stood in the small bedroom off the kitchen and looked at himself
in the mirror over her dresser. One eye was completely swollen
shut, both of them were turning black. There was an egg on the
back of his head that made his hair stand out no matter how much
pomade he smeared over it. He hadn't looked this bad since he'd
been knocked out in the first round at the Golden Gloves when he
was twelve.

Signora Merelli wiped her hands on a dish towel and pulled
down the sleeves of her sweater. "Now," she said, "you gotta go
up. But she gives you any trouble, you come back down, you
hear?"

"She won't give me any trouble."

"She better not. She gives you trouble, she's got some nerve."

Frankie went up the stairs. He could feel his knees where he must
have hit the pavement. Everything was starting to ache. He got to
the fourth-floor landing and saw that his door was shut, not a
good sign. Gracie usually left it half-open, like all the others, held
by a string that looped around the doorknob and attached to a
hook on the wall inside. It was a way of getting some air.

Frankie tried the door but it was locked. He felt in his pocket
for his key, but his pockets were empty. So, he thought, they'd
robbed him, too. He felt a sense of relief, realizing this. It could

have just been a robbery. Sure, he thought, it was just a couple of brazen punks out for a Saturday-night score. There were all kinds of characters in the Village. Sometimes it didn't pay to be so well dressed.

He felt confident, less guilty, victimized. He twisted the big brass key that stuck out from the top of the door and rang like a bell when you turned it. He could hear Gracie moving around inside, the backs of her slippers flapping against the kitchen linoleum. He called her name, softly at first, so his voice wouldn't carry into the other half-open doors, so nobody would know his business. There was no answer, just the blare of a radio, Hank Williams singing "Your Cheatin' Heart," the volume turned to high. He called Gracie's name again, his mouth close to the door, his palm pressed against it. He felt he was forever standing outside tenement doors with his tongue hanging out.

The door stayed shut but he heard Antonella Milardi's door open. Frankie knew she was standing behind it. He could feel her staring at him with her one good eye, the other a dry hole, the eyeball torn out when a firecracker bounced off her windowsill one Fourth of July. Antonella Milardi made everyone's business her own. Thank God, it was said, that she had only one eye, with two she would have seen into your soul. It made Frankie mad that she was witnessing him grovel in front of his own door, whispering to his wife, trying to get into his own house. He stood up straight, cocky, and knocked hard.

"Gracie, it's me, Frankie." His voice was loud, bossy. "I forgot my key." He expected Antonella Milardi to shut her door, her curiosity satisfied, but she didn't. He lost his temper then and started to bang on his door with both fists, misjudged his distance and knocked his head into the brass ringer. His forehead was bleeding. Antonella Milardi's one eye was peering.

Frankie stomped over to Antonella Milardi's door. "You really wanna know what's going on? Let me tell you. I forgot my key. My wife has the radio on and can't hear me. Now you know. Now you can go stick your big pepper someplace else."

At this Antonella Milardi opened the door wide and stepped out. "Listen, you," she said. "If I wanna open my door, that's my business. But I think I gonna close it because this hallway smells." She held her fingers to her nose and stuck her face in his. *"Puzzo,"* she said, and slammed the door. He heard her throwing curses behind it, at him, his son, his mother. For some reason, Gracie was spared. Even Antonella Milardi thought Gracie had it hard enough.

Jeannie Popeye was on the earie, too. She lived in the apartment next to Antonella Milardi but Jeannie Popeye wouldn't dare open the door because her husband would give her a smack for snooping. Without men, women just got out of control, Frankie told himself. His wife's family was a case in point. When Charlie grew up, Frankie was going to tell him a thing or two about being careful where you hang your hat.

Frankie clutched his head, told God and the saints how much he hated women, and then rattled and banged his apartment door until the lock broke but the chain across it held. "What do you think you're doing?" Gracie yelled from inside.

"I'm trying to get in. Can't you hear?"

Gracie came up close to the open slit of the door. "Don't think you can walk in here whenever you want. You left this afternoon. You know what time it is?"

"I was in my mother's. If you open this goddamn door and stop giving everyone a floor show, I can explain." Gracie came to the door and pushed against it with her whole weight to close it. Frankie stepped into the space between the doorjamb and the door. She pushed against his foot, crushing the soft calfskin loafer he had lovingly rubbed with polish in small slow circles with a chamois cloth. He felt a sharp pain in his arch. He bit the inside of his cheek. His voice cracked. "When you see what happened to me, you're gonna be sorry, Gracie. You'll never forgive yourself. Wait and see. Don't let me in. What do I care? It'll be on your conscience."

She opened the door. "Jesus . . . Frankie . . ." She let him inside. "You look like a truck hit you."

He sat down at the table and told her the story, how he was on his way home one minute and flat on his back with his head busted the next. By the time he'd finished, he believed it himself. He put his arms around her waist, buried his face in her belly, pulled her tighter, squeezed tears out of his eyes, burrowed closer. He talked into her skirt, caught the material in his teeth. "I thought I was never gonna see you and Charlie again. I thought I was gonna die on that sidewalk after those guys busted me up."

Gracie pulled his head back. "Who were they?" she said.

"What?"

"The guys that busted you up. What'd they look like?"

"What do I know?" Frankie told her. "They sly-rapped me from behind."

Chapter Fifteen

The next Sunday, Gracie got ready for the nine o'clock Mass, the one the school kids had to make. Charlie said if he wasn't at that one, when Father Linus came to the classroom Monday morning to ask who was there, he always smacked you around in the front of the room if you said you weren't.

"So tell him you were there," Frankie said.

"You can't. It's a trick. Sister St. Bernard takes attendance and she rats you out."

"Christ," Frankie said. "Sister St. Barnyard's still there? She must be over a hundred by now. I had her in sixth grade. She left me back twice."

"She likes when Father Linus hits the boys. I thought he was going to kill Vincent Albanese last week. I thought he was going to make him bleed." Charlie looked at his father. "How come they hit you so hard and you don't bleed?"

"They're smart, that's how . . . like the dicks down the station house."

"Frankie . . ."

"She left you back twice?" Charlie said.

"He's kidding, Charlie. Daddy was smart in school."

"Yeah. I was always good with numbers." Frankie put his hand up Gracie's dress and pinched her leg. She smiled at him because she could tell Charlie hadn't seen. She put a plate of soft-boiled eggs on the table in front of him. She hadn't made toast because she didn't think Frankie could eat it. His face was still swollen from the beating he took the weekend before. If it got any worse, she was afraid he'd have to drink soup through a straw.

Frankie loved Gracie a lot this morning. She was being so good to him. Nothing got to Frankie like attention. His mother had told Gracie early on that he was just a big baby.

Frankie offered Charlie a forkful of egg but he shook his head. He said he couldn't eat because he had to receive Communion. On Monday morning Father Linus asked about that, too.

"Jesus, Charlie, you may as well be a priest," Frankie said. Signora Merelli had tried that with Frankie, sent him to the seminary when he was fourteen. Finding him with Tessie Marscarpone should have been her first clue, but Signora Merelli was determined. She saw herself in Rome in a fur-trimmed coat and matching hat, the mother of a priest. She had filled a suitcase with black clothes she bought on credit from the Jew on Broadway and when Frankie ran away and came home two days later, her sobs could be heard as far as Bleecker Street. When he walked in the door, she'd banged the heel of her hand on the doorjamb and she told him he'd never have any luck.

Frankie touched his jaw and felt up the side of his face, and wondered if his mother had foretold the future that day or just cursed him. Maybe that was his first mistake, running away from the seminary, or was it Tessie Marscarpone? The religious life didn't look so bad to him anymore, no bills, and all those grateful mothers from the PTA just dying to get popped.

Gracie sat down at the table and pulled Charlie between her knees and knotted his tie. She fixed his collar and kissed him all over his face and held him tight when he tried to squirm away. She smoothed his hair to the side with her fingers and rubbed both his cheeks until they were bright pink. "You're so handsome," she said. "You're the love of my life." Frankie pretended he didn't hear. Those were the words he wanted to hear Gracie say to him. Maybe when they were alone, he'd make her say them.

Gracie and Charlie walked on Spring Street together but he ran ahead of her when they reached the corner. She followed him with her eyes as he crossed Prince Street and kept going up Sullivan to St. Anthony's Church. He had to go downstairs in the basement and line up with his class. But after Gracie watched the schoolchildren march in procession up the steps to the main church, she didn't follow, but walked north, up MacDougal Street. She went into Dante's café, ordered a cappuccino and a *sfogliatelle* and sat in the big window and watched the people walk by, all kinds of people. She thought about how different the world was beyond Houston Street. She thought about sometime going to Leroy Street and getting a card for the library. Charlie had one from when the second-grade nun would take the class on Wednesdays for story hour.

A man at the next table smiled at her and she smiled back. She got so shook up at how naturally she had reacted to a strange man's attention that she went to the bar to pay her check and leave before she realized the man was Vincent Violotti, the lawyer with the office on Bedford Street. Standing at the bar, waiting to pay, she saw Ralphie, the neighborhood shylock, at a back table with Joe Stretch. Even on Sunday, she thought, somebody needed a quick buck. Then she really got nervous.

Suppose they saw her and told Frankie? Had they seen her smile at Vincent Violotti? But Ralphie and Joe Stretch were deep in conversation. Gracie felt relief and then anger. Her sisters were right. "You moved to Spring Street," they always told her, "not Sicily." She was going to start doing exactly what she wanted to do. She left a big tip on the table and planned to stop at Vincent's table on the way out and say hello, but he was gone.

She took her time walking to Fourth Street Park, where the nannies in white uniforms minded the babies from the buildings on Fifth Avenue. Gracie found a space on a bench and sat down next to an elegant old couple with a white poodle. No one would have known where she came from, she thought. She was wearing a hat and white gloves, just like the old lady who was saying something to her about the weather. Gracie had stepped through the looking glass for one afternoon. Sitting there she couldn't believe how wide the world was, how she had locked herself into a box of a few city blocks. She petted the white poodle and the old man smiled. "His name is Pierre," he told her. "We live in that building," and he pointed to a brownstone that faced the park. "Do you live around here?"

"Farther down," Gracie told them, "but it must be nice to be on the park."

"Oh, it's lovely," the woman said. "You should consider moving."

Gracie smiled. Why not? she thought. Miracles happened every day.

When Frankie heard the door shut, he waited, five, ten, fifteen minutes for Gracie to be out of the building. He had to figure on her meeting somebody on the stairs and yapping. She was such a *chiachiarese* she could bullshit with a cockroach. When he was convinced she was gone, he slipped out of bed and got dressed. Things were working out. He didn't know how long she'd be, but he didn't need that much time. He just had to get over to Horatio Street and see about Doreen. He felt a little woozy and he looked like shit. He put his collar up and the brim of his hat down.

Despite everything, Frankie's blood was pumping, settling in his pants. To live the fantasy for one swift second, he closed his eyes. In his fantasy, Doreen was always waiting for him, frantic for him, arms outstretched, on fire, begging for him, like the girls in the cheap paper novels she would read aloud to him in bed.

He had no key. That had disappeared with the rest of the stuff in his pockets when he'd gotten brained outside Fedora's Saturday night, so when he got to the apartment he had to knock, but there was no answer. He thought about getting Carmine, the super, to let him in, but on a whim, tried the knob, felt a bolt of excitement as it turned in his hand. The door swung open and he stepped inside.

There was no Doreen. There was no nothing. The place was empty. It had been stripped: the satin couch, the fringed lamps, the marble coffee table from Roma furniture on the East Side that had cost him an extra sawbuck because it was so heavy to get up the stairs. The mirrors shot through with gold had been unscrewed from the wall, the red glass ashtray where he'd put his cigarette while Doreen sat in his lap. Everything was gone.

He heard someone behind him. It was Carmine, the super Frankie had staked three hundred bucks to get the apartment in the first place. Frankie felt a sense of relief, as though Carmine could rescue him, make it all right again, the way it had been.

"Carmine!" he said. "What happened?"

Carmine shrugged, his big meaty hands outstretched. "I don't know what to tell you. I'm as surprised as you. I thought maybe you moved."

"Without saying nothing?"

"Hey, people are funny. I don't ask questions."

"You don't know what happened? You didn't see nobody?"

"To tell you the truth, I went out to Jersey to pick up my wife. She was staying with her sister. I was gone a few days and when I come back, the place was like this."

The truth, which Carmine had told his brother-in-law Funzi, but wasn't about to tell Frankie, was that a redhead had come by, cute as a button. (Carmine had a thing for redheads . . . Rita Hayworth was his idea of a dreamboat . . . he had a picture of her taped up on the wall in the boiler room.) The redhead had been with another dame, a blonde, and they had given him a hundred bucks to get rid of all the stuff in the apartment. Carmine had called a friend of his and picked up another two hundred. All in all, it had been a nice score.

"It wasn't no break-in," Carmine told Frankie. "I found the keys in an envelope in the kitchen." Carmine paused. "Gee, I feel bad about this . . ."

"No, forget it. What could you do?" Frankie said and handed him a pound. "Thanks anyway."

"You okay, buddy? You look pretty beat up."

"I'm fine. I'm just great."

Carmine pocketed the five-dollar bill. "You know," he said, "I don't think I can get you that last month's rent back. The owner's a son of a bitch that way."

"Yeah, sure. Of course not."

"Well, take your time. Just shut the door on your way out. I got a couple looking but they ain't coming for another hour."

Frankie walked back home. Did he have a fucking sign on his back? Did that asshole Carmine think for one minute Frankie bought his cockamamy story? Doreen must have left the furniture, and Carmine had sold it. And he was grabbing the last month's rent on top of it. Frankie had gone for his lungs furnishing that apartment and he still owed on it. He'd bought it all on time.

With his hands stuck deep in his pockets, Frankie made a promise to himself: as soon as he felt better he was going over to the Savannah Club and get himself a stripper, one of those Georgia Peaches, a headliner. He was going to buy her a bottle of champagne and put his hand between her legs when she was between acts. He was through with love. But for now, he was going home.

Frankie swallowed four aspirin without water as soon as he got there, and crawled into his marriage bed.

Chapter Sixteen

Demoralized and humiliated, his body a mosaic of rainbow-colored bruises, Frankie refused to leave his bed. When Gracie shook him awake Monday morning, he only pressed his face deeper into the pillow. He shivered in the bed. He couldn't go in to work; he wasn't feeling so good. He told her that in his condition, he could collapse and die. He mentioned Joe Mosca. It was cold; the wind off the river was brutal. And if a ship came in, he could be working twenty-eight hours at a clip.

Gracie left him in bed, the covers pulled up to his ears. He heard her in the kitchen calling Charlie to get out of bed and telling him to be quiet, to hurry up and get dressed. She wanted him to go downstairs and tell Lena Santulli to tell her husband Dibby, who Frankie shaped up with down the docks, that Frankie wasn't going this morning, that he wasn't feeling so good.

Frankie relaxed under the covers. The beating he took was almost worth it if it saved him from a couple of days carrying them friggin' bananas. "I don't want to go to school. I don't feel so good, neither," he heard Charlie say.

"Too bad. You're going and you're leaving early because you have to stop and tell Lena." Gracie poured Cheerios in a bowl with milk and cut up a banana. She tucked a napkin in Charlie's shirt collar and handed him a spoon.

Charlie left and Gracie listened for him in the hall. If the apartment had faced the front, she would have watched him from the window but she knew Signora Merelli would be out her window. She couldn't rest, she told Gracie, until she watched Charlie join the stream of kids that flowed out the building on the way to St. Anthony's School.

Gracie made another pot of coffee. She took one of Frankie's cigarettes and lit it with a wooden kitchen match. She watched the smoke curl up around her fingers while she smoked. She thought maybe she'd buy her own pack this afternoon. Something with a filter. Maybe after a while, she'd inhale. She counted the change in the sugar bowl she kept on a shelf in the tin cabinet over the sink. Plenty for a pack of cigarettes with enough left over for Mr. Feldstein, who sold life insurance door to door. She'd met him in the hallway and he told her he'd come by to collect her installment. "Better safe than sorry," was Mr. Feldstein's favorite saying, and "Death doesn't take the time to knock."

On Friday, Gracie pushed and poked and called Frankie's name. "You gotta to go to work today. You been in all week. It's Friday. You get paid on Friday."

"You are really crazy," he said, sliding back down into the bed, the sheet just under his eyes. "In that shit job you don't get paid unless you work and I ain't been there. That's why I hate shaping up."

"You get nothing, Frankie?"

"Nothing, Gracie, 'cause that's what I am, nothing." He pulled the sheet over his head and lay there like a corpse. He wondered why the hell he'd gotten married in the first place. He was doing fine before, living with his mother, working a few card games, a few nights here and there behind the bar at one of the Village clubs or the strip joints on Third Street. Soldiers were quick with a buck. He had done okay, but with a wife and then a kid, it wasn't enough and Gracie didn't want him working nights, so when he couldn't get started in business, he'd had no choice but to get himself some backbreaking work. There was always backbreaking work available.

It bothered him that Gracie just couldn't get it through her head that he wasn't like the other guys on Spring Street. He wasn't meant for manual labor.

But Gracie wasn't interested. She loved him with nothing. She'd never thought about the future with Frankie, where she'd be living, how he'd put food on the table. But she expected him to work. He'd had chances for better things but none of his schemes ever worked out. He'd lost a vegetable store and a butcher shop and his mother's life savings. And Gracie never even knew about Ciminelli Trucking.

The problem was Frankie couldn't get it through his head that you had to work a business. He just wanted to be a *padrone*. If you had to work, what was the point? Signora Merelli told Gracie that her son wasn't meant for business. He was born to be a priest.

Gracie shook Frankie's shoulder hard. "Get up. You gotta go to work. Enough is enough." He reached for her, pulled her down to the bed, slid a hand around her waist, ran the other along her thigh. He moved over and put his head in her lap. "Gracie, I can't go back to shaping up, carrying them bananas, every day, every day. Have mercy. You don't know what it's like. They drop those stalks on your shoulder from three feet in the air. You got any idea what a stalk of bananas feels like on your back? What it weighs? I can't take it no more. And what about them spiders? Big like grapefruits, hairy, ugly, hiding in the bananas. Suppose I get bit by one of them spiders? Then what? Huh? What happens to you and Charlie? Whatta you do? Go on home relief?"

"It can't be that bad, Frankie. A lotta guys around here shape up."

"Yeah, but they're losers. You think I'm a loser, Gracie? That's what you think?"

She didn't answer. She felt like smoking one of the filter cigarettes she'd bought in Sam & Al's.

"I'm losing my pride, Gracie. What's a man without his pride? You see how long I gotta stand by that sink scrubbing my hands with Boraxo? I see that goddamn black-and-white can in my sleep. Look at this," and he held out his hands for her to see that he knew what he was talking about.

She rubbed his hands in hers. He was full of shit, she thought. They were still soft. This afternoon he'd go for a manicure. But she knew what he was saying. Frankie was about clean crisp knife pleats in his pants. It was what she had noticed about him first thing; he was all angles, all edges, as though he had been cut out with a pair of hopelessly sharp scissors, nothing left to chance.

"You could talk to your sisters," Frankie was saying. "You could talk to Mary . . . I bet Nick could do something. He's still got the connections down the piers." Frankie stroked her arm. "Your sisters would do anything for you."

She pushed his hand away and stood up. "No," she said.

Charlie was lurking behind the door. Gracie caught him when she came out into the kitchen. "What are you doing? You're gonna be late."

"I don't feel so good."

"Go to school, Charlie. I'm not putting up with you, too. You felt fine ten minutes ago."

"Daddy's still home."

"Daddy's sick. You're fine. Get outta here. Grandma Merelli's gonna be screaming up the hallway any minute if she looks out the window and don't see you."

"I'm going. I'm going. Don't push." Charlie left, his hand to his mouth, forcing himself to cough. "You're gonna be sorry," he called up to her on his way down the stairs.

• • •

Gracie had finished cleaning up the kitchen when Frankie came in, sat down and asked her to make him coffee. She told him she couldn't do everything and left him sitting there while she went to the bedroom to get dressed. "I'm going to my sisters, Frankie, but this is the last time. I'm not asking them for you ever again."

She would go to Anona's. Helen and Mary always went to see the old lady on Fridays. It was a ritual. She would see her sisters and she would ask them about a job for Frankie. She thought about him sitting there in the kitchen smoking a cigarette, asking her to make him coffee. He looked surprised when she walked out the door wearing her hat. He could make his own coffee, she figured, or go downstairs and get some. Either way, Gracie had decided, it was about time he took care of himself. She was annoyed with him, her patience thin. She had one son; she didn't need another. What she needed was a husband.

She was walking up MacDougal Street past St. Anthony's School on her way to the bus stop when Mother Benita's secretary came outside on the school steps and called her name. "I'm so glad I caught you," Mrs. Rotunda said. She was a neighborhood mother who took her job as Mother Benita's secretary seriously. She had to, Gracie supposed, her husband had left her with five kids and run off with a cocktail waitress from the Bon Soir.

Charlie was in the principal's office, she said. Sister St. Bernard had sent him to the nurse when he complained of a stomachache, and the nurse had sent him to Mother Benita because Charlie said that his father was home sick from work with something bad and catchy and he felt really terrible. In Mother Benita's office, Charlie had doubled over and spit up on the floor and Mother Benita told her secretary to call Charlie's mother to come get him.

"Charlie said you have no phone and you know we don't let the children go home alone during school hours."

"How lucky I came by," Gracie said, matching airs. She'd have to talk to that kid about telling people what he had and didn't have. He was a such a blabbermouth. "Can you send him out?"

Charlie came down the school steps and threw his mother a sly grin. "Mamma," he said and ran to her. "Mrs. Rotunda was gonna have to walk me home." He took his mother's hand in his and looked back at Mrs. Rotunda. "Thank you, Mrs. Rotunda," he said.

"Bye, Charlie, I hope you feel better soon."

Gracie smiled until Mrs. Rotunda went inside and then she yanked Charlie's arm so that his head bobbed like a buoy. "What are you doing pretending to be sick?"

"I told you this morning I didn't feel good." He pulled away from her. "Where are you going, anyway? How come you're all dressed up?"

"I'm going to Anona's, and it's none of your business. Who are you, my boss?"

"Can I come?"

"No, you're going home. You wanted to go home, that's where you're going." She turned back toward Spring Street. "And now I'm gonna be late. I'd like to break your head when you do this." She grabbed his shoulder and pushed him in front of her. She twisted his ear.

He started crying. "Why can't I come? Pleasepleaseplease. I'll be quiet. You won't even know I'm there. I'm sick, remember? You can't leave me. You're my mother. Don't you love me?"

Gracie stopped. Love him? She never thought she could love anyone the way she loved Charlie. It scared her how much she loved him. She always pushed it out of her mind. Anona had taught her that to dwell on something you loved was a sure invitation to tragedy. Hide your love so the *malocchio* won't find you.

Look what happened to Emma, Anona said, covering her ears when Helen and Mary said it was the influenza, not evil spirits, that had killed their mother. Millions of people died like Emma, they told her, but Anona wouldn't listen. Doubt brought the spirits, too.

How could Charlie not know she loved him? Gracie stooped to straighten his tie and fix his sweater where she had pulled it out of shape when she yanked his arm. She caught his face in one hand and kissed his mouth. "Of course I love you. I'll always love you, but I'd still like to kill you. C'mon, we're late." He rubbed his ear, which was starting to swell, and ran after her.

Chapter Seventeen

Gracie took Charlie on the Eighth Avenue bus uptown and they got off at Thirty-eighth Street and walked over to Tenth Avenue to Anona's. Helen and Mary were already there, sitting around the table. Anona had the coffeepot on the stove, the coffee percolating into the glass knob of the cover, the aroma filling the kitchen. It might have been the third or fourth pot of the morning. No one walked into Anona's without sitting at her table with a cup of coffee. And there was always a bottle of whiskey on the countertop under the glass cabinets, near the shrine to St. Rita.

Mary got up when Gracie and Charlie walked in. She hugged Gracie and smothered Charlie against her, his head disappearing in the circle of her arms. Her dress was cut in a deep V and Charlie's nose caught between her breasts. She held him there until he thought he would suffocate before she passed him to Helen, whose hug left the imprint of buttons on his cheek. Mary smelled of perfume, Helen of smoke that clung to her as tightly as her dress. He was glad for Anona's casual, "Hiya, sonny boy," and the detached way she turned her face for him to kiss.

Mary pulled out a chair for him and pushed him close to the table. Helen stood up and, cigarette hanging from her mouth, filled a plate with pastries and poured him a glass of milk. Gracie kissed Anona and her sisters and sat at the table. "So," Anona said, putting a cup in front of her, squinting at her. "You good? Everything okay?"

Gracie shrugged and nodded. She held out her cup for Anona to fill.

"Sonny boy's all right? How come he's not in school?"

"He didn't feel good . . . his stomach . . . he threw up in the principal's office."

Mary smiled and ran her hand through Charlie's hair. "You think pastry's a good idea with a stomachache?"

"I'm better. You always feel better after you throw up . . . right, Ma?"

"Signora Merelli tells him that. She prefers enemas but throwing up is a close second," Gracie said. She looked at Charlie. "Two," she said. "Don't eat more than two."

"And how's Frankie doing?" Mary asked.

"He's not so good. He got busted up bad in the Village a couple of weekends ago. You can't believe what they did to him. In fact, he's still home in bed."

Helen looked up. "Ohmygod, poor Frankie!" she said. "Who? What happened? A fight?"

Mary had moved her chair next to Charlie's and was replacing the pastries in his dish as fast as he ate them. She watched Gracie from under hooded lids.

Gracie made eyes at Mary to say she didn't want to talk in front of Charlie but Helen was the one who got the message. She smoothed Charlie's black curls away from his forehead, looking around for a way to divert him. There was a noise in the hall and she had a brainstorm. "Shush," she said. "I bet that's the Hanley kid." She took the half-eaten miniature chocolate-covered éclair out of Charlie's hand and pulled him off the table and over to the door. When she flung it open, Mike Hanley, Jr., was standing outside with a brand-new Schwinn. "I knew it was him," she said to Charlie. "He never goes to school, either. Where'd you get the bicycle, Little Mike?"

"My father. He just gave it to me. I'm just walking by and he comes out of the bar wheeling it. Ain't it somethin?"

"It sure is."

"Who's that?" he said, pointing at Charlie.

"Oh, my nephew from downtown."

"A guinea?"

"Yeah, but he's a good kid."

Helen pushed Charlie in front of her and out into the hallway. "I want you to meet a friend of mine, Charlie. This is Little Mike. Maybe he'll take you downstairs and show you around the neighborhood." Helen took out a half-dollar and flipped it into Little Mike's grimy fist. Charlie forced a half-smile, remembering Jimmy Mulligan's choke hold.

Gracie came to the door. Helen looked over her shoulder. "Mike Hanley's kid is gonna take Charlie around," she told her sister. Gracie forgot about Frankie lying at home in his sickbed and took a long look at Little Mike. She didn't like what she saw.

She knew there was crust behind his ears, dirt wedged into the creases of his neck and maybe a switchblade in his pocket. Irish boys always had big necks lined with dirt. She remembered this from when she was a kid. It didn't look like anything had changed.

"Let him go," Helen said. "Little Mike'll look out for him, no?" Little Mike shook his head yes and motioned for Charlie to follow him. Helen stuck two quarters in Charlie's sweater pocket and went back inside. She didn't know Little Mike would extort them before Charlie was halfway down the stairs, but she wouldn't have been surprised.

"Now," Helen said to Gracie, closing the door. "What's going on?"

"Some guys jumped Frankie in the Village." Gracie turned to Mary. "It was that Saturday we went to Peter Luger's."

"That's awful. Who was it?"

"He didn't see anybody; he never knew what hit him. He said they hit him from behind."

"He's got no idea?"

"They emptied his pockets so he figures it was a robbery. You know Frankie. He always looks like a million dollars."

Helen screwed up her face. "Whatta shame! But he's okay?"

Gracie sat up. She positioned her coffee cup in front of her and cleared her throat. "Yeah, he'll be fine, but you know what? He just can't see himself shaping up anymore, carrying them bananas. The kind of riffraff he works with down the piers . . . Who knows? Who knows who did this to him? I mean, Frankie never hurt nobody. He's an easygoing guy. This work is killing him."

Anona stood up. "Tell us what you want, *cara*," she said. "Your sisters, they'll do anything for you."

"He needs a job, a real one. Something clean, something

where he can feel like he's somebody. It would be good for all of us. Who's Charlie gonna look up to?"

Mary nodded. "You're right, sweetie. You should have told us before. I'll talk to Nick tonight. He'll get him something easy on the piers. Where is Frankie now? Pier 13? Don't even think about it." She came around and put her hands on Gracie's shoulders. "Frankie'll be wearing a suit and tie to work in no time. You can go to sleep on it."

Helen thought for one split second about offering to get Frankie a job in one of the clubs. She knew everybody in the night life, from the Village to Harlem, but she decided to keep quiet. Let him stay on the piers. She didn't believe in tempting fate, or Frankie Merelli. "Sounds like great news, Gracie," she said. "You can press a few more shirts."

"Very funny," Gracie said, relaxing back into her chair. She took a pignoli cookie and dunked it in her coffee cup. "But thanks. I really appreciate everything you've always done for me. Frankie'll be so happy."

Anona went over to the shrine to St. Rita on the kitchen counter. She checked that the devotional candles in the semicircle of dark red cups around the plaster saint were lit. Anona ordered the candles by the dozen, yellow and white. But in the back of the closet in her bedroom, there was a box of black that she used for her magic. She hoped she wouldn't need them but she was always ready to do what she had to do. She accepted the power of fate but she also believed it could be manipulated. There had to be some protection against the world. That's why she had St. Rita and all those candles. Anona would sit in the dark and think. She had done this when she had been left alone to raise the girls. She had decided to stay where she was, in this building with the Irish. She knew it was a way of staying independent. She had given up the support of community and taken her chances. She could have gone back to the Italians on Sullivan Street or Mulberry Street or even uptown on 107th Street. They would have embraced her in her misery and loss. They would have helped her. But they also would have judged her and tracked her every move.

She would never have known the pleasure of a drink at Hanley's at the end of the day. Or the satisfaction of having the cleanest house, the best kitchen aromas, the most coddled patron saint. Anona liked Hell's Kitchen and her neighbors just fine. And she raised her girls to think for themselves. She mumbled in the ancient dialect she had spoken as a child in the village of Bocca al Lupo, blew out the candles and relit them three times. The room was quiet.

"Now," Anona said, after making the sign of the cross one last time. She shuffled over to the stove. "I make some more coffee and we have a few drinks."

"What was all that for?" Helen said, pointing to the shrine.

"I'm just making sure everything works out. St. Rita, she likes candles. She's good to me; I light some candles."

Mary rolled her eyes. "You light enough candles to burn down the building."

"Don't worry about me. Besides, I got a lotta firemen live in this building," Anona said. She counted on her fingers. "McManus and Fitzsimmons on the third floor, Brady downstairs, his sons, Eddie and Johnny . . ."

There was a pounding on the door. Gracie went to open it and there was Charlie, a paper bag of gumdrops in one hand and in the other a charlotte russe with all the cream licked off the top. "Little Mike got pinched!" he told his mother.

"Oh, for God sakes, get inside. I don't believe this, Anona. Nothing ever changes around here."

"I was in the candy store . . ." Charlie held out the paper bag to Anona. "Want some?"

Anona shook her head. "I got no teeth, sonny boy. See?" She flipped out her plate. Charlie gagged. He hated when she did that.

"So, what happened then?"

"Two cops come in and they say, 'Where'd you get that bike,' and Little Mike says his father, and they say, 'You're lying, that bike's stolen,' and one of them takes him by the collar and the other one wheels the bike. They were big cops." Charlie picked out the pieces of gumdrop stuck in his teeth. "What's gonna happen?"

"He's a little boy. They'll scare him and let him go," Mary said, shaking her head. Her bosom heaved. Charlie followed it with his eyes. He thought that when she hugged him goodbye, he would turn his face so his nose wouldn't get caught and then she could hold him forever against those milky white hills that swelled over her dress.

"Forget Little Mike and get ready," Gracie said. "We're leaving."

"I'll drive you," Mary said.

"No, stay. It's early for you."

Anona made a package of pastries and cookies wrapped in wax paper and tied with string for Gracie to take home. Charlie kissed and hugged Anona and Helen. Then he kissed and hugged Mary and wouldn't let her go. He had purposely saved her for last.

Anona leaned out the window to watch Gracie and Charlie come out of the building and up the street. She started to cough and Mary came over and tried to shut the window. "No wonder you have asthma, always sticking your nose outside. Come over here."

But Anona pushed her away and wouldn't go anywhere until

Gracie and Charlie were gone, until she lost sight of them around the corner. When she sat back down, Helen poured rose water on a handkerchief and Anona held it to her face.

"Maybe," Helen said, "Frankie's learned his lesson."

"I hope so, because I don't know what else we can do."

"Gracie could be right. If he feels like a big shot at work, maybe he won't have to stick his pole into every tomato that comes along."

Anona sneezed. "I don't believe the way you talk, the things you say in front of me, an old lady like me, your grandmother."

Helen came over and tugged on Anona's sleeve. "So now you're an old lady? When you go sit in Hanley's and have a few beers, you don't hear talk like that?"

"Whatta you mean? Those boys treat me nice in that bar. They got a lotta respect."

Helen kissed Anona's face until she pushed her away. "You going down after we leave?"

"No, whatta you think, I go there all the time? Once in a blue sky, maybe."

"Blue moon . . . once in a blue moon." Mary got up to get her coat. "If you do go out, you be careful. It's starting to rain. The streets are slippery."

"Anona was walking these streets when they were slippery with blood, right, Anona?" Helen said. "When this neighborhood was really tough."

Anona waved the two of them away with the back of her hand. "Go, go," she said. *"Andate via!"* She sat still while they kissed and hugged her goodbye but after the door closed, she went over to the window to watch them drive away in Nick's big black Cadillac.

Then she put her purse in her pocket, buttoned up her

sweater, and went downstairs to Hanley's Bar. She ordered a beer and asked about Little Mike. When Big Mike got to the police station to get him, they told her, he smacked his son for stealing the bike and smacked him again for telling the cops his father had given it to him. "That'll be the last time Little Mike tells the truth," Jerry, the bartender, Big Mike's brother, said, and they all laughed.

Anona stayed late but she knew to leave before the fights broke out, which they did every night just before closing time. Like Helen said, she'd been in this neighborhood a long time.

Upstairs she sat in front of her statue of St. Rita, not to pray but to watch the small blue flames of the votive candles and remember all those years ago when it was just her and Mary and Gracie and Helen, on their own, with coal stolen from the barges on Twenty-third Street and vegetables scavenged from Paddy's market under the Ninth Avenue El. They'd done good, she thought, although she seldom thought about the past, or the good. It was too precarious and the less attention you gave it, the better off you were. Sometimes an unbruised apple was enough to attract the *malocchio*. It was what she liked about the Irish; they weren't always so ready to put the horns on you. They didn't know how. It made for good neighbors.

1931–1933

Salvatore Maranzano Assassinated
Shot and Stabbed in Gangland Slaying at 230 Park Avenue

ADOLF HITLER BECOMES CHANCELLOR OF THE GERMAN THIRD REICH

World's Tallest Skyscraper

EMPIRE STATE BUILDING OPENS

Chapter Eighteen

Hell's Kitchen in 1931 was all about Vincent Coll, who worked for Dutch Schultz until he decided to go out on his own. The slaughter that followed reminded some in the neighborhood of the days of the Gophers and the Hudson Dusters and the feud with Patsy Doyle that had sent Owney Madden to Sing Sing for eight years.

In June, Coll kidnapped Madden's partner, Big Frenchy, and held him for ransom, and not a month later, he attempted a hit on a hood named Rao and killed a five-year-old boy, a stunt that earned him his nickname, "Mad Dog Coll," and put a fifty-thousand-dollar reward on his head.

Mary was worried about Nick but never said anything except to Helen, who told her if she was going to live the fast life, she'd better forget about worry. It would come and find her when it was ready.

Times were bad, the Depression worsening, but Mary spent her time in places like the Stork Club and the brand-new Waldorf-Astoria Hotel in sequined dresses that Nick brought her by the carload. Prohibition and working for Owney Madden secured the good times that Mary and the rest of the Mallones had been used to ever since Nick Andersen showed up. They went to the pictures to see Jimmy Cagney in *Public Enemy* and when the George Washington Bridge opened, Nick took them all for a ride across to New Jersey with the top down.

But then Vincent Coll was machine-gunned almost in half in a drugstore phone booth on Twenty-third Street near Eighth Avenue on February 8, 1932. Nick Andersen disappeared right after.

Mary sat in Anona's chair by the window and looked down at the street, thinking any minute he would show up in his black Cadillac and white fedora. But Nick Andersen was on the lam. Mary wasn't the only one who was looking for him.

If the police got him, he was facing ten to twenty, which wasn't much for a tough guy like Nick who'd come to America as a cabin boy on a Swedish freighter and jumped ship in New York. He had never wanted a life of hard work and at six foot three and fifteen years old (thanks to a diet of crushed fruit, stale cake, and sugar candy rumored to be made of glue) he made a convincing enforcer. He was built like a "brick shit house" of which there weren't many in Hell's Kitchen, the standard being a wooden shack stuck back in the tenement yards, one for two buildings.

Tarring Jimmy Nelson's mouth shut and tying him to the railroad tracks that ran along the Hudson River established his reputation. Prohibition made him part of history. Nick Andersen could do ten to twenty standing on his head. But it was a long time for Mary Mallone, who was sixteen years old and starting to show.

Mary wore her dresses loose, Anona taking out the waistbands bit by bit. No one could tell for sure, and the Irish women were looking hard. The jackals, Anona called them, were watching. They stood in bunches by the door and parted quickly when Mary came or went, looking, watching, and if their suspicions were confirmed, Anona knew they would have their fingers up, counting, remembering the sequence of events.

Anona wouldn't let Mary go back to the job in the candy factory that she'd had before Nick came along. She said she didn't want Mary standing on her feet all day, breathing fumes and dust. Gracie took her job instead, even though she didn't want to leave school. But Anona said it wasn't getting her nowhere; she might just as well leave now as later.

And Helen went to work in the slaughterhouse. The McGee sisters got her the job after their sister Molly got fired for stealing a ham. It was better than the battery factory, they told her, breathing in all that acid. The work's easy and besides what you can steal, they give you the livers and things they don't want.

The bills Mary had smuggled home in the lining of her coat were safely away. Anona had carefully pressed them flat with the iron she heated on the stove, pressed them one on top of the other and hidden them no one knew where. They would last a long time, she said, and with Gracie and Helen working, she'd probably never even have to pawn her pearl brooch, which she kept pinned on a red silk ribbon next to St. Rita.

The problem wasn't money; it was that baby in Mary's belly. Nick had disappeared without a trace, without a word. Mary kept waiting for some news, expecting one of his gang to let her know where he was, to send for her, to do something, but Big Nick Andersen had vaporized. As Anona told Mary, he could be anywhere. And as she told Gracie and Helen, he might even be dead.

Anona chewed over the options with St. Rita. She could find a midwife who would give Mary something poisonous to drink and insert something foreign into her vagina until the baby, violently disturbed, was expelled. She could say Mary was secretly married, sadly widowed, but who would believe that? It was an old story. Anona never believed it when it was told to her. There was no war, that wonderful widow maker, only a Depression that was getting worse and worse, with people's furniture being thrown out into the street and long lines of jobless men waiting for a handout, Anona explained to the saint. No help there. Too bad.

But Anona did remember to thank the saint for the Mallones' good fortune, all the while patting herself on the back for her prudence and thrift with the money that had come their way. She hoped St. Rita wouldn't be overly concerned about where the money came from. After all, there was nothing virtuous about money. Anona could recite a million parables about the dirty stuff. Money wasn't the problem. It was what to do about Mary.

Anona could see only one way. Marriage, a quick marriage, suitable for these hard times, and like always, a baby. A baby usually followed a marriage. Women knew that, whether they had come from Ireland or Italy or from no place at all. It was a fact of life.

Anona worried about Mary and made pastes for her of powdered seeds and olive oil. Anona would rub these pastes over Mary's stomach and breasts and wrap her with strips of cotton torn from bedsheets. She made Mary eat boiled wilted greens that she found in Paddy's market and alongside the streets, thin weak things that pushed themselves up through cracks in the cement. She learned these things from her Nonna, she'd tell the sisters, when she was a girl in Bocca al Lupo, where these greens grew everywhere. "Hmmm," Anona would say, stirring the pot of beans and escarole. "Better than steak!"

"Let's go back," Gracie said to Anona once. "Can't we? Can't we get on a ship and go the other way from everybody else? Let's do that. Go back and live in Bocca al Lupo."

"You crazy?" Anona said, hitting her forehead with the heel of her hand. "It was hell. We starved. We died from the cholera. We scraped the earth for nothing. Why do you think we came here?"

"Ha," Mary said from the corner, where she was fumbling with knitting needles and yarn. "Whatta you call this? Paradise?"

"You have to die to go to heaven," Anona told her.

"Not me," Mary said. "I'm gonna find a piece of it here. I had it, too. I had it real nice for a while till Nick had to go away." She threw the piece of knitting on the table. "And I hate this. I like things store-bought."

"I don't understand, Anona. One day you tell us it was beautiful in Italy and the next day you call it hell," Gracie said.

"So? Just listen. Why you gotta be so *picayune* and make a big deal. I don't gotta feel the same every day. It's a free country, America, no?"

"Mrs. Murphy came in today when you were out," Mary said. "She was looking at me, right at my belly, I swear, talking about how good you are to us, 'a real saint, your granny,' she said."

"That *pittacuse,* she tries to dig the dirt, the first to throw stones."

"Yeah, her daughter Maureen left after that big fight and never came back," Helen said.

"What left? She threw her out in the street like the garbage. What a thing to do . . . she wears the hat all the time like she's somebody." Anona spat in her handkerchief and put it back up her sleeve. "They throw out their daughters and then they go to church."

"She was bringing men home," Gracie whispered. "They said she was taking money."

"So?" Anona said. "You don't throw out your blood."

Mary started to cry. "What am I gonna do, Anona? I'm gonna have this baby and then what? What's gonna happen to me? I should go jump in the river and get it over with."

"The river?" Gracie shouted and Helen pushed her shoulder to shut her up. Anona came over and pulled Mary's hair. She held Mary's face in her hands.

"Be quiet!" she said, pointing to the statue of St. Rita. "You want her to hear? The saints, they don't forgive despair."

"I can't help it."

"You keep crying, you gonna ruin this baby's eyes. My aunt Sistina cried like that, the baby came out with the eyes stuck shut. Don't worry. Everything works out. We got Helen back, no?"

"It was Nick found Helen."

"Nick, that big dope . . . and who found him? You! No?" Anona dried Mary's face with the hem of her top skirt.

Mary's tears stopped. She scowled at Anona. "Don't call him that," she said. "Nick was good to us."

"Huh, who cares what I call him?" Anona said. "He's yesterday's newspaper." Mary's tears came again. She opened her mouth to speak, to protest, but Anona took hold of her and crushed her in her arms. patted her hair, rubbed her fingers along the back of her neck. "Way before anybody can say anything, you'll be married with a beautiful baby and then they can eat their own crap."

Mary looked up. "Nick's gone. How's he gonna marry me?"

"He's not gonna marry you," Anona said. She reached down to tighten the stockings knotted under her knees. She smoothed down her skirts.

"If he knew about the baby . . . he'd come back and marry me if he knew about the baby." Mary held her stomach and cried some more.

"He comes back here, I'll throw him out," Anona said. "You want to get mixed up in these things he does? You want to have this baby in jail?"

Mary suddenly ran to the cupboard, to the drawer under St. Rita. When she turned to face Anona and her sisters, she had the big kitchen knife in her hands. "I'm gonna kill myself," she said. "I'm gonna stab myself right in the heart." She was calm, which scared them, and she held up the knife and told them to stay away, all of them. Gracie screamed and ran toward Mary but Helen pulled her back by her skirt and pushed her against the wall, all the while shouting at Mary to stop, tears running down her face. "Kill us all, then," Helen said.

Gracie had slid into a heap on the floor, her head hidden in her arms, sobbing. And Anona? She walked right over and stood in front of Mary. Gracie and Helen were afraid when Anona did this, terrified that Mary was crazy, would hurt Anona, herself, the baby in her stomach, but Mary didn't do any of these things.

She let Anona embrace her, walk her to the chair, rock her in her arms. Mary held the knife against her chest and closed her eyes. There was blood on Mary's lip where she had bitten down hard and there was blood on Anona's arm. Gracie and Helen stayed where they were and watched as Anona crooned in Mary's ear, quieted her with the same words over and over. "You don't worry," Anona whispered. "I'm gonna take care."

Anona brewed valerian tea for Mary to drink and the four of them sat around the table.

"How?" Gracie said. "How you gonna help Mary?"

"Is our name Murphy?" Anona said.

"No."

"Appunto," Anona said to Gracie. "Mallone. We're Italians."

"What's that mean?"

"Gesù, I should be raising rabbits. . . ."

"It means," Helen said, "that we take care of each other."

"If Nick knew . . ." Mary said. She started to cry, covered her face with her hands.

"You gotta forget Nick and think about the baby. You gotta get married and give this baby a name."

"Who's gonna marry me like this?"

"I told you. I'm gonna tell you again. Don't worry."

Gracie came over to Mary and kneeled beside her chair. She circled her waist with her skinny arms and put her head in her lap. Helen came over, too, and the three of them held each other until Helen lifted her head and said something had kicked her. "The baby," Mary said and Helen and Gracie pressed their ears against Mary's waist.

Anona said it was too early and all three of them were *pazze* and how broad did St. Rita think her shoulders were giving her three idiots to raise but the next morning she got dressed up like Easter and took Gracie with her to Mulberry Street on the East Side.

Anona wore one of Emma's hats and pinned the pearl brooch to the lapel of her coat. Gracie told her she looked beautiful and Anona smacked the back of her head. Anona hated vanity, but then she stopped to look at herself in the window glass of the downstairs door. "It's the hat," she said. "Nothing makes class like a hat. Emma knew that. She always wore a hat." And she grabbed Gracie's hand and dragged her down the stoop because "We don't got all day."

When Anona and Gracie came home that night, they had a proposal of marriage from Pasquale Ciarello, the nephew of a woman whose family knew Anona's from the other side. This Pasquale had just come over on the boat and was living with his uncle and aunt and six male cousins in a two-room cold-water flat on Stanton Street. The place smelled of dirty clothes, men's clothes. When Gracie pinched her nose shut with her fingers, Anona slapped her hand down and said she was sorry she had taken her. There were too many men in that place for Gracie's taste and back on Thirty-eighth Street, she told Helen and Mary that it seemed to her Pasquale's aunt was glad to be rid of him.

Pasquale's aunt agreed to the marriage contract Anona proposed. The match was *perfetto*, Signora Ciarello said, as Anona counted out the dowry. It was unhealthy for a man to be alone. Pasquale was young, strong. He'd make a good husband for her granddaughter, Signora Ciarello said, putting the bills in her hip pocket, resting her hand over the pocket, disappointed that they didn't make more of a bulge, wondering if she had made a good deal after all. Anona's ironed bills made a very slim packet.

Nevertheless, the deal was sealed and Signora Ciarello spoke to her nephew, who sat morosely in a corner near the stove; then she brought him over to sit at the kitchen table while she served espresso in chipped china cups.

Pasquale kissed Anona's hand and stared at Gracie. He started speaking rapidly to his aunt, who raised her voice and said no, this wasn't the one, and called him a name that Anona said later meant "moron" only worse, in that ancient dialect of Bocca al Lupo and he was quiet after that.

Anona and the aunt set a date for the next Saturday because, as the aunt said, her house was very crowded, and Anona agreed that there was no reason to wait. Pasquale drove a horse and wagon and Anona told Mary when she got home that he wasn't so bad-looking. He had good skin and most of his teeth. "Except he's a moron," Gracie mentioned, and Anona pulled her ear and made her take it back.

"How tall is he?" Mary wanted to know.

"You're fussy, too?" Anona said.

"Why shouldn't I be? You taught me that."

"He's young. You're lucky. If you were in Bocca al Lupo, the best you'd get was some old windbag with bad breath, or maybe a gimp and even then you'd be lucky."

"Geez, Anona," Mary said. "Don't you have any happy stories?" She was reconciling to the idea of marrying Pasquale. He would work all the time and she would have her baby. She would have Anona and Gracie and Helen. "I'm tired," she said and went inside to lie down on the big bed.

Gracie waited until she heard the bedsprings squeak. She moved closer to Anona and Helen. "Poor Mary," she said, "marrying somebody she don't love."

"Ha! Never mind. She should thank God we're here in America. My *gumarra*, Gungetina, back in Bocca al Lupo? She got nobody to marry her. They stoned her on her way home from the fields. Her *innamorato* was there. He threw stones like the rest. They made the baby come early. The baby died. It was cursed. Gungetina threw herself in the ravine." Anona crossed herself.

"How? How was it cursed?" Gracie wanted to know.

"Never mind. You won't sleep."

"Tell us, Anona." Helen wanted to know, too.

"It was a boy."

"So?"

"It had only one arm . . . right here." She pointed between her breasts.

Helen and Gracie gasped.

Anona put her hands together as though to pray but instead shook them in Helen's and Gracie's faces. ". . . And," she added with great drama, "no *piscalico!* There was nothing between his legs!"

Satisfied with the effect of her story, Anona went to the stove and made a pot of espresso. She heated the milk for the caffè latte and poured it into bowls for Gracie and Helen. She made a cross with the knife on the bottom of the big round loaf of bread and held the bread against her chest to cut three thick slices. "A real wedding," she said, "next week. Tomorrow I go see the priest. And we invite all the nosy holes. Shut them up for good." Anona drank her espresso and filled her cup again. This cup she sipped. "I hope it's a girl," she said to Gracie and Helen. "That would be nice, no? A little girl? Eh, a boy would be okay, too, a nice big boy. This is a big country. No place for a small man."

Chapter Nineteen

So Mary and Pasquale Ciarello were married in Holy Cross Church. Anona had gone to see the pastor, a few more of those pressed bills from the lining of Mary's coat crossed palms, and the next Saturday, without the banns being read, Father Flannagan gave Mary Mallone in sacred matrimony to Pasquale Ciarello.

Mary wore Pasquale's aunt's wedding dress, which was yellow in places, but the lace was still perfect, not torn at all and it fit Mary good, because while she was a lot slimmer than Pasquale's aunt, Mary did have a few extra pounds on her. She made a beautiful bride.

Anona poked Gracie in the ribs when Mary came down the aisle. "See them looking?" she said. "But you can't tell nothing. We got them good this time. Let them talk later. What's done is done."

"But when Bridget Kelly got married pregnant, they did it in the back of the church," Gracie said. "How come?"

"That was Bridget Kelly," Anona said. "This is us!"

The veil covered Mary's head and face and trailed all the way down the back of her wedding gown and swept along the marble floor of the church. Anona had bought the silk net and pinned it to Mary's hair under a wreath of wax flowers. There was a party afterward, and the whole building came and anyone who passed by the door was invited in for a drink to toast the newlyweds. Hanley had provided the bootleg liquor and plenty of it, with two bottles of real Irish whiskey for the cops who stopped by when the fighting broke out around midnight. It was Mary's wedding but just another Saturday night in Hell's Kitchen.

In bed that night, Gracie curled against Helen and put her head in the crook of her big sister's arm. They were teenagers: Helen fifteen and Gracie fourteen, but they lay against each other like small children. Both of them missed Mary, who was in an apartment two flights up. Anona had seen to it that Mary would be close so she could watch over her and the baby and make sure Pasquale did the right thing. Anona didn't trust him, even though she was convinced he was a piece of bread, the way a man should be.

Pasquale's English wasn't very good so mostly he was quiet until the one night he came to the door, Mary behind him, calling out for Anona. Mary was big with the baby and Pasquale was confused and surprised and suspicious that she was so big so soon and upset that since the wedding night she hadn't let him near her.

Anona sat him down and explained to him that in America, everything was big, bigger than anywhere else, and his baby was going to be big because his baby would be an American. Here she crossed herself and muttered a quick prayer of thanks before going on and on about how *fortunato* he was that his baby would be born here in this country. His baby, she said, leaning over him, pushing him back in the chair, his son, Pasquale Junior. She knew, Anona told Pasquale, that Mary was carrying a boy, big like America. She could tell about these things. "And what a man you are, Pasquale," Anona told him, watching him forget his complaints and puff with pride. "Just married and your wife already huge!"

And then Anona warned him to keep his hands to himself. When women were pregnant, she said, you had to leave them alone. Think of the Madonna!

Pasquale knew nothing about women and at first he had sought out his aunt, but she had shooed him back to Hell's Kitchen without answering his questions. He was married now, she told him, he had questions he should ask his wife.

There was no mother; there were no sisters, no one to whisper in Pasquale's ear all the dark secrets of females. He had only Anona to tell him the things he wanted to know, to embrace him when the midwife held up a huge blond baby boy six months after his wedding in the Holy Cross Church.

Sonny was so big, Mary almost died having him. She sweated and grunted and cried out and Anona held her hand and wiped her forehead and prayed over her. There were so many candles burning in front of St. Rita, the statue had to be cleaned with alcohol to get off the black soot.

Mrs. Kelly was the midwife. She came with her daughter Kathleen and they made Mary squat between two chairs and they tied her legs to the legs of the chairs and told her to bear down. Anona made sure they washed their hands and she boiled the water herself. But there wasn't a woman in the building who had given birth to less than ten kids and Mrs. Kelly had ushered more than a few of them into the world.

Mary lay in bed for ten days after Sonny was born and Anona had to find a wet nurse because Mary had no milk. Janie Cullen agreed to come nurse Sonny if she could eat at Anona's table. Anona agreed. When she was feeding Janie Cullen, she was feeding Sonny, because after all, like Helen said, "The Irish eat like shit."

Gracie and Helen could hardly get their arms around Sonny, he was so big; it took the two of them to pick him up. They baptized him Pasquale, just like Anona had promised, but they never called him anything but Sonny. Pasquale wondered how come his baby was so big, so blond, so white, until Anona took him aside and told him in English, because she said he had to learn sometime, that a runt of a guinea like him, bandy-legged greaseball that he was, should get down on his knees and thank God for sending him a girl like Mary Mallone, who had just given him a big healthy baby boy with skin like milk and eyes like marbles.

Pasquale understood less than half of what she said and promised he wasn't complaining. As for his aunt, out of respect Anona sent her a gallon of wine and two salamis when Sonny was ten days old.

The wonder baby, Anona called Sonny. She wondered how they'd lived without him. Gracie and Helen would sing to him and take him out for walks in his little carriage that Anona had bought right after he was born.

Life was sweet again for the Mallones after Sonny was born. Pasquale worked long hours down the piers pushing a hand truck for seventeen dollars a week. Anona had moved heaven and earth to get him the job. It was getting tougher and tougher to get a job and the Irish still had the piers sewn up but Anona had been around a long time and she knew just who to ask.

Mary stayed home with the baby and after Pasquale came home, he helped the super stoke the furnace and he carried the cans filled with ash up from the basement for the sanitation trucks to pick up at the curb. Mary would hear the clatter of the ashcans as the building super rolled them back from the curb where the garbagemen threw them after they had emptied the contents into the truck and she would think of Pasquale, black with soot from the coal dust, and then she would think of Nick, big and strong, with a blue sapphire the size of a robin's egg on his pinkie finger, and she would clench her fists into balls and tell herself that Nick was coming back for her and Sonny, that this life she lived now was not her life, that Nick would come and change her life again, the way he had the first time.

Mary didn't see Pasquale until late at night and then she was usually asleep or in Anona's house with her sisters, playing cards at the kitchen table while Sonny slept in his cradle next to them. She would leave food for Pasquale, because Anona insisted that a man had to eat or he couldn't work, food that more often than not, Anona had cooked, because Mary complained that Sonny took all her strength. In the afternoons, Mary would sit with Anona on the stoop and let Mrs. Sweeney and Mrs. Murphy and all the rest of them pinch Sonny's cheek and compliment her on his size and his beauty, all the while searching his face for resembling features.

Anona had pinned a medal of St. Rita to Sonny's undershirt, right over his heart. The *malocchio* wasn't getting this baby boy, not like the other one, she said, that little boy that Emma had loved so much it killed her when he died.

They were sitting around the kitchen table one night making silk flowers, Gracie and Helen and Anona. Sonny was tied with a belt into one of the kitchen chairs, sucking on a *biscotti*, his face covered with wet crumbs.

Mary came through the front door, emptying a sack of apples on the table, polishing one with the hem of her skirt, handing it to Anona, who told her to get a knife and peel it but Mary took it back and bit out a big piece. "Takes too long," she said defiantly.

Anona looked down at the silk flower stem she was tying. They had graduated from tags. Flowers paid better. Mary pulled out a chair, sat down and chewed the apple, her mouth open. She got up, paced the kitchen, pitched the core out the open window then stood in front of St. Rita's statue, ran her fingers over the plaster saint, from the top of her white veil to her naked toes peeping out from beneath her blue gown.

Walking over to Sonny, Mary chucked him under the chin and he grabbed on to her finger. "Cute, ain't he?" she said, eyes hooded, looking over at Anona, ". . . and strong, just like his father."

"Whatta you talking about?" Anona said.

Mary sat back down in her chair. "Nick's back."

"Back where? Where'd you hear this?" Anona said.

"Somebody told me."

"Who? Who told you?"

"One of his crew, Louie Lump. He just came up to me on the street and told me. He's the one gave me them apples."

"Yeah, what'd he say?"

Mary shrugged. He said, "The Swede's back in the Kitchen. The heat's off. He's looking for you."

"*Porca miseria* . . . Like we need him now. Where was he a year ago?" Anona threw down the flower she was working on and the green silk thread unraveled as it rolled across the table. "Well, you tell him to get lost."

Mary leaned over to undo the belt around Sonny's waist. She plucked him out of the chair and sat him on her lap. He started to cry.

"You think he's gonna come here?" Gracie said. "What's he gonna do when he finds out?"

"Finds out what?" Anona said.

"About Pasquale. About Sonny."

"Ha! He goes away and Mary gets married and has a baby. What's to find out?"

Mary kissed the top of Sonny's head. "When he sees the baby, he'll know," she whispered. "Look at him!"

Anona snorted. "Ridiculous, Don't you know from 'white seed'? It's Pasquale's baby. You're married. That's all Nick needs to know. That big dope." These last words she said to herself, under her breath.

Mary said she wanted to get out of the house, needed to take a walk, and she bundled up Sonny and they all went down, Gracie and Helen and Mary and the baby, and they put Sonny in the carriage and strolled around the Kitchen, all eyes and ears.

The streets were crowded; they always were. There was no space in the tenements, no air. The streets offered excitement, action. Something was always going on. They walked past speakeasies, the ones you could see and the ones hidden behind storefronts where the kids bought candy. The speakeasies made Mary long for Nick. If she saw a pair of two-tone shoes, her eyes would move up. If the man was tall, if he looked strong and powerful, with fair skin and blue eyes, she'd let herself imagine it was Nick. She would stop herself from looking carefully at his face, partially hidden beneath the brim of his fedora.

She would let herself think it was Nick. It could be Nick, she told herself. It could be. He was here, back in the Kitchen. She'd heard the rumor. She could find him if she wanted, but she'd wait for him to find her. She had to be sure he still wanted her, a married woman with a son, even though it was his son. She had to be sure.

"Whattya gonna do?" Gracie asked Mary, a hand on her arm. "You scared?"

"Scared? Na, I'm better off than that poor horse, no?" Mary

pointed to a scrawny pinto that had fallen dead in the street. It lay in the gutter, waiting for the wagon that would carry it away. A crowd of boys and one little girl jumped on its swollen belly. Helen called the little girl over and gave her a nickel. The boys swooped to take it from her.

"You're always starting trouble," Mary said, annoyed that the attention had been taken away from her, that Helen had been so easily distracted from Mary's dilemma.

"You're gonna get that poor kid a beating. Look at the size of her. They'll kill her for that nickel," Gracie said. It was one of the reasons, unlike her sisters, she stayed close to home. She liked the quiet, the way she had liked the order of school, the neatness, the straight lines they made when they walked through the halls, the slot in the desk for the pencil, the round hole cut out to hold the inkwell.

"No they won't. Watch her," Helen said, and Mary and Gracie turned to see the girl raise a skinny arm, the hand a fist, and then run, losing her pursuers in the people milling around the stoops, crowding the sidewalks. Helen laughed, put an arm around each of her sisters, pulled them close. "I know a tough kid when I see her. Besides, if she couldn't handle them, I would have jumped in and wrung their dirty necks. I could use a good fight."

"With little boys?" Mary scowled.

"Well, it would have been at least five to one. Them's fair odds. Anyways, who said anything about fair? Where do you think we are? Fifth Avenue with the swells?"

Mary laughed and then got quiet. She bent down to take the ribbon from Sonny's hat out of his mouth. It had come untied and slipped up over his chin and he was happily chewing it. "We lived like that when Nick was around, didn't we?" Mary said. "Poor Sonny," she said. "If you had your real daddy, you'd be dressed in silk and satin."

"You should stop that," Gracie said. "If Anona ever heard you talking like that . . ."

Mary turned to Gracie. "Ah, don't get me wrong. Pasquale's not so bad and Sonny's such a sweet baby. But I was meant for Nick. There couldn't ever be anybody else. Not for real. And who knows? Maybe nothing will happen. Maybe Nick won't even show up. But you know"—and here Mary tilted her head, formed her mouth into a sweet circle—"he's crazy for me." Helen was far ahead of them by now. Strolling babies was not her idea of a good time, even though she thought Sonny was the cutest baby ever born. She had found a stickball game and bullied her way into hitting a few before her sisters caught up to her.

When Nick Andersen did come by, it reminded Gracie of that first time, except he wasn't driving a big car. He just showed up at the door, all six foot three of him, thinner in the face but just as powerful and he took Mary in his arms and lifted her up in the air like she was the baby, not Sonny. She was dizzy when he put her down and thrilled a little too.

"You took good care of my girl," Nick said to Anona and for the first time the sisters could remember, Anona's tongue dried right up in her mouth and she had nothing to say.

"She did. Anona took care of everything," Mary said, and she went over and lifted Sonny out of his cradle and gave him to Nick, who blinked as if to say, "What's this?"

Anona got out of her chair and slammed the door shut and it was the only closed door in the building. Every door on every landing had popped open to hear what was going on.

Anona admitted later that the three of them did make a picture. Mary so small and dainty and Nick so big and strong and that big blond baby right in the middle of them.

"Give me a chance," Nick said. "I'll do the right thing. Mary belongs to me . . . and now the baby . . . both of them are mine and I'm gonna take care of them."

"Sonny ain't your baby, and we take care of ourselves," Anona said, folding her arms across her chest. "This is a good country, America."

Gracie tugged on Helen's sleeve. "What's gonna happen? What about Pasquale?"

"Shh," she said. "One thing at a time."

Nick had been away, "all over," he told them. He'd been to New Orleans and he'd been out West to San Francisco, and he'd been to Chicago. He'd been working for Owney Madden. And he wasn't just another triggerman, not just another strong-arm. Madden liked Nick, had pulled him into the inside where the money was, and Nick had plenty. He wanted Mary and he wanted his son. He could afford to take care of all the Mallones, he told Anona, who looked heavenward or closed her eyes altogether while he spoke. No more of them worrying where the next buck was coming from, he said. They'd all live in luxury now Big Nick was here.

Anona was not happy to see Nick Andersen. Mary had a husband who worked, an apartment in the building, and a beautiful baby with a legitimate father. She'd been married in church. Who was this *jabone*, this *lambajul*, this *shambayone*, to come here and mix everything up? Anona compared Nick to cholera, to the Spanish influenza, to the Triangle Shirtwaist Fire, but no matter what she said, Mary insisted she was going with Nick. They'd be a real family, she told Anona.

"He's not Pasquale's son. You know that. You can pray to that saint until you're blue in the face, you ain't gonna change that. No weaselly little greaseball could make a baby like this. Ask anybody."

Gracie sat without saying a word. She shivered in the face of Anona's wrath and Mary's determination. Helen took it all in stride, wondering out loud if maybe she could work for Owney Madden. She could drive a truck out of the Colonial Garage on Fifty-second Street and deliver the beer from the Phoenix Brewery. But Nick told her things were changing. Prohibition was on the way out and when Madden got out of jail this time, more likely than not he was gonna hang up his hat.

After Nick showed up, Mary was just sullen, rocking Sonny on her knee. Pasquale was unsuspecting, falling into bed exhausted, eating his meal in silence, a hot one if Anona had cooked, some bread and cheese and tomatoes if she hadn't. He would hold the baby and she would soften for just a moment before she got angry and weepy again. This wasn't her life, she told Anona. She didn't belong in this hellhole with this little wop and she didn't care how hard he worked.

"*Povero lui,*" Anona said about Pasquale. "He thought he got a nice Italian girl, he told his aunt, but no, he doesn't know what he got. It's just that he loves the boy. His aunt told me this, she came here and told me this herself. He went to her crying. He begged her to help him."

"And what'd you say?" Mary said. "Did you tell her how rotten I am?"

"You think I would talk against my own? *Che strunza!* No, I told her it's different up here. The girls aren't slaves."

Mary put her arms around Anona. "You're wonderful," she said. "You know everything."

"I know this," Anona said. "You do what you want, but don't think you're not gonna pay."

Nick came on a Sunday to get Mary and Sonny. Gracie and Helen were quiet, surprised at Anona saying nothing, doing nothing. They were waiting for all hell to break loose. "Whatta you gonna do?" Gracie finally asked when Anona had turned from the window. "What's gonna happen now?"

Anona waved Gracie away. "I done what I could. Mary's making her own table."

"Bed, Anona, Mary's making her own bed."

Anona stood in front of St. Rita and blew out the extra candles. She threatened to change saints, even though she didn't mean it. Anona knew St. Rita didn't believe her, but she had to get mad at somebody. "Children always pierce your heart," she said to the saint. "Maybe there's nothing you could do. I'm gonna believe you did your best."

The building was quiet. It felt like the whole neighborhood had quieted down, too, waiting to see the drama unfold, waiting for Pasquale to confront Nick Andersen. The Sweeneys and the Flannagans and the McMichaels, every family in the building was on the "earie," their heads cocked, their doors open. There was nothing the Irish loved more than a good fight, but while this one wouldn't be much of a match, there were hopes it would be bloody. "Never liked that little dago anyways," Mrs. Sweeney told Mrs. Kelly behind her hand. "Wouldn't mind seeing him thumped."

But the Flannagans and the McMichaels and the Sweeneys were disappointed in their desire for a good brawl, for the familiar sound of a head banging down the hallway steps, some blood on the front stoop. It ended quietly. Pasquale Ciarello wasn't there and no one would ever see him again.

The police came to talk to Mary. Pasquale's aunt had put them wise. Pasquale had been staking her all the time he was married to Mary, enough that she was interested in what had happened to him. "Imagine," Mary said, when she found out, "taking bread out of the baby's mouth and never telling me a thing." But for the police, who came to talk to her in Anona's kitchen, Mary held Sonny and cried and cried until her eyes swelled shut.

Anona just sat in her chair wearing all her skirts and made faces to indicate that she knew nothing. She didn't even blink. Gracie sat very small in a corner and Helen mugged and shrugged her shoulders. The police questioned the neighbors, who said they knew nothing, saw nothing, heard nothing. This was the Kitchen, after all, Anona said, hunched over the table winding green satin ribbon to make stems for the silk flowers. No one was going to talk to the police, she said, not for some poor dago who couldn't even speak English good enough to have a civil conversation or buy a neighbor a glass of beer.

If something had happened to Pasquale Ciarello, it was unfortunate, but people disappeared in this neighborhood all the time. Who could keep track?

Mary and Nick skipped the wedding and had their honeymoon at the Traymore Hotel in Atlantic City. Mary loved Nick. He was no choirboy, she knew, and that was most of why she loved him. He made up for all the men that didn't exist in her life. Helen never needed a man to feel safe. The cheese stands alone, Anona said about Helen. Men entertained Helen, gave her gifts, made her laugh and sigh with pleasure, but she could do without them. But

Mary had never known how much she longed for the protection and devotion of a man like Nick until she had him in her power. It was the way she loved to drive his car, all that machinery purring under her gloved hands.

To her, Nick was Hercules, the strongest man. Even when she lost Sonny, when he got so sick that he wasted away in front of their eyes, she could bear it as long as there was Nick, and after Sonny died, she never wanted another child. She said she couldn't have any more children, that having Sonny almost killed her, that she wasn't made to bear children, but the truth was she only wanted Nick. Nick Andersen was all she had ever wanted.

And Pasquale? Mary didn't ask Nick about Pasquale. She wondered but she didn't want to know. Nick told her to forget about him. Mary knew Pasquale could be dead but she preferred to think of him as gone, maybe back to Italy. He was back in Italy, Mary told Anona, even though Anona didn't ask, and he could have been, Mary reasoned.

She never knew that Nick had plucked him off the street one night and walked him into an alley and told him that he was taking Mary and Sonny. He told Pasquale to go away and forget all about them.

Pasquale Ciarello was no fool. He knew this man could back up his threats. Nick Andersen showed Pasquale a gun and he showed him a wad of bills in an envelope and he told Pasquale to choose.

1952–1953

Summer and Smoke Opens In Greenwich Village

TENNESSEE WILLIAMS PLAY DEBUTS AT CIRCLE IN THE SQUARE PLAY-HOUSE IN GREENWICH VILLAGE

Playboy *Magazine Debuts With* *Centerfold of Marilyn Monroe*

BRITAIN TESTS ATOMIC BOMB OVER THE MONTE BELLO ISLANDS IN AUSTRALIA

Chapter Twenty

They did it, of course. Nick did it. He got Frankie a decent job. All Mary had to do was ask. Owney Madden had retired to Hot Springs, Arkansas, in 1935 and married the postmaster's daughter, but Nick still knew people in high (and low) places. Nick went back a long time and so did his reputation.

The Italians controlled the piers up to Number 42, which was where the Irish took over. Nick made the connection for Frankie to work as a checker on Pier 13 on the East River, where the Standard Fruit Company boats came in from Central America filled with bananas. Standard Fruit had the monopoly on bananas for the East Coast and the Genovese family had the piers and the trucks that carried the bananas off the piers. During the war, the banana trade had shriveled up with the ships busy elsewhere. But come 1952, Don Vidone was back from Italy and business was booming. Millions of bananas were coming in every week.

So Nick made a call and Frankie Merelli was no longer one of the shape-up crew hoping for work when a ship pulled in; now he had a union job and he went to work clean, if not exactly in a suit. He wore slacks, a flannel shirt buttoned to the top, a cardigan sweater. He wasn't, after all, the president, although he told Gracie that she made such a big deal about asking her family for the job, he should have been. Frankie did manage to wear his gold watch and his Siegel shoes that he got on the cheap from the store on Eighth Street because he knew a salesman who'd hold a few pairs on the side for him.

And he didn't have to carry bananas anymore and wear a canvas apron to protect his shoulders and neck from the tarantulas and scorpions that hid in the stalks. All he had to do was stand on the loading dock and count the stalks the men carried off the conveyor belt and onto the trucks. He counted for two trucks, standing between them, pumping once on the mechanism under his foot for every stalk loaded until each truck held a hundred stalks. And he ate in a nearby restaurant even though Gracie gave him his lunch every day.

For the first week, he took the brown bag with the sandwich wrapped in wax paper and the piece of fruit and the napkin and he gave it to a bum sleeping in a cardboard box on the Bowery, but after a few weeks he told Gracie not to make him lunch anymore. He could have told her he wouldn't be caught dead walking around carrying a paper bag. He could have gotten mad at her for even thinking a guy with his kind of class would carry his lunch in a brown paper bag. But instead he kissed her mouth and said she had enough to do taking care of Charlie and the house.

Gracie didn't have that much to do taking care of Charlie and the house. The apartment was three small rooms and Charlie was in school so she saw a lot of her sisters, who, as Anona said, never let the grass grow under their hands. Gracie could only clean so much, and she was egged on by Helen and Mary, who saw no reason to slave over a house. And Gracie never forgot the time Jeannie Popeye, not the cleanest, had passed by her door one afternoon when she was pregnant and on her knees scrubbing, the door open so the floor would dry faster. Jeannie Popeye had poked in her head and made a face. "That floor will be here long after you're gone," she told Gracie. "Whatta you wanna go kill yourself for?"

Gracie bowed to the greater wisdoms. She liked getting dressed and going out to lunch with Helen and Mary. They would pick her up downstairs in the car, Mary driving the big Cadillac, or in the good weather, when the stoop was filled and the folding chairs were out on the sidewalk and she didn't feel like parading past, she might meet them up the block or around the corner. Sometimes she took Charlie and threatened him under pain of death to keep his trap shut and not to tell his father where they'd been. Charlie would hold this over her head when he couldn't get what he wanted and she would tell him if he talked he would die like a dog and that kept him quiet because Charlie was not a tough kid, but a *gagasorte,* a shit-the-pants, afraid of everything, which Anona said made him exactly like his father.

Gracie would alternate between smacking Charlie and bribing him, depending on how vulnerable she felt to Frankie's demands and expectations that she stay home and clean the house and press his shirts and "keep her lip zipped." Frankie hated gossip, and he should, Anona said, because a lot of it was about him.

Gracie was hanging kitchen curtains when she heard Sam from the candy store calling her name in the hallway. "Your sister's on the phone," he yelled up. "She says be downstairs for eleven-thirty."

Right on time, Helen pulled up in a powder blue Lincoln Continental convertible and beeped the horn. The men hanging around outside the building gaped at the scene and when Helen leaned over to push open the door for Gracie to get in the car, Helen waved at them. Gracie looked straight ahead until they hit West Broadway and stopped at a red light.

"Where'd this come from?" Gracie said, rubbing a hand over

the dashboard. She adjusted the radio. "I was expecting Mary in the Cadillac."

Helen patted the blue leather seat. "I thought we could use a change from that old clunker."

"Nick or the car?"

"Don't let Mary hear you," Helen said, leaning over to kiss Gracie's cheek.

"C'mon, you know I'm kidding. I love Nick. He's been great to us. Frankie's back to work steady. . . ."

"That don't make Nick the Pope. You're too grateful. You got to expect things and then you get them."

"Blue Lincolns?"

"Is the color a killer or what? I just mentioned I liked blue."

"Whose is it?"

"Can't tell. Not yet."

"You getting married again?"

"Don't you think once is enough?"

"It wasn't your fault. You can't help bad luck."

"Luck? Mick Mullen drank himself to death."

"He did not. He got hit by that Schlitz beer truck."

"Oh, that's right. I get mixed up. You're right. That's how I got the insurance money, but don't forget that he was dead drunk when the truck hit him."

"Anona told you not to marry Irish. You never listened."

"If I'd listened to Anona, I'd be over there right now putting on her slippers. Besides, the Italians are so morbid. And I hate to cook. Who in their right mind would want an Italian husband? Can't complain about them as boyfriends, though. I gotta give them that."

"Yeah," Gracie said. "I should have followed in your footsteps."

"Why you saying that, honey? What's he up to now?"

"Nothing. "I'm just talking. Frankie's fine. We picking up Mary?"

"She's meeting us at Salerno's."

"Helen, I gotta be back. Charlie comes home for lunch at one."

"Don't worry about Charlie."

"The kid's gotta eat."

Helen slammed on the brakes, put the Lincoln in reverse and backed up two blocks, pulling in to the curb at 196 Spring before Gracie said another word, and for a minute Gracie thought she was being made to go home again, punished, like a child.

Charlie did have to eat, she told herself in her own defense. Helen didn't have kids. She didn't understand the responsibility. But then Helen touched her arm before she opened the car door and said, "Wait here," and Gracie relaxed. She was happy to let go, to let Helen take charge.

Helen got out of the car and went into Sam & Al's. Al was behind the counter and she handed him a five-dollar bill. "When Charlie Merelli comes in, make him a sandwich," she said.

Al held her hand when he took the money. "That's a lot for a sandwich."

Helen smiled. "And give him whatever else he wants. Oh, and tell him to eat it here"—Helen pointed to the wooden bench against the wall near the red Coca-Cola icebox—"that his mother'll be back later."

Al nodded and put the bill under the register. "Anything you say."

"Thanks."

Al watched her get into the Lincoln. His partner Sam was by the window straightening the cans holding miniature American flags on sticks and boxes of sparklers that had been there since the last Fourth of July. "What a looker," Sam said, twirling his index finger at the corner of his mouth, his thumb extended in a gesture that indicated perfection.

"Charlie's taken care of," Helen said.

"What'd you do?"

"Left a pound note with instructions. He'll be fine. Let's go before Mary has a hemorrhage." Helen pulled the car away from the curb at forty miles an hour. She fumbled in her bag for her cigarettes with her free right hand and handed a gold cigarette case to Gracie. "Light me one, will you?"

Gracie took out one of the gold-tipped black cigarettes, turning the case over in her hand. "Nice," she said. "Where did this come from?"

"Enough questions," Helen said. She winked at her sister and pushed the bag closer to Gracie. "There's a matching lighter in there somewhere."

Gracie shook her head, smiled. She found the lighter, lit the cigarette, put it between Helen's lips.

"Have one," Helen said.

"I don't smoke."

"C'mon. Enjoy yourself. Besides, men like women who smoke. Think Bette Davis. If they wanted nuns, they'd all be hanging out in the convent."

Gracie lit one for herself. She waved it around and held it on her bottom lip but she wouldn't inhale. She leaned over into the rearview mirror and admitted that she liked the way she looked.

They drove to Salerno's on the East Side. Helen pulled the car up in front of the restaurant and seemed to know the guy who took the keys. Mary was waiting for them in a booth in the back, drinking whiskey and soda. Gracie was nervous that someone who knew Frankie would see her because Frankie hung out on the East Side but Mary told her to relax. "Frankie never takes you out, so how's anybody gonna know who you are?"

"You're right," Gracie said and she took another cigarette from Helen's cigarette case and lit it with the gold lighter. The lighter felt heavy in her hand and she closed her fingers around it, thinking she should take off the red nail polish before Frankie came home and that she probably shouldn't be drinking in the middle of the afternoon, but when the waiter asked her what she wanted, she told him a whiskey sour. Helen ordered appetizers and entrées and salads and when Gracie got up to call Sam & Al's and check on Charlie, Mary nudged Helen with her shoulder.

"So what do you hear?"

"What can I tell you? Nothing. Maybe getting caught like that straightened Frankie out."

"I still don't trust him."

"Listen, she's happy and he's happy."

"Why's he happy?"

". . . the new job. Gracie says he's doing good down the pier. She really appreciates Nick setting it up."

"Yeah, it was no big deal and, you know, Frankie's got his good points. He sent Nick a couple of ties that must have cost him two weeks' pay."

"*Bene rieg*," Helen said. She emptied a shot glass of bourbon. "What else is new? It's always the same thing."

"Except with you. What's going on?"

"Ask her about the blue Lincoln Continental parked outside," Gracie said, back from the pay phone.

"Blue Lincoln? Whose?"

"I asked her the same thing but she's not talking," Gracie said.

"Okay, okay, it belongs to Joe Black," Helen said.

"Joe Black? Skinny? Flashy dresser?" Mary said.

"Who's Joe Black?" Gracie said.

"Joe Black. Short? Bald? Old? He's old, Helen!" Mary said. "I remember him from the Cotton Club."

"Look who's talking about old. Nick's as old as the hills."

"We're not talking about Nick. We're talking about Joe Black."

"You see us getting a check? He owns this restaurant and some other places, too. A lot of other places."

"I know who he is. Where'd you find him?"

"I went for an interview for a hatcheck girl at the Copa and there he was."

"You looking for work?" Mary said.

"You know, keeping busy. Schlitz was generous but not that generous and Mickey wasn't insured. Well, he was, but they kept saying it was suicide and I had to settle. Why we rehashing all this again?"

Mary tossed her head. "You brought it up. I thought you were through with men. Anyway, I was just asking about the car. Why a Lincoln? Nick won't buy nothing but a Caddy."

"Nick's from the stone age. And it's not my car. I didn't buy it."

"I liked your husband Mickey," Gracie said. "But he drank too much."

"What can you do? It's in the blood. Aren't you lucky to have a hot Italian instead of a drunken Irishman?" Helen said.

Gracie put her hand over Helen's. "Maybe this is the one," she said.

"How's Charlie?" Helen said.

"He was on his second sandwich when I called Sam & Al's—mortadella, I think."

"Did you talk to him?"

"No, the bookmakers needed the phone."

• • •

Friday was payday and checkers on Pier 13 made nice money. Especially on weeks like this one, when three ships came in. Frankie was in Milady's with a sawbuck on the bar. He had the money for Gracie in one pocket and he had a wad in his other pocket that was all his, part from his pay and the rest from the little side venture he'd worked out with Pauly Russo, one of the truck drivers. It was a perfect scam. Frankie's foot would miss a few times when the stalks of bananas were being loaded and at the end of the day, when Pauly had finished his deliveries, there'd be bananas left over in the truck. Pauly'd sell them for cash and give Frankie his cut the next morning.

Frankie was convinced his luck had changed even if his horses kept losing and his number never hit. Things were working out better than he expected.

He'd go to the Savannah Club tonight around eleven and look around. No more Midwest blondes for him. No more Doreens, although he got a pain where he thought his heart was when he remembered her. He still had that picture where she was wearing the fuzzy sweater. He kept it in his locker down the pier, just for old times' sake.

Frankie rapped on the bar and the bartender poured him another drink. He lit a cigarette and fingered the bills in his pocket that were just for him. He'd already taken out a couple of bills for the *busta*, his secret stash.

By the time he went home to change his shirt, Charlie was asleep in the hideaway bed in the kitchen. Gracie heard him come in and when she called his name he went into the bedroom and sat down on the bed. He touched her shoulder. She turned away. "Jesus, Frankie, it's eleven o'clock. Where were you? I thought you just went down to get your pay."

"I did, but I stopped by Milady's to have a few drinks. I'm under a lot of pressure. This job ain't no picnic."

"You wanted this job."

"Don't get carried away. I didn't exactly want *this* job . . ."

"Oh, this job ain't good enough for you? Whatta you want now, Vito Genovese's job?"

"Forget I said anything. It's a great job. I love it. I just want you to understand that I got responsibility now, making sure all them bananas get counted. It ain't easy." He moved to the closet, took out a shirt.

"What are you doing now?"

"I'm changing my shirt. I'm going out."

"It's eleven o'clock."

"So what am I? A pumpkin? It's Friday. I broke my ass all week. I need a break."

"You broke your ass? You got it easy. You got the best job on the pier."

"No, Gracie, the best job on the pier is the sweeper. That's how much you know. He don't even have to show up. Don't listen to your sisters, or that big Swede. I'm on my feet all day in all kinds of weather. You think that's a piece of cake? Try it sometime." He rubbed his neck. "Anyway, there's some people I got to see. I'll be back early."

She was sitting up now. He could tell she was mad. Her cheeks went pink. Maybe his mother was right. Maybe she was Irish. He'd never seen an Italian girl whose cheeks got pink like that. He came over to her. Her nightgown was sleeveless and he circled the top of her arm with his fingers. He bent down, kissed her shoulder. "I'll be back, early, okay? I promise. I just gotta take care of some things. I'll be back soon."

Gracie watched him getting ready through the open doorway.

He was tying his tie in the shaving mirror near the kitchen sink. Even just knotting his tie, Frankie was graceful and smooth.

"I left your money on the table under the sugar bowl," he called to her when he was finished. He blew her a kiss and flipped the light switch near the door before he went out. The kitchen went dark.

She lay back down but after a while she got up and went into the kitchen. She made coffee and counted the money he'd left for her. There was some extra. She figured it was overtime. She figured she didn't have anything to complain about but then why was she sitting up watching the moonlight slice across the oilcloth that covered the table?

"*Mollica,*" Anona called her, "the inside of the bread . . . soft."

Gracie sat in the dark kitchen and stirred her coffee. She watched Charlie breathe. There was more out there, she thought, more than she was getting.

Chapter Twenty-one

The Savannah Club was just heating up when Frankie walked in. He sat at the bar and watched the line. The girls were beautiful. Andy Mosiello liked them from south of the Mason-Dixon line. He held auditions every Wednesday; the girls got a cut of everything and nobody bothered them. The club was famous from Atlanta to New Orleans.

Frankie didn't make a move when he saw his favorite "peach" go over to another table. He wasn't in the mood right now and a girl had to eat. Besides, he'd sworn off getting involved. One woman was as good as the next. His mother had tried to teach him that. She had held up her hand, her thumb holding down the last two fingers, the fingers left forming a V, like the victory sign. "Look at me, Frankie," she told him, the V of her fingers under his nose. "And remember. You turn a woman upside down, they're all the same." Frankie remembered but he'd learned the hard way. From now on, he was going to keep it short and sweet.

After the show, Frankie went up to the Copa with Andy and some of the neighborhood faces to catch the lounge act. They sat at the bar and Frankie listened to the singer and watched himself in the mirrors behind the banquettes and played with the ice cubes in his drink. Andy asked him why he was so quiet but Frankie never answered. He was thinking about some new shirts he wanted, custom with his initials stitched on the cuffs and maybe a new pair of cuff links. He remembered the gold ones in Maurizio's bag of swag the night he picked up the bracelet for Doreen. The cuff links were black onyx, square, with a diamond in the center. He was thinking that he should have taken them and skipped the bracelet. Talk about no return on your money.

He bought a pack of Camels he didn't want from a redheaded cigarette girl who stood very close to him when she said "Cigars, cigarettes," and at five o'clock in the morning in the taxi on the way downtown he asked Andy if he knew anything about the cigarette girl with the red hair.

Andy made a long face. "Oh, please, Frankie. Who knows anything about those broads? One week they're here, next week they're gone. They all look good and they all cost money. They're hoping for the big score, you know? The garment-center Jew, the Hollywood producer, the wiseguy who'll sit them ringside for

Sinatra on Sunday night. What a joke! The same guy's there opening night with the ball and chain, and the girlfriends end up marrying sax players and bartenders. But, hey, that's life. It's tough, you know?"

"I didn't ask you for the history of the world, Andy. I asked about the redhead."

"Do yourself a favor, Frankie, and forget it. Me, I get the urge, I buy a hooker."

"That's degrading."

"You think so? I know this place on Twenty-third Street, clean, quiet . . . I got a girl there, she's always happy to see me."

They were on Houston Street when Frankie told the cabby to pull over. "You getting out here?" Andy said. Frankie nodded. "Okay. Me too. I'll walk you around to Spring." They cut down through Sullivan Street and crossed Prince. "So how's it going?" Andy asked.

"Good, it's going real good."

"It must be. I saw your wife get in this big blue Lincoln yesterday."

"Not my wife."

"Yeah, your wife . . . yesterday afternoon, pulled up right in front of your door. Ask Sam."

Frankie shut his eyes halfway. He breathed out. "Oh, yeah, I forgot. My brother-in-law traded in the Caddy."

"Rich relatives, huh?"

"Yeah, fat lotta good it does me."

Gracie was asleep when Frankie came in. It was almost 6 A.M. He took off his tie and his shirt, hung up his jacket, and then he sat on her side of the bed and shook her until she opened her eyes.

"What? What time is it?"

"Never mind what time it is. What's this crap about you in a blue Lincoln? Who's picking you up in the middle of the afternoon?" His weight on the bed had pulled off her covers and she reached to put them back over her shoulder.

"Leave me alone."

"I'm asking you a question."

"Listen, Kefauver, you keep your voice down. You wake up Charlie and I'm really gonna get mad. You got some nerve, coming in here"—she leaned over to pick up the alarm clock—"six in the morning and asking me about cars."

"Don't change the subject. Who do you know with a Lincoln?"

"Oh, only you know people?"

"Nick sold the Cadillac?"

Gracie was awake now. She adjusted her pillow against the headboard and sat up. "You know Nick won't drive nothing else. Owney Madden told him in 1922 that Cadillac's the only car to buy and he's had one ever since. Mary says he misses the running boards, though."

"Who cares about Nick? I'm asking who picked you up in a Lincoln."

"Helen."

"In a Lincoln?"

"Yeah."

"I don't believe it."

"What's so hard to believe? You should see it, powder blue, dark blue interior . . . a convertible to boot."

"Don't you care what people think? Getting in a car like that in the middle of the afternoon? Did my mother see you?"

"I don't give two pins if your mother saw me. I was with my sisters."

"Your sisters . . . your sisters. They're always up to something. When you gonna get it through your head you can't be like your sisters. They're crazy. You're a married woman. You got a kid." Gracie lay back down and pulled the covers over her head without saying anything. "So where'd Helen get this car? She killed another husband?" Gracie threw the covers back.

"You better shut up, Frankie. I had enough out of you for one night."

"No, tell me. Where she'd get the car?"

"A friend of hers."

"And where'd you go?"

"For a ride."

"Yeah?"

"You heard me."

"Where?"

"I don't remember, some restaurant on the East Side."

"The East Side? Everybody knows me on the East Side!"

"So what?"

"And Charlie? The kid comes home, you're not here? That's how you take care of your kid?"

"Now he's my kid? He's not your kid?"

"Listen, Gracie, I don't want you running around all over town with your *stroush* sisters."

"Frankie?"

"What?"

"I'm going back to sleep."

"You got the money I left for you?"

"Yeah, thanks." She turned her back, shoved him off the bed. He stood up.

"You don't have to thank me, Gracie. Whatever I got is yours. You know that. It's you and me. Don't I always tell you that?" He wanted to get under the covers, push against her, but first he had to take off his pants and hang them up. He always envied those guys who could throw their clothes on the floor and just go at it.

He sighed, took off his pants, folded them carefully over the hanger, lined up the cuffs. The he lay down next to Gracie and he ran a finger from her cheek down along her neck. He leaned over and bit her shoulder. He was a little drunk and he didn't want to fight anymore. She made a sound but he covered her mouth, put his tongue between her lips. He took her hand and put it against himself under the covers. "Feel that, Gracie?" he whispered in her ear. "It's like a bat." She looked over her shoulder in invitation. She'd decided she could be mad at him and still enjoy his weight on top of her, his hands pinning down her wrists, or like now, his coming into her from behind. He wasn't always gentle and she didn't always mind.

Frankie closed his eyes and the redhead from the Copa was in his arms.

Chapter Twenty-two

Frankie couldn't get the redhead out of his mind. He tried, he really did. He'd go uptown with Pauly Russo for a few drinks and they'd pick up a couple of girls, airline stewardesses, cocktail waitresses, hatcheck girls, even schoolteachers, nice enough girls, even though sometimes, Pauly said, they smelled like old fish fillets. These girls were easy to impress with a trip to the Village. A drink at Chumley's, a dish of paella at El Faro, maybe a steak dinner at Peter's Backyard. Frankie and Pauly knew nothing about the artists and writers that had made the places famous, but when it came to restaurants and clubs, they knew Greenwich Village.

But Frankie kept seeing that redhead with the cigarette box around her neck in the Copa lounge. He'd stand between the trucks on Pier 13, he'd push down on that button with his foot and he'd look up at the clouds through the skylights and he'd think about her and how he wanted to wrap his hands in all that red hair, twist it around and around his fist, fill his mouth with it.

Then, to be fair, he'd think about Gracie. He'd promised himself after Doreen that he'd play straight, not get involved, but he always came back to thinking about the cigarette girl and all that beautiful beautiful red red hair.

Gracie pressed his shirts, starched the collar and cuffs just the way he liked them. She cooked his dinner, put up with his mother, took care of his son. She was warm in bed whenever he wanted her. He loved Gracie. It was domestic life that was killing him.

Like his mother always said, he was never the type. And his mother had warned him. Signora Merelli had told Frankie she would take care of him until the day she died. And then, she said, he could have the apartment in the front all to himself. A man could always get a woman. A man was never too old. Why he had to tie himself down young, she still said every time Gracie would leave him to stay with Anona, why he had done that to himself, she never understood. But once he'd gone and done it, once he'd had Charlie, she wouldn't give him right, no matter what.

Even though Signora Merelli called the sisters *puttane,* she never said anything bad about Gracie except that Gracie embarrassed them (her and Frankie or "the Merellis," which is how she thought of herself, her beloved only son, and of course Charlie, who would carry on the name) with those sisters, never knowing what they would do next, like pulling up on Spring Street in a powder blue Lincoln Continental convertible. She had seen it with her own eyes, she told Frankie. It was why she liked living in the front. "Noisy, but I see everything. Everything!" she told him.

She never stopped talking about all those quiet girls from good families. "Beatrice . . . you remember Beatrice? She was crazy for you, but no, you gotta go find a girl at some dance. So she had blue eyes, so what? She was a pretty little thing, but her family's a bunch of nuts . . . gangsters, insurance frauds. I tried to save you, but no, you always gotta find out for yourself."

"Frankie, you counting, or what?" It was the foreman, standing there, watching his foot. "What the hell you doin'?"

"Sorry," Frankie said.

"Listen, you can't handle this job, there's plenty of guys that would kiss my ass for it."

"I was thinking about something," Frankie said.

"Yeah, well, nobody's paying you to think. Just count those stalks and press that button with your foot, you got it?"

"Sure," he said. He smiled but his lips were tight. "Cocksucker," Frankie said under his breath. He flipped his cigarette out over the loading dock and tried to pay attention.

But the next morning Pauly Russo grabbed him outside the gates to the pier. He told Frankie there were forty stalks of bananas left over in the truck when he finished his deliveries. "Pigs eat, Frankie. Hogs choke. Whatta you doing? It's too much. I don't like it; it makes me nervous. We gotta be careful. We got families to feed."

"So what'd you do with the bananas?"

"I offed them, what was I supposed to do? Give them out for Christmas? Here," and he handed Frankie the most money he'd seen since they started the scam. Frankie could taste that red hair.

"Not bad," Frankie said.

"No, it's terrific, but forget doing it again. We gotta go nice and slow. A little bit at a time, and no one'll care. We get caught doing this, we're fish food." Pauly shivered. "Ugh, the thought of going down in that filthy river . . . You ever take a look at the stuff floatin' in there? Garbage, old rubbers . . . Whatta you think? They throw you in alive? Or they kill you first?"

"Who knows what the hell they do?" Frankie didn't like this conversation.

"Well, I don't wanna end up in that river . . . no river, for that matter. I don't wanna end up no floater. I wanna die in bed. Didja ever see what a body looks like after it's been in there a few days? The head swells up and the eyes are just sockets, the fish . . ."

"Will you shut up, Pauly? You wanna see my breakfast? I'll be careful. I had things on my mind. I'm okay now." Frankie put his hand on the outside of his pocket, the pocket with the bulge of money. It felt as good as touching his dick.

"I just don't want to blow a good thing."

"We won't. Don't worry."

Frankie felt bad for Pauly. He was always up to his eyeballs. Between the girls and the racetrack, Pauly was always into somebody for something. And on top if it, he had a bad heart. He'd had a heart attack last year and there were twenty shylocks around his hospital bed checking if he was going to make it. Twenty guys who cared about Pauly's health because he owed them money.

The loan sharks were the ones who got Pauly the job on the pier. He was in such a hole, he couldn't even keep up the vig, so they helped him out. They got him a job and took most of his pay. They got their cut first. In fact, Pauly told Frankie that what he made on the side was almost all he got to keep for himself.

Frankie couldn't figure guys like that, always on the run from somebody. When Frankie had it, he played it, but he always put that little bit aside and he stayed far away from the loan sharks. The loan sharks made his father disappear at forty-three even though his mother told a story about how he had died rescuing a baby from a tenement fire in Chinatown. They still talked about him at the Golden Dragon Restaurant on Mott Street, Signora Merelli said. This was true. They did talk about Frankie's father in the Golden Dragon, but it had nothing to do with Chinese babies. They still remembered him from the fan-tan games in the basement, the only white guy who played there, the one who always raised the stakes.

Gracie was setting the table when Frankie got home. He took off his shirt, washed up at the sink. Frankie sat down, poured his wine, opened his napkin, and put it across his lap. Charlie came in and Gracie made him stand in front of the sink. She stood behind him, washing his hands in hers under the stream of water. She dried them carefully with the dish towel, finger by finger, then held out his chair, wiped his forehead, kissed his mouth.

When Gracie sat down, she asked Frankie about the docks. He said things were fine. She asked Charlie about school and he said he hated it and he hated Sister St. Bernard, who hated his guts and gave him *F*'s on his tests even when he passed. Frankie put his knife and fork down.

"*F*'s?" Why you getting *F*'s?"

Charlie shrugged, swallowed. "I told you, she hates me."

"She . . . Who's she?"

"Sister St. Bernard."

"Then say Sister St. Bernard, not she. So why's she hate you?"

"She hates Italians."

Frankie wiped his mouth with his napkin. "So, what are you worried about? Tell her you're half-Irish."

"I am?" He looked at his mother. "Nana Merelli says that sometimes. When she's mad, she calls Mamma a mick."

"Nice," Gracie said.

She looked at Frankie but he ignored her, picked up his fork, put a slice of steak in his mouth. He chewed slowly, reached over and pushed back Charlie's hair. "No, kid, you're all Italian but Sister St. Bernard don't have to know that. You got blue eyes, no? That's a start. That don't work, tell her something else."

"What?"

"Tell her you want to be a priest."

"But I don't wanna be a priest," Charlie said.

Frankie raised his eyebrows, pleated his lips. "She's only gonna know what you tell her," he said.

"That's right," Gracie said. "Teach him to lie."

"That's not a lie. He could be a priest."

"He just told you he don't want to be a priest."

"He's a kid. He don't know what he wants."

"I do too. I want a car like Uncle Nick's or maybe Aunt Helen's. Yeah, Aunt Helen's, a convertible."

Gracie got up and started clearing the table. "Don't start," she told Frankie, but she didn't have to say anything. Frankie wasn't going to touch that, the sisters and their cars. Tonight he had plans.

"I'm gonna quit," Charlie said.

"Quit what?" Frankie said.

"School."

"You can't quit school. You want to stay stupid? And don't get left back either or you'll get stuck with the old battle ax for another year."

"Did she leave you back?"

"Me? Na . . . where'd you get that from?" and he cuffed Charlie's ear before he took his head in his hands and kissed him. Frankie was an affectionate guy.

Gracie stood by the sink, doing the dishes. Frankie came up behind her. "Good you told him," she said.

"What?"

"About not ever quitting school." She leaned back against him, nuzzled her head into his shoulder. He put his arms around her waist and rocked her side to side. He kissed her neck, bit along the edge of her ear. This was all she wanted. She folded like a cheap suitcase, Helen would say. When Gracie had Frankie close, when he said things to Charlie that a father should say, when he put his arms around her like this . . .

"When you gonna finish?" he said.

"Why?"

"I need the sink. I gotta shave and get out of here."

She stopped mid-dish. "Where you going?"

"Out for a little while. I gotta see some people."

She didn't answer. She just took her time. She washed a dish. She dried a dish. Frankie sat at the kitchen table in his undershirt, his belt undone, smoking one cigarette after another, turning the pack over and over, slipping the cellophane off, slipping it back.

"You want coffee?" she said.

"No, just finish the dishes, will you?"

She did. And then she cleaned the sink, sprinkling Bon Ami on a rag, scrubbing around the drain, washing her hands, drying them on the dish towel, putting out a clean dish towel. She knew just what she was doing. And she was enjoying every minute, the feeling that she had power over him, that she was in control. He wasn't going anywhere, wasn't moving, until she allowed it, until she was good and ready.

She moved away from the sink and he stood up but when he took a step forward she was back at the sink, running the water.

"What are you doing now?"

"I'm making coffee."

"I don't want coffee."

"I want coffee."

"You can't wait? You got all night."

"Why should I? I want it now."

He made noises of exasperation, sat back down and started blowing smoke rings. He waited until she was sitting at the table, coffee in front of her, before he got up to use the sink. She was watching him, he could feel it. He enjoyed her watching him. He knew how she felt about him, how she looked at him. He felt like he could reach out and touch the way she felt about him. He tightened the muscles in his back and leaned over the sink from his waist. He could feel what she wanted to do, come up behind him, put her arms around his waist. Charlie was downstairs, out in the street, eating sunflower seeds and drinking Pepsi, cashing in his credit at the candy store. Frankie stood very still, waiting, but Gracie didn't move except to reach over and take a cigarette from his pack. He heard the match strike and he looked over his shoulder. She blew out a long stream of smoke.

"You smoking now?"

"Once in a while."

He hated that. He hated when women smoked, women like Gracie, anyway. She chain-smoked while he shaved, lathering his face, sliding the blade from bottom to top along his cheek, around his chin. He had to turn from the mirror to rinse the blade in the sink behind him and with every turn, he saw her. She wasn't going to get to him. And she was trying hard.

When he was finished shaving, he shut the hot water faucet and dried his face and neck, then wiped the blade clean. He opened the medicine cabinet, put away his razor and shaving brush and splashed on Old Spice cologne. And while he combed his hair, bending his knees so he could see all of himself in the medicine cabinet mirror, the teeth of the comb making furrows as he pulled it through his hair, he wondered about the cigarette girl's name. He got dressed and on his way out, picked up his pack of Camels from the table. It was empty and he crushed it and left it there. He didn't say what time he was coming back and Gracie didn't ask.

Frankie waited to count his money until he was outside in the hall. Plenty for a night at the Copa and a pack of cigarettes from the redhead. He'd give her a pound and say keep the change. She'd remember him as a sport. Those kinds of girls liked guys who were good with a buck. He whistled for a cab on Sixth Avenue. "Sixtieth Street," he told the driver, "off the Park."

Helen saw Frankie walk in. She was sitting ringside at a table with Joe Black and his cronies. She swiveled around in her chair, moved it back a little behind one of the palm tree columns, straining her eyes in the darkness, wanting to be sure. Oh, it was Frankie all right. From what she could see, though, he was by himself.

Joe Black said something to her and she turned toward him. He was asking her about the car. What'd she think of that Lincoln? How'd it handle?"

When she turned back, Frankie was gone. "That son of a bitch . . ."

"What?" Joe Black said.

"What?"

"You said something?"

"No, sweetheart. You're hearing things." She puckered her lips. He touched them with a finger, leaned over, kissed her.

"Whatta you wanna eat? Chinks?"

"You order for me." She held his hand for a minute before she excused herself and got up. She walked back up to the balcony and looked out over the club. She didn't see Frankie but the Copa was a big place. She walked around and checked out the crowd. Nothing. She went up the stairs to the lounge—bingo! He was sitting by himself, dressed to kill, up to no good, she was sure. What neighborhood guy came to the Copa lounge by himself?

She was back at her table with Joe Black when she saw Frankie on the balcony talking to one of the cigarette girls, leaning up against the wall. She watched him put money in the girl's hand, hold it too long. Joe Black was talking to her. Did she want duck sauce? Definitely, she told him, lots of it. She was grateful when the lights dimmed and the show started, relieved of the effort of keeping an eye on Frankie. She hardly watched but twisted her napkin into such a tight spiral she was embarrassed when the waiter took it. She ordered one scotch after another and leaned against Joe Black when he whispered to her in the dark. She'd end her night on Varick Street, but for now . . .

Chapter Twenty-three

The redheaded cigarette girl was from South Carolina. Her name was Miranda. There was nothing happening where she came from, she told Frankie. The best she could do was the son of the guy who owned the local hardware store. That was making it where she came from. Could he imagine? Frankie couldn't but he told her she could have sold a lot of screws.

She paused, laughed, showed big white teeth. Like a horse, Frankie thought. He couldn't wait to ride her. She told him that she'd come to New York for her career. As what? Frankie asked but he didn't have to because he knew the answer. She was an actress, she told Frankie. She could dance. Never had a lesson in her life, but she had this natural talent. Ya know?

"Yeah," Frankie said. He knew.

And she could sing—again, no lessons, she was a natural. Of course. She just needed a break, had to get lucky, meet the right people.

Frankie understood. He told her he knew a lot of people in the business. Oh, Miranda said, he did? She looked at him more closely, like they all did when he told them that. She straightened her shoulders and leaned forward a little bit more.

When her break was over, she got up to leave. Frankie told her how much he liked talking to her and what time did she get off? Four? Well, good. He knew a place close by where they could have a drink. How was that? She tilted her head and smiled and he said he'd be waiting for her next door in Norby Walters Bar.

At 5:15 A.M. he was arm in arm with his redheaded dream girl waiting for a cab on Fifth Avenue to take him to the Gold Key

Club, an after-hours joint on Fifty-second Street. It was a private club, he explained, flashing his gold key at the doorman. She was impressed, he could tell. She hadn't been in the city long, she told him. This was all new to her except for the couple of times she'd gone out with . . . Frankie closed her mouth with his lips. "Don't tell me about anyone else," he said, his voice low, hoarse. "I don't want to think there's ever been anybody but me."

They got a quiet table in a dark corner that cost him, these things always did, and he let her talk, listened to her like she was speaking eternal truths, and he held her hand the whole time, kissing her long thin fingers, holding them to his face. He noticed she wore no rings and he thought about putting one on her finger, nothing too expensive, a nice stone, a couple of baguettes on either side.

He said he'd never seen a girl as beautiful as she was, and he'd seen a lot of beautiful girls, because, he told her, he hired the showgirls for the Savannah Club down the Village. Miranda was impressed. Did he think she could be a showgirl down the Village?

In a minute, Frankie told her, she could be a showgirl down-town in a minute, but that wasn't the way to go. She was working the top nightclub in New York. You couldn't get better than the Copa. If she was looking for the Big Time, she was in the right place. His fingers were on her shoulder, her neck, behind her ear. "With your looks and that natural talent . . ." Frankie moved his chair closer. His tongue followed his fingers. He was whispering now. "Believe me, it's only a matter of time."

He dropped her off at the apartment on Third Avenue that she shared with three other hopeful new-to-the-city-girls she hardly knew and he promised he'd see her soon. He wrote her phone number on the inside of a Gold Key Club matchbook.

The sun was up when he got to Spring Street. Sam was just

opening up the store. Frankie bought a newspaper and drank a cup of coffee with three sugars before he went upstairs.

That same morning, Helen showed up on Spring Street. She drove down in the blue Lincoln that Joe Black had officially given her last night at the Copa. He had handed her a small blue velvet drawstring bag sometime between the spare ribs and the lobster Cantonese. The keys were inside, on a gold monogrammed chain twisted around a strand of pearls the size of gumballs.

Helen had already been to see Anona, bringing her a case of beeswax candles to burn in front of St. Rita.

"I think I've found my man," she said, puffing on one of her black cigarettes.

"Again?" Anona said, pouring anisette in her coffee.

"You're drinking at breakfast now?"

"I'm not drinking. I'm giving the coffee some flavor. Better than sugar, sugar's bad for you. At my age, you gotta worry."

"At your age you should be having cornflakes and milk in the morning," Helen told her, "maybe a banana . . ."

"That's a good idea. I like that. Give me a banana."

On Spring Street, Gracie was washing sheets in the tub in the kitchen. The door was open and Helen walked in. Gracie turned, holding up her soapy hands and forearms and Helen came and hugged her around the waist. Gracie thought of Frankie, the way he came up behind her at the sink, the way he excited her and then made her so mad. Water and soap suds dripped on the linoleum floor.

"Surprise . . . where's the kid?"

"Charlie? He went down. You didn't see him in the candy store? He always hangs around there on Saturdays. Joe Lima and the bookmakers pay for all the soda the kids can drink. Sam & Al put the icebox out on the sidewalk and they let the kids have whatever they want."

"Maybe he was inside," Helen said. "I couldn't see. It was dark. The lights were off. What are the old geezers doing, saving electricity?"

"Joe Lima gives them money for the electric bill, too. According to Frankie, they leave off the lights and pocket the money. But who can believe what Frankie says? He can't stand them. He calls them washwomen."

Helen took a handful of grapes from the bunch in the fruit bowl on the kitchen table. "Mmm, these are good," she said. "Remember when Anona put that wax fruit she won at the raffle in Hanley's Bar out on the table and Nick bit into the apple?"

"How could I forget? She's still got the apple with his teeth marks in the fruit bowl." Gracie dried her hands and forearms on her front apron. She didn't wear housedresses like the other women on Spring Street. She knew Frankie appreciated this about her. She didn't do it for him, but she might have given in to the ease of a button-down-the-front cotton flowered apron dress with two front patch pockets if Frankie didn't always comment on how glad he was she didn't.

Helen started to laugh. "And then Mary says, 'Nick chews glass, a wax apple ain't nothing.'"

"Are we gonna pick Mary up?"

"No, it's just us. I parked the car on Thompson Street."

"Thompson Street? Where? Frankie gets crazy if I walk up Thompson. He says one of those guys decide they like you, they don't care if you're married."

"Which guys?"

Gracie pushed the tip of her nose sideways with her index finger. "The guys with the bent noses. They're always outside the club on Thompson Street."

"Frankie's too jealous," Helen said. "I don't know why you let him get away with it. Me, personally, I can tell you there's worse things than catching a wiseguy's eye."

Gracie didn't answer. How could she tell Helen that she even liked Frankie's jealousy. If he was so afraid of losing her, he must love her all the more. She didn't understand Helen's easygoing nature when it came to men, but she also didn't know about Helen's life with women. She knew that Helen dressed up sometimes, but Helen had done that as a young girl. Gracie could not begin to imagine the things that went on just steps from her door. She had gone from Anona's kitchen to her own, but Helen? Helen was what Mary called a "free spirit." Nothing stood in her way.

"I'm glad you didn't see Charlie in there," Gracie said. "Maybe he's outside doing something. Playing ball, climbing fences."

"Why you want him to do that? You're always worried he's gonna get hurt."

"I know, but Frankie says a boy's supposed to do that stuff. Don't ask me why. Who ever got anyplace climbing fences?"

"Yeah, unless you're running away from the cops. Where is Good-Looking anyway?"

"Frankie? He's sleeping."

"He got home late last night?"

"Why?"

"Oh, nothing. Just making conversation. It's a beautiful day. Want to go for a ride? Shopping? We could go shopping."

"You got the car again?"

"What got? It's mine."

"He gave it to you?"

"Last night at the Copa." Helen held up the keys, turned the key chain around so Gracie could see her initials. "And . . ." Helen held up the string of pearls.

"Oh, Helen . . ."

"They're yours, anytime you like . . ."

"Where would I wear them?"

Frankie came out of the bedroom, buckling his pants. Helen waved a hand in his direction. "The next time lover boy takes you out."

"Hey, Helen," Frankie said. He hadn't heard her. "What brings you downtown? Slumming?" He came over to her, bent down, and kissed her cheek. Gracie's sisters drove him crazy but secretly Frankie loved them. Frankie loved women. He loved the way they moved and the sweetness of their voices and the smoothness of their skin. He loved the way they smelled, the way they looked up at you from under long black lashes. And so he loved Gracie's sisters, but they just wouldn't give him a break; they wouldn't give in to him the way women usually did. He felt like they had his number, they were always one step ahead of him, and they were too smart, not the way women were supposed to be. So they attracted and repelled him both, and because they were his family, his sisters-in-law, they filled up his life, and because they were so close to Gracie, sometimes he felt like he was married to all three of them.

"I didn't think of it that way until just now," Helen said. She followed Frankie with her eyes and he could feel it. It was as though she could read his thoughts. He always felt guilty around the sisters. If it had just been Gracie, he thought, if she'd been an orphan or something like that, his life would be a whole lot easier.

Gracie moved between them. "Joe Black gave Helen that Lincoln, Frankie, as a gift, last night at the . . ."

Helen stood up suddenly and took Frankie's arm. "Yeah, it's parked downstairs." She sure as hell did not want him to think for one moment that their paths crossed, ever. If his brain was in his head, rather than down the front of his pants, he would know that he couldn't hide, that Helen was all over the city, from the bohemian clubs to the strip joints to the Stork Club and the Copacabana, but Frankie's tragic flaw, as Helen saw it, was that he didn't know, because he didn't think. He took the easy way and when trouble came, he was always surprised. "A real *Napoletano,*" Mary said, quoting Anona. "He's always got his head up his ass."

"Whatta you, *spoustade*?" Frankie said to Helen as she pulled at him. Where'd you park it? . . . In the alley?"

"Cheez, I forgot you live in the back!"

"If we lived in the front, I could see it out the window. That horse's ass Verducci . . ."

"Don't start him off, Helen. Shut up, Frankie. Forget the front. When she dies, we'll get the front. The super promised."

"I'm gonna die before her, and the super, too."

Gracie put out coffee cups and told them both to sit down.

"Well, then it don't matter, does it?" Helen said to Frankie. "Anyway, it's around the corner on Thompson Street." She laughed, but her eyes narrowed. She looked him over. What was he doing in the Copa last night? Was she giving him a bum rap? She was staring at him, not meaning to, but when he looked back at her she made up her mind. It was a snap judgment: Frankie was up to no good. She wasn't even going to tell Mary yet but she would watch him on her own. If he was up to something, this time they'd nail him good. She put out her cigarette in the ashtray Frankie had brought with him from the bedroom. He pushed it closer to her so she wouldn't have to reach over. She noticed his hands, the long beautiful fingers. He didn't look like he came from peasants who toiled in the sun of the Mezzogiorno, but of course he did.

Frankie eyed Helen. "You're looking good, Helen. Life's treating you okay?"

"I make my life, Frankie. You know that. And when you do the right thing, you got nothing to worry about. Everything takes care of itself. And you?"

Frankie turned down the corners of his mouth. "I can't complain."

"I come to get Gracie out of the house for a while."

Frankie reached up and put his hand on Gracie's hip. The kitchen was small; everyone was an arm's length away. "That's good. She should get out more. She never wants to go anywhere. Always worried about the kid, the house. She's gold, my wife, fourteen karat. I got lucky." He pulled Gracie down and kissed her, but he watched Helen from the corner of his eye.

Helen looked away. She wasn't won over by Frankie's show of affection but she could see Gracie was enjoying the attention even if she pretended to be annoyed and pushed him away. Helen lit a cigarette and Frankie turned back to her. He put his elbows on the table, rested his chin on his folded hands. "When you gonna stop smoking those foreign stinkers?"

Helen smiled at him. "Some things," she said to Frankie, "are tough to give up."

Shit-house Mike kept the dockworkers from taking too long a crap on company time. He was keeping an eye on Frankie and Pauly who were having a conference in one of the stalls about holding off on their sideline business for a while because the bosses were watching the count. Frankie threw Shit-house Mike a deuce when they left the bathroom but he knew it wouldn't mean much. Mike was a company man. At least he'd keep quiet about him and Pauly being in the same stall.

That left Miranda out for a while. He couldn't cut into Gracie's house money and he couldn't impress Miranda on a budget. He had to have a roll in his pocket to show her a good time. He worried that someone else would move in on her while he was jerking off but he couldn't worry about everything. He'd try to stay home a few nights. Take it easy. Pamper himself.

So Frankie spent three weeks playing happy husband and when he and Pauly Russo finally got the banana scam going again, Frankie felt like a released prisoner of war. He'd been to the East Side, played some pinochle in the club, had a few drinks, but he'd gone home every night.

Frankie never hung around Spring Street. Those guys just didn't have his style, Joe Pretzels, Pauly Russo. They were strictly working guys who spent their time checking the racing sheet and the ball scores and bullshitting. But from what Frankie could see, they never did nothing and they never hit big.

They were never gonna either, Frankie was convinced. You had to act like it had already happened before Lady Luck noticed you. And some of the luck you had to make on your own.

He met Pauly in a bar on Barrow Street for the cut-up and went right to Maurizio's and picked up those onyx cuff links with the diamond in the center and a big aquamarine ring for Miranda.

And that Friday night he kissed Gracie goodbye and went up to the Copa with a pocketful of money. She didn't pay much attention to his leaving. She was starting to get wise and had some plans of her own.

Helen had invited her to the Stork Club, told her that Joe Black had a table reserved, that she should get dressed, all dressed up, and have some fun for a change. See how the other half lived. "You're beautiful," Helen had told her that very afternoon, standing behind her at the mirror opposite the sink where Frankie shaved every morning and in the evenings when he was going out. And Helen had pulled back Gracie's hair, away from her face while Gracie looked and Helen kept talking. And then she sat Gracie down at the kitchen table and stepped back. Helen went into her purse and pulled out a satin bag and laid it on the table. She tweezed Gracie's eyebrows and colored her cheeks and her lips. She took a small red plastic case of mascara and slid it open, wetting the little brush inside, coating Gracie's lashes. "Sit there," she had said, and rummaged through Gracie's bedroom closet, which she shared with Charlie and the coats.

Frankie had his own armoire, and on a whim Helen opened it. Inside, carefully spaced, were four suits, carefully pressed shirts, hats lined up on the shelf above, spit-shined shoes underneath. She closed the double doors and took a breath. Back at the bedroom closet, she pulled out a chiffon dress from a gray garment bag. It had a sweetheart neckline covered with sheer black chiffon that shirred to the waist and then billowed out. "Beautiful," Helen said to herself, even if the smell of mothballs made her wrinkle her nose. "This is it," she told Gracie, coming into the kitchen. "I want you to come tonight and I want you to wear this."

"Oh, Helen, how can I do that? If Frankie even sees this stuff on my face, he'll scream like a stuck pig."

"Don't overestimate him," Helen said. "And think about what you're saying. Where is your precious Frankie? I don't see him. You think he's gonna be home with you tonight?"

Gracie half-closed her eyes. She shrugged one shoulder. "You're probably right," she said. "I'll tell you what: if he leaves, I'll leave."

Helen was surprised. Maybe her baby sister wasn't so much *mollica* after all. "So you'll come?" Helen said.

"I told you. But it's complicated . . . I got Charlie . . . and how am I gonna go uptown? The only thing I know about the Stork Club is what I read in Walter Winchell's column."

Helen laughed. "C'mon, Gracie. You can figure it out. Maybe you should walk up Thompson Street," she teased. "Maybe you'll get lucky and one of those wiseguys will take you away from all this."

"Helen."

"Okay, forget I said that. You're a respectable woman. But listen, I'm gonna stop by Anona's first. So I can wait for you there. Nine o'clock, nine-thirty, then we'll go together to the club. I told Joe Black I'd meet him there. I don't like to be picked up and ferried around. That's why I like the car. That's why Joe gave it to me. He listens when I tell him what I like. And there's nothing I like better than . . . whatchamacallit"—she hesitated—"mobility."

Gracie kept her head down when Frankie kissed her goodbye. Helen had called it right, Gracie thought. Frankie wasn't staying home with her, and even when she caught him off guard, kissing him full on the mouth instead of the perfunctory peck, he didn't notice anything different about her, not the glow on her cheeks or the heavy black of her eyelashes. He was too involved in his own plans.

• • •

She put on the chiffon dress that accentuated her waist and the curve of her breasts and she did up her hair in a French twist and tucked in the loose ends with bobby pins. She sprayed it until it was stiff, put on more lipstick, grabbed her coat and was out the door. Charlie would stay with Signora Merelli, which he loved because she fed him anything he wanted, starting with pepper-and-egg sandwiches and ending with a carton of Schrafft's ice cream in three flavors covered in Hershey syrup, and if he was lucky, served on top of toasted plain cake from Sutters Bakery. She thought about stopping to kiss him goodbye but changed her mind when she bumped into Dibby Santulli in the hall and he whistled at her and smiled. If her mother-in-law had a heart attack, who would take care of Charlie?

She took a cab up to Anona's. Her shoes hurt. She hadn't worn them since Frankie's cousin LuLu's wedding. They were pointed and very high-heeled. When she rested a foot against the folded jump seat in front of her to steady herself as the cab turned a corner, she admired the shape of her calf and the line of her instep in the black satin shoe. She realized she never looked at herself, never thought about herself as anything but a wife and mother. She gripped the leather loop on the side of the door and sat back. She couldn't believe she was actually going out, uptown, on the town. When the driver asked her where to, she said the Stork Club but she had to make a stop first.

Helen was there, combing Anona's hair, twisting it into the long skinny gray braid that went down Anona's back. In the morning, Anona would wrap it into a bun in the back of her head with the hairpins she kept in a cut-glass covered dish. "Ah, you're here!"

Helen said, when Gracie walked in. "Look at her, Anona. How beautiful she is." Helen bent down and rubbed her cheek against Anona's. "You, too, you're beautiful. Where's a mirror? I want you to see. I could put some rouge on those old cheeks and take you dancing tonight."

"Pshew," Anona said. She never looked in a mirror. "For what? I know who I am."

"Is Mary coming over?" Gracie asked.

"She is, but to play cards with Anona. Sometimes I think she's as old as Nick."

Anona looked up. "She's not coming with that *moltedevane,* is she? I was hoping for a nice night."

"I don't know," Helen said. "But if she brings Nick, you be nice to him. He's always doing something for you. You're never grateful."

"A man like him, he's lucky I even let him in my house."

"Boy," Helen said, "you don't look to throw him out when he shows up with the booze and the beer and the candles and the olive oil every week."

"You know," Anona said to Helen, "you're a smart cookie. If you had kids, they'd tear your heart out. This way, you can be as much trouble as you like."

"I'll leave the kids to Gracie. She can pay the piper."

Gracie felt a twinge of guilt: dressed to the nines, red lips, black lashes, high-heeled shoes, and her son downtown, unsuspecting, eating his way through a carton of ice cream, Signora Merelli wiping his mouth after every spoonful. Helen saw it in Gracie's face. "Don't go soft on me," she said. "You deserve a night out."

"She's right," Mary said from the doorway. She held a brown paper bag that obviously held a liquor bottle, the bag had been shaped around the bottle, the black cap peering over the serrated edge of the paper bag.

"Mary," Helen said. "You coming tonight? Joe Black's got a table at the Stork Club. Where's the old man?"

"You know Nick doesn't like to go out anymore. He thinks they're still looking for him."

"For what? Why would they be looking for Nick?" Gracie said.

"Why not?" Anona hurumphed. "There's gotta be a list as long as your arm."

"Ignore her," Mary said. "Nick still thinks it's 1932. He worries all the time. 'Who's gonna take care of you, babe, if I get sent up?' He's always saying that. It's very cute."

Anona made some kind of suspicious noise and Mary went over and stood in front of her. "You stop now," she said. "Or I'm gonna take my bottle and the deck of cards in my purse, and leave you alone."

"Go ahead," Anona said. "I'll go downstairs."

"I told Hanley not to give you anything anymore. You're too old to be drinking in bars."

"Why? The Irish are better than me? I do what I want."

"Stop teasing her," Helen said. "She gets all excited and then she has an asthma attack."

"She hasn't had an asthma attack since 1923."

"Then I guess I can have a cigarette," Helen said. She held one out to Gracie, who took it but refused a light.

"Practicing?" Mary said.

"Yeah, for her big night on the town," Helen said. "We should go. I don't like to keep Joe waiting too long. You know who's gonna be there?"

"Don't make me nervous . . . who?" Gracie said.

"Impellitteri . . . the mayor, Joe knows him good."

"Geez, Frankie would die . . ."

"Forget Frankie," Helen said. "This is about you."

Chapter Twenty-four

Miranda walked past Frankie and put her nose in the air. He came up behind her and put his hand on her ass. She kicked back, fast, like a horse. The tip of her stiletto heel scraped down his shin. When he let out a yell, she looked around. He was bent over, errant hand on his leg, grimace on his face. He raised his eyes, waited for a sign of remorse from her but she kept walking, hips swinging, head high.

She stopped at a table of fleshy well-dressed men and they bought Cuban cigars and she smiled at them until Frankie thought her face would break and fall in their dishes of pork lo mein. She bent over the table, tits in their faces, bills changing hands. Frankie was boiling now. The ring in his pocket, the aquamarine he had picked so carefully from Maurizio's bag of swag, was a colored piece of cut glass Frankie wouldn't give his worst enemy. He leaned back against the wall and watched Miranda parade. She moved between the tables: smile, bend, tits, money. The spangles on her costume glittered blue-black, her long white arms and legs shimmered, luminescent in the artificial light of the cabaret.

The place was jammed. He didn't even know who the headliner was since he had only come to see Miranda. He waited for her break, right before the comedian came on, and he came down off the terrace to stand behind her while she took the strap off her neck and put the box of cigars and cigarettes down. She took the wad of money from the pocket sewn into the top of her costume and Frankie got a pain over his eyes. Suddenly all he wanted was to set her up somewhere so she could put down that cigarette box forever. He could put her in Queens, maybe the Bronx . . . It would be good for him, too, to get away once in a while, see some grass, a few trees. That's what went wrong the last time, with . . . what was her name? Donna? Denise? Doreen, the blond cheerleader. He'd been too close to home that time. He must have been out of his mind.

Frankie knew he was made for better things, that he wasn't cut out to be another working stiff. But people kept getting in his way, keeping him from his real life. He knew how to live. He just needed the cash. The money he was making from his scam with Pauly Russo, plus what he'd been squirreling away all these years, was building up pretty good. It was waiting for him in a safe deposit box in the Emigrant Savings Bank on Varick Street. He'd gotten friendly with the guy who made you sign the card when you went in the vault, so he didn't have to sign the card—the things you could do with a sawbuck in an envelope at Christmastime—so there was no record that he was down there once, twice a week, and he liked it that way. It didn't look good if you were always sniffing around your safe deposit box.

Frankie was looking at Miranda's back. She was rubbing her shoulders, the thin pink line where the leather strap had cut into her skin. He put a hand out to touch her but remembered the heel in his shin and drew back. If she did that again, he'd have to get mad and he didn't want to. He felt tender; he wanted to stay that way.

Miranda was putting her tip money into her locker. The truth was she easily made his salary and more, her thigh rubbing against an arm in a custom-made silk suit, red-tipped fingers touching fat wrists and fingers that stuffed a double sawbuck into her hand in exchange for a pack of Lucky Strikes.

The pain over Frankie's eyes circled his head. He'd worked himself up and down his ladder of dreams and was ready to walk out, go back to the neighborhood, have a few drinks, check out Hortense, the "Georgia Peach" from Alabama who stripped at the Savannah Club, and then go home to Spring Street, sandwiched between his wife and his mother, in the building where he was born. But then Miranda caught his eye and he stood there, staring, like a second-story man caught in a cop's flashlight.

"Whatta you looking at?" she said. Her girlfriends were standing around her. He figured she was showing off and decided to let it pass because he didn't want to go back downtown anymore. He wanted to make nice.

Frankie straightened his spine, smoothed his hair with one hand. He knew she was his. He could tell. She had it for him or she wouldn't have said anything at all. Frankie knew women. Now she'd be a little snotty, pretend she could care less, but she wouldn't let him walk out. When it looked like he was going to leave, she'd reach out and he'd have her better than he had her before. It always worked that way. Once Frankie had it figured out, it was so easy. What wasn't easy was the money, the oil that kept the machine running smooth.

"The most beautiful girl in this joint," Frankie said.

"Oh, brother," one of Miranda's girlfriends said, pulling up the front of her costume and walking off. "I'll catch you later, Miranda. I got a weak stomach."

"She's cute," Frankie said. "What zoo did she escape from?"

Miranda moved close to him. "Doris don't mean nothing. She's just looking out for me. She don't want me to get hurt."

"Me? Hurt you? That's what she thinks?"

Miranda shrugged. She put her hands on his shoulders. "Where've you been? I thought I'd never see you again. I was even getting used to the idea." Frankie leaned toward her, but she pulled back. "Something's wrong, Frankie. Me, you. Something smells bad. I can't afford to waste time. I'm not stupid. I ain't gonna look this way forever and it's all I got. I make good money here but it costs me, too. Makeup and facials and manicures and the kickbacks. That's what Doris's been telling me. I got to find a guy who's gonna put me in some nice house in the suburbs, let me hang up my high heels."

"You found him, doll. My purpose in life is to take care of you, take you outta here. Rub those sore shoulders, put you in silk and lace." He moved to kiss her, hold her, cement his good intentions with body heat.

"Not here, Frankie. You wanna get me fired on top of everything else? Just talk to me. What's going on with us . . . for real?"

"I just told you what I want to do."

"Yeah, but wanting and doing are different things. Doris says you're a loser. She called you something"—Miranda bit one manicured fingernail—"a *spiccone.*"

"She called me a *spiccone?* That cheap . . ."

"What's a *spiccone?*"

"Ask Doris. She knows everything."

"She says you probably got a wife and three kids stashed in some tenement downtown. She says I'm going nowheres with you."

"Well, she's got a lotta frigging nerve. What the hell's she doing here, she knows so much? How come she ain't on Park Avenue running charity balls?" Frankie took Miranda's hands and held them. Her perfume was in his head. He touched her hair. He couldn't believe the color of her hair. He'd never seen anything like it.

"Listen," Frankie said, "why we wasting time talking about Doris, what Doris says, what Doris thinks. I'll wait for you tonight when you get off. We'll go out. I'll make you forget all about Doris."

"I don't know . . ."

"Look, baby, I mean what I say." He crossed himself, swore on his dead father's grave that he loved her. She didn't understand how serious that was, so he figured it didn't count. "I'll take you to Rumplemeyer's for breakfast, or wherever you want to go. You can tell Doris all about it tomorrow night. You can make her head spin."

"But Frankie, where you been? For real?"

"I been busy, Miranda. You know what it's like to be in business, one thing after another."

"What's your business anyway?"

"Import-export."

"You're an executive?"

"Executive? I own the company! But, hey, forget business. Look . . ." Frankie took out the ring. The stone caught the light; Miranda caught her breath. Frankie could hear it and felt a pull of disappointment at the predictability. They were all alike, he thought, slipping it on her finger, her ring finger, left hand. He knew they liked that. It had, well, significance.

Frankie took Miranda's hand in his, stroked her fingers. "It matches your eyes," he said.

"My eyes?" Miranda squinted, took back her hand, looked more closely at the stone. "It's a blue diamond?"

Frankie rubbed his mouth with his hand. He bit down on his bottom lip. "It's an aquamarine. I was gonna get a diamond, but I saw this one, and all I could see was your eyes."

Miranda made a small disappointed sigh. "It's beautiful, Frankie. I love it: Thanks." She held her hand out in front of her, fingers splayed. Frankie looked at it, too. It looked pretty good, he thought. It was a big aquamarine. He put an arm around her.

"One kiss, Miranda, before you go back."

Doris pushed in the swinging doors. "Podell's counting girls, honey. Another minute and you're gonna get bounced."

"I'm coming right now," Miranda said. She picked up the cigarette box, balanced it on her hip, held the bottom with one hand and slipped the strap over her head. "Doris," she said, after she had adjusted the weight of the box, "take a quick look . . ." Miranda held out her hand.

Doris took Miranda's hand in hers. Frankie thought she held it longer than she had to. "Hmmm . . . Nice . . ." Doris said. She let Miranda's hand drop and faced Frankie. "Last of the big-time spenders."

Frankie took a step forward. "Listen, Miranda, you want to see me tonight, I'll be next door when you get off."

He left without giving her a chance to say anything, had a few drinks in the lounge and split, went down to Jimmy Kelly's. It was tough to score with all the uniforms around, but he managed to fondle some girl at the bar and at four o'clock, instead of going back to the Copa to meet Miranda when she got off work, he packed it in and went home to Gracie. She was always there waiting for him. Frankie was very fond of women waiting for him, his arrival, his touch. For Frankie Merelli, his anticipating their anticipating kept the earth turning on its axis.

Gracie was asleep when he came in. He got undressed in the kitchen in the dark, hung up his clothes and went into the bedroom. He lay down next to her, put his arm around her waist. "Gracie," he whispered in her ear, "Gracie? Wanna play hide the banana?"

Chapter Twenty-five

Mary and Helen were in Anona's house. They came to see her often. For Gracie, it was more complicated. If too many weeks went by without Gracie, one of them would just go and pick her up no matter what she said or what she was doing and when they came to get her, she always went. But today it was just Helen and Mary.

"So, have you seen Frankie?" Mary said. "You're out every night, the Copa, the Blue Angel, El Morocco. You're in every joint in town with your new beau. Have you seen Frankie anywhere?"

"I saw him at the Copa, in the back, up on the terrace." Helen was looking out the window at Thirty-eighth Street. "But to be honest, I couldn't tell if he was doing anything he shouldn't be doing, and you know, Gracie's not complaining."

Anona filled the pipe that had belonged to Nonno, the pipe she had kept all these years. Nick got her the tobacco. "Who cares?" she said. "She comes back here, I'll take care of her." She lit the pipe with a wooden match from the box near the stove.

"I think you got something besides tobacco in that pipe," Mary said.

"And why in God's name are you smoking?" Helen said. "I thought you had asthma. You're always saying you can't breathe." Anona ignored her, busy fumbling in a cookie tin.

"What are you looking for?" Mary came over to the oilcloth-covered counter and stood next to her.

"Mind you own business," Anona said.

There were strange things in that tin: dirt from the village of Bocca al Lupo that Anona wanted put in her American grave, some dried herbs and seeds that should have rotted decades ago but hadn't. Mary called it rarefied air. Anona called it magic. Like the roll blessed on St. Anthony's feast day that she kept in the back of the closet and replaced every year. That Anona called a miracle. A year in the back of a dark closet and no green mold. A miracle.

"Ah . . ." Anona said. She'd found a piece of thick black thread and carefully wound it around the top button of her dress.

"What's that?" Mary said.

"For my asthma. You reminded me."

"So now you can smoke?" Helen asked her.

Anona didn't answer but sat down in the upholstered rocker that Nick had brought her just last week. Helen came over and rubbed Anona's temples. "You like this chair, huh? Nick's good to you, isn't he?" she said, looking over Anona's head at Mary.

"Stop teasing her," Mary said.

Anona closed her eyes.

"It was nice of Nick to get it for you, no?" Helen said.

Anona shrugged.

"Give it up," Mary said. "You're still trying to get her to give Nick a fair shake. Forget it. Anyway, if she started now, the surprise might kill him. He's not a kid anymore. Leave well enough alone."

Anona was snoring. "She loves Nick," Helen said. "You know that."

Mary shook her head. "Let's face it, Helen. It's not just Nick. Anona hates men." She pulled the blanket that had slipped off the old lady's legs back onto her lap.

"Not your grandfather. Nonno . . . he was a real man," Anona said, suddenly awake.

"What about our father?" Mary said.

"What father?" Anona said and closed her eyes.

Chapter Twenty-six

Frankie was in his undershirt drinking espresso at the kitchen table. Gracie was across from him, buttering toast for Charlie, who was leaning on one fist, eyes half-closed. "You gonna put it in his mouth and chew it for him?"

"Shut up, Frankie. Your mother would've digested your food if she could have figured out how to do it."

"Gracie, when are you gonna stop with my mother?"

"Never, Frankie. Not ever."

"We were having a nice Sunday."

"We're still having a nice Sunday. I'm just buttering Charlie's toast."

"You're right, I started. Now I'm gonna stop. Okay?"

"Fine."

Charlie opened his mouth to say something but Gracie put the buttered toast into it. "Finish that, Charlie, and I'll make you more."

"We should get a car," Frankie said.

"A car? How we gonna afford a car?"

"You buy it on time, so much a month. I'm working steady now. We should have a car."

"I don't know, Frankie."

"Your sisters have cars. I want you to have a car, too."

"What are you talking about? Since when am I keeping up with my sisters?"

"That's not fair, Gracie. If you did what your sisters did, you'd have ten cars by now."

"What?" Charlie said, swallowing the last bit of toast, butter on his chin. "What did Aunt Helen and Aunt Mary do to get them cars?"

"You see how you start?" Gracie said to Frankie. "You think

the things you say go over his head? You gonna stop with my sisters? If it wasn't for my sisters . . ."

"Oh, excuse me for mentioning your sisters who have done so much for us, which is why we still live in this hole in the back and they have brownstones in Brooklyn."

"Since when does where we live have anything to do with my sisters? Like you'd leave your mother if someone *gave* you a brownstone in Brooklyn, like you'd ever get out of here . . . off this block. Don't make me laugh!" Gracie took two more slices of toasted bread off the stove.

"You're making this kid into a blimp," Frankie said. "Why d'you keep feeding him all day long?"

"Charlie, take the toast, go inside. Listen to the radio."

"And you make him eat inside? Do anything he wants?"

"You don't like it?"

"No, I don't like it. You know I hate crumbs. You're not supposed to eat in the living room."

"Frankie?"

"What, Gracie? What?"

She waited until Charlie was sitting on the floor in the living room, legs crossed, in front of the radio, before she came around the table and leaned down close to Frankie's ear.

"Frankie?" she said.

"What, for Chrissakes?"

"Go shit in your hat and tell your mother it's your false curls." She went out the door. She could hear him calling her all the way down the stairs until the hallway door closed behind her and she was out on the stoop.

"She's gonna meet us here?" Mary said.

"I told her we'd be here today," Helen said. "I spoke to her twice this week when I stopped by to see that adorable kid. I love that Charlie. Frankie made some kid." Mary was quiet and Helen saw the anguish in Mary's face and bit down hard on the inside of her mouth. She knew Mary was thinking of Sonny, who would have been a big boy by now if he had lived; he would have almost been a man, but Helen said nothing because they never spoke of Sonny to Mary. If Mary said his name, they would listen, but it had evolved that only Mary was allowed to do that, bring up Sonny's name or his memory.

Mary closed her eyes. She wasn't going to cry. She'd stopped crying years ago. Mary had pictures of Sonny everywhere, but again, she was the only one. Everyone else had to pretend he had never existed. That was the way Mary wanted it. On Sonny's birthday, Mary stayed in her bedroom with the shades drawn and didn't eat or drink or speak. She did the same on the anniversary of Sonny's death. He had died when he was only four years old. There was something in his throat, the doctors said—an obstruction, they called it. He couldn't swallow and he lay there, Mary remembered, and day by day disappeared in front of her eyes. When there was no way to feed him, they had put sour balls in his rectum to keep him alive. There was nothing else to do, the doctors said. Nick could not believe it. He had money, he told them. He would give it all to them. He could get more. He thought about killing the doctor who had first told them that something was wrong with Sonny, as if that doctor had made it all happen, as if his diagnosis had sealed Sonny's fate.

Anona made novenas and followed processions barefoot and on her knees until her skin was raw. She prayed to every saint she could remember and then she tried to blame Nick, but Helen shushed her. Helen drew the line when Anona tried to say it was divine retribution, and a bargain at that, one small soul for all that carnage, all that ill-gotten wealth and prosperity. Helen made her stop. "Then why did Emma die?" Helen shouted at Anona. "And Nonno and the baby and everybody else?" She put her hand over Anona's mouth and Gracie would never have believed that Anona would allow this but that was how Sonny's death had turned their lives upside down.

When they waked Sonny, Anona insisted it be in her house, and the undertaker came and set up the chairs and the stand for the little blue coffin with the pan underneath where the ice dripped. He brought the lamps and a curtain to cover the windows and make a backdrop for the coffin. Helen remembered the curtain. It was gold velvet, not shiny but dull, and it fell in heavy folds, covering the windows, shutting out the noise and the light from Thirty-eighth Street, making Anona's kitchen dark and quiet and somber, appropriate for mourning.

From the first day, there were so many flowers that they spilled out of the apartment and into the hall. They lined the staircase and choked the air with their scent. Owney Madden sent a five-foot-high bleeding heart of red roses and a toy train of violets and lilacs.

Anona sat in front of the coffin day and night. She dozed in the chair, waking with a start, terrified that Sonny's soul had escaped when she wasn't watching. Mary lay in the bedroom, in the bed the sisters had slept in all together. For the whole week, she lay there drugged and inconsolable. Nick sat on the bed and kissed her face when he wasn't outside in the makeshift funeral parlor that was Anona's kitchen, receiving the long line of mourners who came to pay respects. The names of the people who came to see Sonny were in the history books, and for years after, Mary would ask Nick to tell her who was there, the famous and infamous who had come to see Sonny waked in his white satin suit, and when she asked, Nick would recite the litany of names he had committed to memory.

Mary never had another child. She couldn't, she said, even if no one asked. One was all she had in her, she said. And Helen? She had never wanted children, never felt any pull to be a mother, to swell, to nurse, to nurture. She was content to be the eternal aunt. There was too much to do. The domestic life left her cold. In this, she understood Frankie. This they had in common, but she couldn't excuse him for marrying her sister, having a child, and pretending it wasn't so.

Mary and Helen sat at the bar on Varick Street where Helen was more than a casual patron. Helen liked it here, she told Mary. No drunken guys drooling over you, trying to pick you up when you wanted to sit by yourself at the bar.

"What about the girls drooling over you?" Mary said.

"When I come in here, Mary, I'm usually in a nice pin-striped suit, a pair of wing tips, and I sit all by myself at the end of the bar, or at that table near the phone in the back. I've met some nice people in here. You'd be surprised. Just last week, I was talking to this girl takes pictures at the Copa. You know, the girls that go around with the camera and ask you if you want a picture of your table for a price that breaks your legs but the guys are too afraid to look cheap so they say, 'Sure, go ahead'? Doris . . . big good-looking blonde." Helen sighed. "If I was six feet tall, I could've got a job like that. I could've raked it in."

Gloria, the owner, came over to make sure everything was okay. She sent them a drink on the house. Her father was connected so she didn't have much trouble with the cops who regularly raided gay establishments in the Village, even though they were on the take. Gloria's was down a cellar and Varick Street was dark and quiet once the printers who worked in the buildings on Seventh Avenue went home. When it got noisy down Gloria's, there was no one to complain. After five o'clock, the street was a ghost town.

"And tell me before Gracie shows up, anything with Frankie?" Mary said.

Helen shrugged and ordered two more Seagrams and soda. "Relax. And you know, Mary, maybe we should get off Frankie's back and mind our own business. Gracie told me he's bringing home the money, sometimes gives her extra, and never stays out all night."

"I don't like the sound of that."

"You're awfully suspicious, Mary."

"Goes with the territory. Waiting for Nick to get popped all these years made me careful."

"Mary, he's been out of commission almost twenty years."

"What can I tell you? He still looks over his shoulder. I figure it keeps him young."

"We survived everything, didn't we?" Helen said.

Mary nodded. They clinked glasses. *"Salute,"* Helen said. *"Cent'anni."* They drank and called for another round.

Frankie was on his back. Miranda was over him, one long leg on either side. He thought he'd died and gone to heaven. He was never looking at anything but redheads ever again. But maybe this was the one, this was the redhead. He'd promised himself he wouldn't get involved, no more *gummaras,* but what the hell?

You only live once. He could afford it. The scam with Pauly Russo was going better than either of them had expected and he was even doing a little loan-sharking on the side. The guys down the docks were always getting bagged up. It wasn't much, but the vig was heavy. It added up. Frankie let it get around that he was tied in with some big guys. He never said anything direct, just let gossip take its course. He didn't expect any trouble. It was small potatoes, he told himself. Everybody has to eat.

So the money was coming in nice now. Gracie was getting hers and once in a while he'd give her some extra, nothing steady, he didn't want to spoil her, get her expecting it every week, but he wanted to keep her happy so he could be happy, too.

His end was good enough to get over to Belmont when he got the urge and put a double sawbuck on a number and rent rooms like this one whenever he could get away. Miranda was crazy about him but why should she be any different than the rest? Sometimes he closed his eyes and conjured up all the women he had known and imagined them in his very own personal Miss America contest. Miranda always got the crown. She always beat out all the rest.

Except she was always bothering him about the future, their future. He'd made the mistake of letting her think they had a future. Miranda had no idea about Gracie and Charlie and he wasn't planning on telling her anytime soon. He didn't feel too bad; it was a sin of omission. He'd tell her when the time was right, convince her that they could still be together, just not the way she thought. He would make it up to her. Then he could have everything. His family down on Spring Street and Miranda in a house somewhere, painting her toenails, petting her poodle, waiting for him.

He was going to tell her, he promised himself, but not right now, not when she was naked on a double bed in a room on the twenty-first floor of the St. Regis Hotel.

Miranda put her tit in his mouth. "Whatta you thinking, Frankie?" she said. He didn't answer, but rolled her over and starting at her neck, kissed her all the way down to the toes on her left foot and back up her other side. He thought about tying her up, imagined those long white arms crossed at the wrists above her head, but the only thing handy was his tie, 100 percent silk, from Sulka. There was no way he was going to use his tie; she would just have to wait for another time.

Chapter Twenty-seven

Miranda was pushing, pushing, every time Frankie saw her and he saw her a lot. He started to worry about getting caught again. It would be just his luck. Miranda . . . It wasn't enough worrying about the sisters, especially Helen, who'd hooked up with Joe Black who owned half the clubs in the city and ran the East Side, but then there was the lesbo Doris, Miranda's self-appointed guardian angel.

"She's got it for you," he'd tell Miranda. "Can't you see what's going on? What'd you learn down there in South Carolina, anyway? She wants you for herself, that train car. Why dontcha tell her to get lost?"

"You got a dirty mind. Doris cares about me. She worries about me like a sister." Frankie shivered. Just what he needed, another loving sister in his life.

Miranda would pout, then move in for the kill. "She thinks you're a shit-heeler, Frankie, a broken-down valise, a rubber boot."

"Anything else you wanna add? So what the hell you doing with me anyway? You wanna go believing that bull-dyke? Is she gonna take you outta here? Put you in a house somewheres like I am?"

"I'm all alone in New York, Frankie. I ain't got no friends. Just you and Doris, and for her I got a phone number."

"Big deal. I told you, I ain't got a phone. I told you that a million times."

Miranda's eyes slitted. It was always the same thing. "How come, Frankie? How come a big shot like you don't even have a phone?"

"You wanna hear it again, I'll tell you again. I need some peace and quiet. If you got a phone, you got every Tom, Dick, and Harry calling you up and busting your balls."

It was always the same thing, over and over. He'd put his arms around her, bite the tip of her ear. "I wish I could be just an ordinary Joe, just for you, baby, but I'm not. I got serious obligations. I'll take care of you. Trust me. Just stick with me and you'll never have to worry. You'll have a rock on your finger the size of a chicken egg before I'm done. You won't be able to lift your hand."

They were in the back room at the Copa. He was getting into it, his words garbled, his tongue pressing into Miranda's neck. He thought they were alone. He heard a snort and he closed his eyes. He didn't have to look around.

"You should be on stage, honey," she said. "Your talents are going to waste back here."

Frankie stood up, fixed his tie, his cuffs. "I thought they kept horses in stables," he said.

Doris didn't answer him, but moved toward her locker. She pushed him as she passed. She was a big girl, and Frankie realized—not that it would come to that, not that he would ever hit a woman, not that Doris was a woman—that she could probably break his ass.

Times like these made Frankie want to give it up, but when he did, at least once a week, and stayed away, it got worse. The pier, the bananas, Spring Street, Gracie, the kid . . . it all got too much to take.

And then when he went back uptown, Miranda was wild, contrite. She'd do anything for him. He'd go home exhausted, bowlegged, convinced that he had to make a move, a big move, and then he'd get to Spring Street and Charlie would climb up on the couch next to him and hold on to him and there'd be the smell of garlic cooking in oil and Frankie would close his eyes and wish, really wish, he'd never been born.

He was getting nervous, too, about robbing the bananas. When he really thought about what he was doing, not just robbing bananas, but who he was robbing them from, he'd lose his balance, see points of light in front of his eyes and have to put his head down, like when he was a kid and would almost pass out in church from the heat and the incense. He was slipping more and more, his Siegel Brothers–shod foot missing that steel button more and more, and more and more uncounted stalks of bananas were going into the back of Pauly Russo's truck every day. Pauly had reduced his protests to a steady whine, because, Frankie knew, Pauly was barely keeping his head above water. The more Pauly had, the more he gambled.

The pile of hundreds in Frankie's safe deposit was growing in direct proportion to his troubles. Sometimes he'd stand between the trucks on the pier and his leg would shake so bad he'd have to sit down on the stool that he usually just leaned against. His fingers were stained yellow from smoking too many cigarettes and Miranda started talking about them going to California together. She could send for her mother in South Carolina. Her mamma made biscuits like nobody's business.

Miranda started talking about leaving all the time. It got so she'd just say "California" and Frankie'd lose his hard-on. He said "great" to everything, even the biscuits, even though he never heard of anybody but dogs eating biscuits. When Miranda said, "When?" he'd say, "Soon," and anytime he bumped into Doris, who made a point of knocking against him in a show of strength, she'd lean in close and whisper, "So tell me, lover boy, how soon is soon?"

Frankie could feel the noose around his neck. He knew he had to slip his head out before somebody pulled.

"This is it, Frankie," Miranda said. "I'm getting tired. You tell me we're getting out of here, then you disappear for a week. Doris says I'm getting taken for a ride. I don't want to end up looking like a dope. I get other chances, you know. I'm not gonna keep blowing them for some . . ."

Frankie put down his cigarette and reached over for her but she moved away. "I'm serious," she said. "I want plans, real ones. Dates, tickets. I want it all laid out."

"What tickets? We're gonna drive, no?" Frankie said, jumping up. He started singing, "Get your kicks on Route 66." He had a good voice. His mother said it was a dead ringer for Sinatra's but her Frankie was better-looking.

"Get out of bed. Let's go." He was thinking that if they checked out before noon, he wouldn't get stuck for another day. These St. Regis rendezvous were getting expensive. When he first brought Miranda here, he thought it was a one-night stand or at the most, a special night to remember. He didn't think she'd start to see it as her personal hotel.

"What?"

"Get dressed. We're gonna go look at cars right now. What was I thinking? Poor baby, on your feet in that smoky club. You should be stretched out in the warm sun, by the pool. Oh, we're gonna have a great time, Miranda."

"We're gonna go buy the car now?"

"I told you, didn't I? How're we gonna get to California without a car? Get dressed. Make sure you look good. I don't want the salesman to think we're a couple of nobodies wasting his time."

"You've got to drop me off home, then. Look at me."

"There's no time, Miranda. You wanna go get the car or what?"

"But you said I had to look . . ."

"You look beautiful." He ran his hand through her hair. "Look at this." He grabbed a handful, rubbed it over his face. He stepped back and pointed to his crotch. "Look what you do to me," he said. "Look at me. No, forget it, get dressed. We'll never get out of here." Frankie looked at his watch. They could still make the checkout time. He leaned over her, kissed her face, bit the fleshy part of her arm. "Hurry up. I'll be downstairs."

Frankie told the front desk to add last night to his bill. The front desk told him he had to clear his account and gave him the bill for last night and the week before. Frankie mentioned a few names, tossed them out like rice at a wedding, Genovese, Tony Bender, Tommy Rye. The clerk behind the desk looked at him. "Shall I call the manager?" he asked.

Frankie muttered under his breath and took out the cash from his back pocket, paid the bill and broke himself. He gave the clerk a five-dollar tip to show there wasn't any hard feelings and he sat

down in one of the big club chairs with the newspaper to wait for
Miranda and tell her he was a little short, that they'd have to wait
to buy the car.

Because Frankie was reading the newspaper, he didn't see
Helen and Joe Black coming out of the coffee shop but Helen saw
Frankie. She looked at the clock, checked her watch and steered
Joe Black into a jewelry store in the lobby. Joe Black bought her a
bracelet while she watched Frankie through the store window. Joe
Black said something and Helen smiled but she wasn't listening.
She was watching a redhead make her way across the lobby to
where Frankie was sitting. Helen couldn't see the woman's face,
only a mass of red hair but she saw her lean over Frankie and she
saw Frankie move up to kiss her. She watched them for a few
more minutes before she took Joe Black's arm and led him out the
door into the street. The new bracelet was on her wrist, the blue
velvet box at the bottom of her pocketbook.

Helen was at the bar at Gloria's that night, drinking and thinking
hard about where she had seen that redhead. A big blonde sat
next to her at the bar. It was Doris, from the Copa, and then
Helen remembered the cigarette girl, the one with the hair even
redder than her own.

Helen bought Doris a drink and invited her to try a black-and-
gold-papered filter cigarette and asked her about the Copa and
the redheaded cigarette girl.

"Miranda? You know her? Well, hands off. She's a doll, ain't
she? But she's as dumb as the rest of them up there. Hooked up
with some downtown loser. Keeps promising her the world but I
don't believe a word of it."

Helen asked Gloria to bring them a bottle and some ice. She
liked Doris. She really did. She liked her enough to tell her she

thought she knew that downtown loser Miranda was seeing. His name was Frankie and he was married to her sister.

"Shit, Helen, they're planning to go away together!"

Helen took a long slow drag on her black French cigarette. "When?"

"He keeps telling Miranda 'soon.' They're going out to California, she says. It's all I could do to keep her from quitting her job last week to get ready."

"Doris, could you do me a favor?"

"Ask me."

"Don't say anything to Miranda. Just let me know when they're leaving."

"You won't do anything to her, will you? She's a sweetie, Helen. Just got mixed up with the wrong guy. If she knew he was married. . . ."

"Doris, I wouldn't do anything to anybody. I just want to protect my sister and this way works out for you, too. You can be there to pick up the pieces when she finds out what a snake Frankie is. You tell her now, she won't even believe you. There's nothing like a woman in love."

Doris leaned over, put her arm around Helen and kissed her hard on the mouth. "You got a deal," she said.

Chapter Twenty-eight

Gracie stood over Frankie, shoving his shoulder, rocking him back and forth in the bed. "What do you mean, you're not going to work? You gotta go to work! You're not sick. What is this?"

"Hey, Gracie, what are you, my mother? Go bother Charlie. Go get him up."

"Charlie's up. Charlie's going to school." Gracie could see Charlie in the kitchen, brushing his teeth at the sink, wetting his hair with his father's black comb.

"Gracie, if I don't feel like going to work, I ain't going and it ain't the end of the world, okay? There'll be other ships. They been coming in three a week. Whatta you worrying about? I can let this one go. Let some other *jabone* make a buck today. You think the most important thing I got to do is count bananas?"

"What other things you got to do, Frankie? What? You got a job, that's what you got to do. You lose this job, you're finished. I told you, I'm never asking for you again."

"I ain't gonna lose no job for one day off."

"No, but you're not gonna get paid. If you were sick, I could see it."

"Okay, I'm sick. I feel sick." Frankie gagged. He coughed. "I'm so sick I think I'm gonna die."

From the floor below, Mary Franchetti banged her broom on her ceiling. She yelled up the steam pipe. Her voice came through the opening in the floor, the hole around the pipe where there should have been a steel ring but there wasn't. Frankie sat up in bed. "Bang back," he told Gracie. "You old whore," he shouted at the floor. "Drop dead. We put up with your loudmouth husband all hours of the night."

"Frankie, she can't hear you."

"You go tell her, then. Go over by the steam pipe and yell down."

"Cut it out, Frankie. You gonna get up or what?"

"I'm not. I'm not getting up. I'm sick. I told you. You want me to tell you again? *I'm sick and I'm not going to work.*"

"Well, then, I'm leaving. You think I'm staying around here putting up with you, you're sick in the head."

"Oh, good excuse. Go ahead. Where you going? Your grand-mother's? To meet your sisters? Go ahead. Make a big deal outta nothing. Talk about me. Make me look bad. Why don't you report me to The Swede? Why don't you do that?"

"Don't talk about Nick like that. He's been good to us."

"Yeah, Gracie. Thanks to Nick, I don't carry bananas no more; I frigging count them. You know what your problem is, Gracie? You got no faith in me. You don't give me no credit. If I was a different kind of guy, I'd be in California right now. I'd be enjoying myself!"

"Yeah, that's why you're right here on Spring Street and you're gonna die on Spring Street, like a dog."

"I'm on Spring Street because I never got no encouragement. I always sold myself short, listening to you. Get a job . . . Get a job . . . Who cares what kind? Just so's you put food on the table. I shoulda been outta here a long time ago, before I got roped in. Look at Jimmy Jumps. He did it. He's out in California."

"Yeah, Frankie. So's Clark Gable."

"Never mind. Jimmy Jumps ain't counting bananas. He's walking Errol Flynn to his table right now. I coulda been doing that. I look better in a tux than Jimmy Jumps."

Charlie was at the kitchen table eating his seventh piece of toast. Gracie had made a pile of toast and buttered it before she had even gotten him out of bed. "Hurry up," Gracie called to him from the bedroom, turning away from Frankie, "or you're gonna be late."

"It's early," Charlie called back.

"So be early. Make a good impression."

"I'll have to wait outside."

"Good. Get some fresh air. You'll be first in line."

"Yeah," Frankie said, turning on his side, turning his back to Gracie. "The early bird catches the worm."

She gave his shoulder one last shove before she went into the kitchen and stood behind Charlie. She held his shirt while he slipped in his arms and then she turned him around and buttoned every button from top to bottom. Between buttons, she held his face in her hands and kissed his mouth. She tucked his shirttails in, back to front, and when she finished, she handed him his book bag and pushed him out the door. She stood at the head of the stairs listening to him go down and then she slammed the door behind her and went over to Jeannie Popeye's apartment across the hall.

Jeannie Popeye made Gracie sit down and she poured her coffee and pushed a dish of crullers across the table. Jeannie Popeye's husband was the first one in Canapa's every morning. He made a special trip up Sullivan Street on his way home from his night watchman's job at a warehouse on West Broadway and got the crullers right when they came out of the oven. Then he walked down to Spring Street, came upstairs and went to sleep. He slept all day. "But you don't have to be quiet," Jeannie Popeye always told Gracie. "Nothing bothers my Gerry."

"Everything bothers Frankie," Gracie told her.

Jeannie Popeye nodded. "He's a nervous guy, Frankie. Look at his mother," she said. "You ever see such a nervous wreck?"

Gracie nodded back.

"It's a good thing he found you," Jeannie said. "Me and Gerry always say it. 'When Frankie found Gracie,' we always say, 'he found gold.'" Jeannie Popeye pulled the dish of crullers back toward herself and picked one out. She looked at the ridged dough before she put it in her mouth. "Yeah, me and Gerry always say that. Frankie's mother should kiss Gracie's feet. She should kiss the ground Gracie walks on."

When Gracie left Jeannie Popeye and went back into the

apartment, Frankie was gone. Gracie thought she'd won. She thought he had gone to work.

"Oh, baby . . . oh, baby . . . oh, baby. . . ." Frankie's face was in Miranda's snatch. He thought he would burrow inside her, curl up inside, all the way up and never come out again. He reached down to touch himself but nothing was happening.

Miranda was pulling at his hair, her hands balled into fists. He bit the soft flesh on the inside of her thigh and followed the faint line of reddish-blond hair that ran up the center of her stomach. He bit and licked all the way up until he found her mouth but his dick stayed small, curled up, nested against his leg. After the news he had gotten this morning, he wasn't surprised.

He lay on his back staring at the ceiling, his eyes unblinking. Miranda was over him. She started talking to him but he didn't answer. He couldn't. He didn't want to. He wanted to just lie there. What was it about him that women just couldn't leave him alone? His mother, Gracie, her sisters, Miranda, Doris, all of them. He could feel himself getting mad. Shut up, he wanted to say but he didn't. Instead he squeezed his eyes shut until he saw colored circles of light.

He thought about how he had called Miranda at 10 A.M. from the phone booth on the corner of Houston and Sullivan and told her to meet him at the St. Regis. "Room 869," he'd whispered into the phone and hung up before she could answer. He'd woken her, he knew. She worked until four in the morning and never got up until the afternoon. But he also knew she'd be there. Some things he could depend on.

The phone booth was across the street from the church. He'd crossed himself. The church doors had been open and he could see inside to the gilded altar. He had touched his fingers to his lips and then up to heaven and with those same fingers, those same lips, he had whistled for a cab to take him to the St. Regis.

Miranda was there when he arrived and he knew she'd gotten up out of bed and come right over because she was crazy about him and would do anything he asked. Except shut up. She was lying across him now, one long red nail drawing pictures on his chest, and she was talking about California, about their going away, about their getting married in Vegas.

He covered his eyes with his arm. All he could think about was what he'd heard in Sam & Al's this morning when he'd gone in to buy a pack of cigarettes. It was Johnny-Bag-of-Doughnuts told him, casual as anything. Pauly Russo was gone. He'd skipped town, run away. It was a common enough occurrence when a guy, especially a gambler, got bagged up, but Frankie had to take it personally. He was in bed with Pauly. They were robbing the bananas together and now Pauly had cut out. But Frankie knew he'd come back; they always did. And Frankie also knew that to save himself Pauly had only one out. Give somebody else up. Turn somebody else over. And Frankie knew who that somebody else was. It was Frankie Merelli.

Frankie had stood there and opened the pack of Lucky Strikes, torn the cellophane carefully, tapped out a cigarette, lit it, exhaled. He'd moved slowly, listened to some crap about Joe Lima having a heart attack with some broad who threw him in a cab and told the driver to take him to Spring Street, and then he left.

"You're not listening." Miranda poked him in the center of his chest. "You're not paying attention. What's going on, Frankie? We never got the car. What's holding us up?"

But he was deaf and dumb.

Miranda got up and went over to the window. She pulled aside the curtain, so heavy it was like night in the room and Frankie could see by the light that it was getting late. She called room service and ordered a couple of steaks before she got in the shower. Frankie was glad to have her out of his sight. He had to think. When Pauly gave him up, and Frankie would have sworn on his father's grave that Pauly would, Frankie's life wouldn't be worth two cents. They'd kill him for sure. All that money he'd put away in the safe deposit box in the bank . . . no one would even know about it. It would never help anybody.

Frankie brought tears to his own eyes, imagining his wake. His mother crying in Nucciarone's. Gracie in black clutching a handkerchief. She'd have to buy Charlie a suit for the funeral. Frankie imagined everybody talking about him, whispering about him. He worried for a minute about the turnout, hoping for the big room. He remembered Vinny Feets's wake, where nobody came, his widow sitting alone for three days in the front row.

He stopped thinking when room service arrived. Frankie watched the guy wheel in the cart. He tipped him a pound and the waiter backed out the door. Frankie thought it could be his last meal. He lay on the bed and picked up the newspaper that was complimentary with the room.

Miranda came out of the shower, naked and wet, a white towel on her head like a turban. She sat down in the brocade chair and pulled the cart over to her and uncovered a dish. She cut the meat in pieces and ate them with her hands. Frankie looked at her over the newspaper but he wasn't hot anymore. He was a married guy in a hotel he couldn't afford with a woman who wasn't his wife. He lived in a tenement on Spring Street and went to work every morning on Pier 13 hoping the sun would shine but not too much and that the tarantulas had stayed in Central America. And that was the good part. Now he was going to be looking over his shoulder for the guys who were going to come and kill him.

He put the newspaper down. He looked at Miranda again. Her mouth was shiny with grease.

"Miranda . . ."

"What?"

"C'mere."

"I'm eating."

"Just c'mere a minute?"

She got up. She walked over, sat on the bed, took the towel off her head, bent over and started to dry her hair.

"What, Frankie?"

"We're leaving."

She lifted her head. "For real?"

"Yeah. This is it, baby. We're out of here. We're going to California."

"Oh, Frankie . . . Oh, my God." She started to cry.

Frankie felt better already. He rolled over on his back. "Kiss it, Miranda. You wanna just kiss it for a little bit?"

Afterward he asked her what time it was and she said she didn't care. He sat up then. "You've got to go to work."

"Work? Why? I quit! I don't have to go back there."

He jumped up, put on his pants, pulled on his shirt. "Listen," he said. "We got to do this right. Act normal, like nothing happened."

"Why? What's the big deal? We're not doing nothing illegal."

"It's just that I got things to take care of before we go."

"What things?"

"Miranda, just trust me, okay? Just do what I say. This is the last weekend. Put that goddamn box around your neck like you do every night. Friday, Saturday, Sunday. Monday we'll blow this town. And screw the car. We'll take a train. Go in style."

"You don't want me to tell Podell I'm leaving so he can get another girl?"

"Podell? Screw Podell." Frankie could feel the sweat break out on his forehead. "Don't tell Podell nothing. Don't tell nobody nothing. I'll call you Monday at the club when I've got everything straightened out and that's it. Turn in your spangles and we're gone." He threw some money on the table next to the bed and told her to pay the bill.

When he left, Miranda sat back down in the chair, finished her steak and started on Frankie's. She was thinking about California and about how long it would take for the marks on her neck to fade away, the marks from the leather strap of the cigarette box she'd been carrying around all these months, waiting for her big break.

Chapter Twenty-nine

Gracie wasn't talking to Frankie when he got home that night. She acted like he was invisible. She had had it just about "up to here," she decided. Her sisters were right. There was no excuse for him to go gallivanting all over the place whenever he felt like it. Was she jealous? Yes, she realized. She wasn't only jealous that he might be with another woman, but she was jealous of his time, his attention, for her and for Charlie. Who did he think he was? If he wasn't going to grow up he could go back to his mother. And if he pushed her one more inch, she was going to tell him that. She might even take all his clothes out of his closet and put them outside the door. She was starting to question her life with Frankie: fighting in the kitchen, making up in the dark of the bedroom and nothing much in between.

"Where's the kid?" Frankie said to her when he came in the door. Nothing. Silence. "Where's the kid?" Frankie said again.

Gracie picked up the plate of food she had covered for him, opened the window and threw it out into the yard.

"Was that my mother's dish?"

She shut the window. The glass rattled in the frame.

"The dish she carried all the way from Italy?"

He stared at her but she turned her back. He sat down at the table, took the pack of cigarettes out of his shirt pocket and lit one. "So, now you wanna tell me where's Charlie?"

"He's with Mary and Nick. Nick was taking him to a ball game."

Frankie got up and opened the window. He flipped out his cigarette and looked down into the yard. "That was my mother's dish, wasn't it? You think she carried that dish all the way to New York so you could fling it in the alley like some piece of junk?"

"It was a piece of junk."

"You think you're gonna get me mad? You're not. You wanna act like this, that's your business. Me, I got better things to do." He looked around, at the hole around the steam pipe where he could see the light from Mary Franchetti's apartment, at the cheap tin cabinet where Gracie kept her cooking pots. He tried to imagine leaving here and never coming back. He closed his eyes. He cursed Pauly Russo. The last thing he wanted to do was leave. He had never wanted to leave. Gracie was in the bedroom arranging her handkerchief drawer. She did that when she was nervous. She folded and refolded her handkerchiefs until they were lined up perfectly along one side of the drawer. Her underthings were on the other side but these she never rearranged. He wondered why. There were a lot of things he didn't know about her, that he had never tried to find out. He was sorry now, this very minute, and he came up behind her, started kissing her face and neck and eyes. Gracie turned in his arms and pulled his face down against her body. She took his hand and put it up under her dress, along the inside of her thigh, the way she used to do all those years ago against the wall down by the piers when they were keeping company. But it was different now. She was different. She loved Frankie. She loved his hands on her, his mouth, his breath, the marks his teeth left but she was starting to understand that, like Helen said, he wasn't the only man in New York City with something between his legs.

"Took you long enough to come to," Mary had said, when she told her sisters she was getting fed up with Frankie and his ways.

Anona shook her head. "Aggh . . . you live too long and you learn too late."

But Helen winked. "Don't listen to Anona," she said, pinching Gracie's arm. "It's never too late."

Mary agreed.

"Charlie's gone for the whole night," Gracie told Frankie. "We don't have to be quiet."

After, when Frankie was falling asleep, Gracie was telling him something about getting a job, at Schrafft's, as a waitress, but he

wasn't paying attention. He was too tired and very very scared.
Poor Frankie.

The ladies' room in the Copacabana was a beautiful place. It was
pink marble from floor to ceiling and the help was not supposed
to use it. But two long-legged women in black net tights and
sequined costumes were breaking the rules. The big blonde was
saying how bad her feet hurt. The redhead complained about her
neck and her shoulders.

"That feels good, Doris," the redhead said, leaning back as
Doris rubbed her shoulders. "I keep telling Frankie I'll be glad to
see the last of this goddamn box."

"And I'm telling you, Miranda, this guy's a loser. Sure, you get
a couple of nights at the St. Regis but that ain't gonna help you in
your old age."

"You got Frankie all wrong, Doris. I'm gonna be out of here
before you know it and it ain't just promises this time. It's for real."

"Oh, honey, these guys are all the same and this Merelli character is the biggest jerk I seen in a long time. Believe me. They
throw around some money and get you thinking they're gonna
take care of you for the rest of your life, but you know what,
they're already in harness. You're just another Saturday night. I
wish you'd wake up before you waste any more time."

"Doris?"

"Yeah?"

"You got Frankie pegged all wrong."

"I wish I did, honey.'"

"No, really."

"I know what I'm talking about."

"Doris, I'm not supposed to say nothing, but . . ."

"What?"

"But I guess you'd find out sooner or later. I would've written to you. I wouldn't have just left you up in the air like that . . ."

"Miranda . . ."

"This is my last weekend."

"What?"

"For real. Frankie's taking me to California, just like he promised."

"You believe him, doll?"

"Of course. Why should he lie?"

"Because he's probably been lying to you all along."

"Now I feel bad I said anything. I thought you'd be happy for me."

"Oh, I am, sweetheart. I don't mean nothing. I just worry about you. I love you. You know that. I'm glad you told me. I would've been worried sick if you didn't show up."

Doris put her arms around Miranda and pulled her close. She kissed her very close to her mouth and quickly turned her face and held her, their cheeks touching. Then Doris stepped back and held Miranda by the shoulders. "When you leaving?"

Miranda turned to the mirror to reapply her lipstick, ran her pinkie along her bottom lip. "Monday. He's calling me Monday afternoon and we'll be on our way."

On her next break, Doris went into her locker and found the matchbook from Gloria's club on Varick Street. Inside was Helen's phone number.

Helen picked up on the first ring. Not long after, she got dressed, went out, and got into her Lincoln, which was parked across the street. She drove straight to Mary and Nick's.

They were playing cards for chips when she got there. It was past midnight. "Early for you, isn't it?" Mary said.

"We gotta talk" was all Helen said.

"Sit. Talk." Mary put down her cards. Helen made a face. Mary put a hand on Nick's arm. "Poppa, why don't you make Helen a highball?" she said.

Nick went downstairs and came back up to the kitchen with a bottle of Chivas Regal and a glass filled with ice. He poured with a heavy hand. "Where's Mary?" he said.

"Getting dressed," Helen said.

Nick sat down and slid Helen's drink over to her. "What are you up to?" Helen leaned over to touch his cheek. She got up and kissed him. "You know, Nick, you're still a good-looking guy."

He laughed at her. "You gonna tell me what's going on?"

"Nick, you don't wanna know. It's women's work," she said, picking up her glass. She and Nick were on their second scotch when Mary came down the stairs. Helen made a face. Mary nodded.

"We're going, Poppa," she said. "Don't wait up." She put on her coat while Nick shuffled the cards and when he looked up, she and Helen were gone.

Outside, the two of them got in the powder blue Lincoln. Helen started the motor, pulled out into the deserted street and stepped hard on the gas. "Frankie's leaving town with the redheaded cigarette girl from the Copa."

"Leaving? He's actually leaving or this broad thinks he's leaving?"

"He's leaving," Helen said.

"I trust your sources, Helen, but I gotta tell you. It's hard to believe. Where's he getting the money? How could he leave Gracie? The kid?"

"Why, it's never been done before? And that ain't the point. The point is he can't do this to Gracie. We can't let him."

"So?" Mary said. "Whatta we do?"

• • •

On Thirty-eighth Street, Helen parked the car in front of the tenement where they were born. They got out on either side and went into the building and up the worn narrow stairs.

Anona was snoring in her chair and they shook her awake. "I'm getting too old for this," she said when she saw them.

"You were born old," Mary said, getting out the dishes and napkins. Anona started setting out food she pulled from everywhere and told Helen there was a gallon of homemade wine in the cupboard under St. Rita.

"Where'd that come from?" Helen asked.

"I got friends," Anona said.

"You're a devil, you know that?" Helen said.

Anona shook her head more than once. "You never listen to me until it's too late," she said.

"It's not too late, Anona," Helen said.

"It's never too late," Mary added. "That's why we're here."

"What?" Anona said. "What's going on? I'm old, you know. I have to be careful. Pretty soon, I'm gonna have to answer for what I do."

"You don't have to do anything then, just listen. And I don't want to hear all your I-told-you-so's. That and a token will get us on the subway." Anona opened her mouth and Helen raised a finger to her lips. "First listen, and then you can say what you want."

"So, it's our baby sister, right?" Mary said. "She's married to a no-good guy who takes her for granted."

Helen nodded. "And no matter what she does for him, he never appreciates it."

Anona rocked. She had made them pull the rocking chair close to the table. She couldn't sit up in those vinyl chairs for very long . . . that space between the seat and the backrest . . . it stabbed her in the kidneys.

They started eating. Mary picked up the thread of the conversation, her mouth full. "She cooks, she cleans, she takes care of Charlie. She's a good wife, and what does she get? Nothing."

"Wait," Helen said. "Let's be fair. He works. He gives her money to run the house. He's good-looking."

"Are you trying to convince me we should let this go? Or convince yourself? You like Frankie, don't you?"

"I do—more than you, anyway. I just don't want to paint him completely black. There's plenty of women that would die for a guy like Frankie."

"Ha!" Anona said. "Not once she got him home."

"I don't know. I think Gracie's pretty happy with him in bed." Anona leaned over and hit Helen's leg. It was the only part of her she could reach without toppling out of the chair. Helen ignored this and so did Mary.

"In bed? Where does that fit in? You're the one that calls her the wooden kimono."

"Yeah, but something's got to keep them going and with Frankie it's all I can think of."

They fell quiet. They drank wine. "He's planning to run away," Helen finally said to Anona. "He's got a girl and he's going to leave town, just like that." And Helen snapped her fingers in front of Anona's face.

"*Porca miseria! Che trabatz!*" Anona went on, going deeper into her dialect, farther back into her past. She called him words they only knew in hell. When she finished, Mary held the arm of the rocker and kept it still. "Does he deserve whatever he gets?"

". . . The dirty dog, sonofabitch, rat bastard . . ." Anona looked up from her tirade, her trance broken. "*Certo!*" she said.

"You talked the same way about Nick," Mary said.

"Not fair," Helen said. "Nick came back. Don't forget that. He came back to take care of you, of all of us."

Anona put her hands together as if she were praying. "Nick, he had to leave. What could he do, poor fella? They were gonna put him in jail. He didn't run away with some *stroush*."

"Yeah," Helen said. "Frankie deserves no mercy. It's up to us. We just have to figure out exactly what to do and how to do it."

Anona stood up. "Me, I'm gonna bed. I need my beauty sleep. I don't wanna know. And keep it down because I don't wanna hear neither." The sisters exchanged looks. They waited until they heard the bedsprings sigh under Anona's weight and the sound of her snoring and then they pulled their chairs close and they talked into the night.

Frankie woke up not knowing who was asleep on his arm until he looked down and saw Gracie. He sighed and looked up at the ceiling, at the crack in the plaster that looked like a face, the face of Jesus Christ, no less, in that picture where he was holding the heart with the knife through it, the one where he had blue eyes and long brown hair like a girl. That picture always bothered Frankie and that crack . . . that crack bothered him, too. It had been plastered over every three years since they'd moved in, but it always came back. It was always there waiting for him, every morning and every night when he looked up from this bed.

He moved his arm out from under Gracie little by little, careful not to wake her and when she turned over on her side, he slipped out of bed. He got dressed in the kitchen, threw water on his face, and went downstairs. He got a newspaper from Sam & Al's but didn't go inside, just took the paper from the pile stacked outside on a wooden bench and left his money on top, next to the piece of wood that held the papers down.

The sun was shining and he lifted his face to it. He said good morning to all the *pittacuse* standing outside and walked up Sullivan Street to the Caffè Reggio and ordered a double espresso. He opened the paper and leaned his chair back against the wall. He tried to relax. This time next week, he told himself, he'd be in California where the sun shone every day. But he couldn't stop the sweat that was starting under his arms and along the back of his neck. He kept his eyes down unless someone passed very close to his table and then he looked up and smiled. He realized that maybe it was a bad idea coming to the Café Reggio. Maybe he should go back up the house and stay there the rest of the weekend. He had to wait until Monday to get to the safe deposit box. Maybe the less he was seen, the better.

When the waitress passed, he asked for another *doppio* and the check. He threw back the coffee in one gulp when it came, left a deuce under the sugar bowl and walked back to Spring Street. He avoided Sullivan and Thompson and MacDougal, following Sixth Avenue, staying at the edge of the neighborhood, hoping to elude anyone who might be looking for him.

Monday was only two days away, Frankie told himself. He could make it. Monday morning he'd go to the pier. Pump on that goddamn button for the last time in his life. At lunch, he'd go over to the bank, pick up the cash, call Miranda, and tell her to meet him at Pennsylvania Station. He wouldn't even pack a bag. With the money from the safe deposit box, he could buy whatever he needed. They dressed different in California anyway, and Frankie always had to look right. New life, new clothes. That was the way to do it. Frankie wiped at the saliva foaming on the side of his mouth. He bought coffee cake in Canapa's before he went upstairs. Gracie was crazy for Canapa's coffee cake.

Chapter Thirty

"Just take care of this for us, will you, Nick?"

"What's going on, babe?" Nick looked from Mary to Helen. "What are you two cooking up?"

"C'mon, Nick, you know better than to ask us questions. You're a tough guy. Tough guys don't ask questions." Helen took a long drink of beer from the bottle she was holding. "If we thought it would do you any good, wouldn't we tell you?"

"Maybe I can help you."

"You can help us, Poppa." Mary smoothed his hair, what little was left. "Call up Smash Nose Pete and tell him you're sending two guys to shape up down Pier 13 on Monday and then forget about it."

"What two guys?"

"Just two guys, not too tall. But tell him they're strong. They'll have red handkerchiefs around their necks. Okay? You can do that, Nick?"

Nick leaned over and lit Helen's long black cigarette. "Since when was there something I couldn't do for the Mallone girls?" he said, blowing out the match. Nick knew about allegiance, but never to women, or girls, which was what the Mallones were when he found them, or they found him. For him, they would always be girls in high-button shoes but as tough as anyone he'd ever met in Hell's Kitchen. Mary looking for Owney Madden as if he were a social worker and not a man whose nickname was "the Killer," and Helen, refusing to tell who she was or where she lived, even though she was days away from being sent on a train to the Midwest, another orphan picked up on the streets of New York City and adopted for cheap farm labor.

· · ·

On Monday morning, Frankie was out of bed before the sun came up, sitting at the kitchen table, his fifth Pall Mall burning down to his fingers. He'd given up Lucky Strikes. The target on the package was turning up in his dreams. The espresso pot was on the stove. He'd boiled the milk. He went inside and woke up Gracie. He didn't want to be alone. Gracie came into the kitchen and he kissed her. "Sit down. The coffee's made," he said.

"What's with you?"

"What's that supposed to mean?"

"I'm usually dragging you out of bed. You didn't go in Friday, now you're up early."

"You know what your trouble is, Gracie? You're always digging up the past and you're a grudge holder, just like the rest of your family."

"Please, Frankie. If my sisters didn't forgive and forget, you'd be dead by now."

The word "dead" made Frankie go quiet.

Gracie poured the coffee and the milk, cut a slice of yesterday's bread and put it in the oven. "So what is it? You can't sleep? Something on your conscience?" She laughed and reached out to touch his hair.

"Gracie . . ."

"This coffee stinks, Frankie." She got up and poured her coffee down the sink. "I'm going back to bed. I didn't sleep so good." She stood framed in the doorway. "I'm going for that interview at Schrafft's today, while Charlie's in school."

Frankie heard her but he didn't know what she was talking about and he didn't answer because it didn't matter. He wondered what she would have said, how she would have acted if she knew that she wasn't going to see him again. He felt like crying.

The pack of cigarettes was empty when Frankie woke Charlie

up for school. Gracie was still fast asleep. The world was upside down. It felt to Frankie that nothing was right. He told Charlie to be quiet, that his mother didn't feel good. "We'll get something to eat downstairs," he said, kissing Charlie's ear. They left the house together, like thieves. They went into Sam & Al's and Frankie bought another pack of cigarettes and ordered a coffee. Charlie took a Coca-Cola from the ice chest and two packages of Yankee Doodles, his favorite, three cupcakes to a package.

They sat outside on a wooden bench. "It's nice without your mother once in a while, no?" Frankie said. "You don't wanna grow up to be no Momma's boy. You gotta be careful around women all the time. You be careful, you hear? You promise?"

Charlie nodded, his mouth full.

"And you gotta stay in school, Charlie. Promise me that. You don't wanna grow up and be just another moron. There's enough of them around here."

Charlie looked up at his father. "You gonna go to work?"

"Of course I'm going to work. Don't I always go to work? Whatta you think I am, a bum? But you know what, one day when it's nice, we'll skip out together, go to Coney Island or something." He kissed the top of Charlie's head and took a dollar out of his pocket. "Don't tell your mother," he said. "And buy something besides food. Spend it on a girl."

When Smash Nose Pete came outside the gates of Pier 13, there were thirty, forty guys waiting to shape up. The regulars were already inside. Smash Nose Pete climbed up on the loading platform and looked out over the huddle of men. "I need twenty-five," Pete said over their heads and he started pointing. "You and you and you." He was looking toward the back of the crowd, where the bigger guys usually congregated but he also checked the front because those men were the most willing.

There was a scuffle at the edge of the platform and Smash Nose Pete looked down. There were two guys, small, elbowing their way to the front. There were others trying to hold them back. Pete saw the red handkerchiefs around their necks. The two men wore gray pea caps pulled down so he couldn't see their faces. He motioned to them anyway. "You two," he said. "Inside."

The crowd closed around the space they left and Smash Nose Pete finished counting off. He took one extra guy in to make twenty-six because the guys with the red handkerchiefs looked awfully small to him. He didn't mind doing The Swede a favor, whatever was going on was none of his business, but he still had to get those bananas unloaded.

The ship was in from Panama. It was starting to rain. The workers put on their canvas aprons, lined up to walk up the plank to the hold of the *Loco Grande*. The river was rough today and the ship moved with the waves. Depending on the tide, the ship would be higher or lower than the pier. Today it was both, up and down as the river slapped against the pilings. There was a guy already puking over the side just watching.

Frankie Merelli was pissed as hell that he had a whole morning to get through. It wasn't raining hard, but a fine drizzle that meant his shoes would get wet. Frankie hated when his shoes got wet. He looked around at the line of men hunched under the stalks of green bananas, the weight curving their backs and tried to count his blessings but it wasn't easy.

The first thing he saw that made him wish he'd never been born was Jimmy "The Dick" Cuciaro and Matt "The Pepper" Rizzo, hanging over by the watchman's shed. They were Vito

Genovese's stooges. They belonged to him like everything else belonged to him: the piers, the bananas, the trucks, the barges, the tarantulas. The thought of Vito Genovese made Frankie Merelli's balls shrivel up into his body. He only wanted to hear that lunch whistle. A few more hours and he'd be in the vault in the bank taking those piles of cash, his cash, out of the metal box. He felt for the safe deposit box key deep in his pocket.

Frankie was coming from the bathroom when he noticed the two guys walking together, small for dockworkers. They must be shape-up guys, he thought. Brothers, maybe. They had the same walk. If he were five feet tall, he'd be looking for a job in a barber-shop or a restaurant. Some guys had no sense. They were proba-bly greasers right off the boat.

What did he care? In no time, he'd be gone from here for good. And good riddance to seagull crap and water rats. It might be the last day for those two *jabones,* too, if they survived that long. They'd feel it tomorrow. They'd have a hard time standing up straight tomorrow.

His mother always told him to look at the ones worse off, but Frankie thought that was rotten advice. He'd never tell his kid that. Why shouldn't he look up? Why was he always supposed to look down? Why was he supposed to be satisfied with any old crap?

He walked along the edge of the water on his way to the trucks and thought about how this was the very last time he'd walk this pier, how he'd never again, in his whole life, be on this pier.

When Frankie looked up, he noticed that the line to the trucks had stalled. A cluster of men had come out of the ship and they were waiting to unload their bananas. They were waiting for the checker to count their stalks so they could take them off their backs. They were waiting for Frankie, who was standing near the edge of the water next to the plank leading into the hold of the ship. The mist turned into a light rain and the men who had dropped off their loads weren't coming back for another but were standing under the shelter of the loading dock.

The plank was empty, bobbing with the waves, moving up and down with the ship. Frankie stood in the rain and stretched out his arms like it was a glorious day. He suddenly didn't care about the rain, about his clothes or about his shoes, because he was starting over. He was gonna get a whole new life.

He saw the two little guys, the greaser brothers, walking together, coming toward the ship, separate from the pack of men. He couldn't see their faces because their heads were down, their pea caps pulled low against the rain. Christ, they were small. Imagine going through life with your nose in everybody's balls. If he didn't know better, he'd have thought they were girls.

Chapter Thirty-one

Frankie Merelli reached in his pocket and took out a cigarette. He was smoking too much; his throat was raw. This was his last one, and he crumpled the pack in one hand and threw it into the dark water of the river. The greaser brothers walked past him. The first one started up the plank.

Everyone else is hanging back, Frankie thought, and these two, they're gonna keep going. They're gonna go back down the hold. Little guys . . . Frankie shook his head, put the cigarette in his mouth and lit a match, his hands cupped to shield the flame from the wind. He bent forward, toward the flame, had a feeling of someone standing near him, behind him. But before Frankie could turn, before he might have blown out the match, the flame moving dangerously close to his fingers, a quick blow to the back of his head ended any feeling he might have had, in those moments and forever. A shove followed, and Frankie stumbled, tumbled, fell unconscious into the putrid water between the ship and the pier. One small man came down the plank and joined the other. Pea caps pulled down, collars pulled up, they walked away from the edge of the water. They walked until they were through the gates of the pier. No one saw.

The rain came down heavy then and the men knocked off for a while. It was almost lunchtime, anyway. It was after one when they started working again. The sun had come out and the river was calm.

Giuseppe Paisano was the one who saw him. Giuseppe was coming down the plank with a stalk of bananas on his shoulder when he looked down into the water and saw something floating, something larger than a rat. He yelled bloody murder when he saw the hand.

Men came running. Giuseppe pointed into the water. "Look! Down there!" he said. They all looked, hands behind their backs, hands on their waists, peering into the water. It was hard to tell; it was a dirty river. But there was something floating down there and it had a hand.

They came in twos and threes until everyone on the pier was leaning over, looking into the black water.

"There's something down there!"

"It's a man!"

"Get him out!"

"Hurry up!"

They shouted and they ran around and finally threw a life preserver near the floating hand and Junior Marchesi yelled for the man to reach out for it, to reach for the white circle and save himself. Matt "the Pepper" Rizzo looked over into the water and sniggered. "Forget it, Junior, that ain't a man, it's a corpse. That hand ain't gonna reach out for anything ever again." Rizzo would know. He'd seen enough dead bodies. He'd thrown a few in this river himself, but his bodies didn't float, they sank like stones. "You better get him out," he said, "before there's nothing left."

The body was caught on one of the pilings and they had to let one of the men down with a rope to tear it loose. Giuseppe Paisano got the job because somebody said he had been a coral diver in Naples. They gave Giuseppe a piece of rope to tie around the body, under the arms, and they hoisted it up.

Dibby Santulli was near the front. He reached out to help pull the body onto the pier, and when he saw it was Frankie Merelli, his head cut open, absolutely dead, he cried, they said, like a woman. Frankie and Dibby had lived in the building at 196 Spring Street since they were kids. Dibby had known Frankie all his life.

"Geez," Smash Nose Pete said. "First Pauly Russo disappears and now this." The dock boss came over to see what was going on. Dibby was kneeling by the body. He held Frankie's hand until the crowd of men broke up and the ambulance came and took Frankie's body away.

The union delegate came to 196 Spring Street before the cops but Gracie Merelli wasn't there. He stopped in the candy store to ask for her and Sam explained that her sisters had picked her up about an hour ago. Her sisters did that a lot, took her out for lunch. He should see her sisters, real lookers, Sam said. Al agreed. They offered the union delegate a cup of coffee, a cold drink, and brought him a chair so he wouldn't have to sit on the wooden bench outside. What did he want anyway? they asked him. Anything they could pass on?

"Her husband . . ."

"Frankie?"

The delegate looked at the paper in his hand. "Frankie? Yeah, it says Francesco right here . . . that's the same, no?"

"What about him?"

"They found him floating in the river between the pier and a Panamanian ship. They figure he fell, hit his head and drowned."

"Oh, my God!" Sam said.

"Jesus Christ!" Al said.

"Yeah, never made a sound. No one heard a thing. Nobody saw nothing, either. Them piers are a whole lot more dangerous than people think."

"Poor Frankie," Sam said.

"Well, don't say nothing," the union delegate said, "because it looks like the widow don't even know she's a widow."

"Our lips are zipped," Sam said, dragging his thumb along his mouth.

Al nodded. "Absolutely," he said. "Sealed tight as drums."

In the meantime, the cops showed up. They found a Mrs. Merelli and told her the bad news. It wasn't Gracie they spoke to, but the signora, Frankie's mother. By the time Gracie and Helen and Mary pulled up on Spring Street in the blue Lincoln Continental with the top down, a crowd filled the street.

The residents of Spring Street, all of them, from West Broadway to Sixth Avenue, were standing outside the building. They rushed to the car, the men waving their arms, women crying, kids who should have been in school yelling Gracie's name.

"What's happening?" Helen said.

"Who knows?" Mary said. "Leave it to the Italians. With them, everything's a big deal."

Two women broke through the throng surrounding the car, dragging Frankie's mother. They were holding her under the arms. She was limp, like an old black rag. Signora Merelli was already dressed for the tragedy. A veil covered her face, black. She wore pearls, black.

"Grace," she screamed, her head lolling. "Gracie! *Figlia mia!*"

"What the hell? What's going on?" Mary leaned out the side of the car.

"What is this?" Helen said.

"I'll get out. Sit here," Mary said, opening the door and pushing into the crowd.

"Gracieeee! Where is she? The daughter I never had?"

"She's right here, Mamma. Take it easy," Mary said, grabbing one of her arms.

"My Frankie! My Frankie! Dead! He's dead!"

"What?" Gracie shouted from inside the car. "What's she saying?"

"He fell . . . hit his head . . . drowned . . ." someone said.

Gracie climbed out of the car and was surrounded, engulfed. Signora Merelli put out her arms, hung on Gracie's neck like a scapular. Sam and Al had tears in their eyes. "I feel terrible," Sam said. "Just this morning he bought a pack of cigarettes."

"And a Coca-Cola and two packages of Yankee Doodles for Charlie," Al said. "Awful. This is awful."

Mary pulled her sister close, whispered in her ear. "Gracie, sweetheart . . ."

Gracie pulled back, looked at her sisters. "What the hell are they talking about?"

"There's was an accident . . . down at the docks. Frankie's . . . gone."

Gracie's face contorted, then softened into a blank stare. "It can't be," she said. "I don't believe it."

The crowd was working its way around the car. "Gracie . . ." Signora Merelli was shouting. "Our Frankie . . . Our Frankie . . ."

Gracie looked down at her mother-in-law, who had stepped back and was pulling at her clothes. Signora Merelli tore her hair from its roots with both hands, screaming Frankie's name.

"Oh no . . . no . . ." Gracie said, and she folded her arms in front of her face.

Mary motioned to Helen to come help and Helen climbed over the closed door of the car into the crowd and they moved to circle Gracie, to fend off Signora Merelli. "These Italians," Mary said, annoyed, her mouth pleating.

"But we're Italians," Helen told her.

"Hard to believe if you ask me."

The union delegate shouted to Gracie over the din. He couldn't make it through the crowd. "Mrs. Merelli," he said, "Local 54 sends its condolences. We're terribly sorry this happened."

"Sorry nothing," Helen shouted back. "Standard Fruit is going to pay through the nose. Don't think you're pulling the wool over anybody's eyes with your sorrys and those big funeral bouquets." She turned to embrace Gracie. "You're not gonna have to worry about a thing," she said. "Frankie might be gone but he'll be taking care of you from the grave."

Frankie's mother clutched at Gracie. "What will we do?"

"We'll be fine," Mary said, pulling off Signora Merelli's fingers. "Let's get upstairs. Helen, you get Charlie. The poor kid'll come home from school and won't know what hit him."

They went up the stairs, and Signora Merelli followed, held up by the Bruschetta cousins, who were mortally offended when Mary shut the apartment door in their faces. Mary turned the lock and hooked the chain. Signora Merelli unhooked the chain. Mary closed her hand over Signora Merelli's. "People want to pay their respects," Signora Merelli said. "You can't shut them out. It's not right. Everybody loved Frankie."

"Frankie's dead," Mary said. "Gracie's alive. She needs some peace and quiet. She just lost her husband, for Chrissakes."

"And me? What about me? I lost nothing? My only son!"

Helen came in holding Charlie by the hand, his face smeared with dirt and tears. Gracie called Charlie over and buried him in her arms, cried into the soft rolls of his neck, the rolls she had cultivated with loaves of toasted bread and store-bought cakes. "Oh, Charlie," she said. "Daddy's dead."

Charlie started to cry. "He was gonna take me to Coney Island. He was gonna let me cut school and everything. But he said he had to go to work. Now we'll never go. Never!"

"I knew it," Signora Merelli said. She came at Gracie, arms raised, fists flailing. Helen grabbed a handful of material at the back of the old lady's dress and held tight. "You sent my son to his death," Signora Merelli screamed at Gracie. "Always pushing, pushing . . . you pushed him right into death's arms. *Strega!*" she called out, breaking into sobs.

Gracie's eyes were already dry. She narrowed them at her mother-in-law until they were slits and said nothing.

"Wait, Mamma, please. You're upset," Mary said. She put her arms around the old lady, pulled her down with her into a kitchen chair. "How can you blame Gracie? She loved Frankie, too."

"*S'fachime!*" Signora Merelli yelled. She pulled away from Mary, grabbed a pot of lentils off the stove and threw it across the kitchen. The pot bounced against the wall. The lentils went everywhere.

"Good," Charlie said. "I hate lentils."

Helen pulled back her arm and slugged Signora Merelli, who went down like a stone. Mary and Gracie and Charlie came over to take a look at her. She was out cold, her dress hiked high above her knees. "It was the only way," Helen said. "She was hysterical. Help me get her inside. We'll put her on the bed. She won't remember."

Signora Merelli was a small woman. Her feet didn't touch the floor when she sat on the bus but the four of them together couldn't pick her up so they covered her with a blanket and went to sit in the living room.

"I still can't believe it," Gracie said, sitting on the couch. "How could Frankie be dead? I was fighting with him only this morning." She wrapped her arms around Charlie, pressed him against her. "And Charlie . . . look at him," she told her sisters. "What's a boy without a father?"

"My ear, Mamma . . . You're smashing my ear."

Mary pulled Charlie by the arm. "Let me see . . . He's right, Gracie. You bent his ear, it's practically hanging off."

"Now it's gonna stick out. Everybody's gonna make fun of me."

"Don't be stupid. Nobody cares about your ears. You think people have nothing better to think about than your ears?"

"Besides," Mary said, "they can be very attractive. Your uncle Nick's ears stick out."

"Where is Uncle Nick? I want Uncle Nick! Where is he?"

"You see how he misses his father? Frankie . . . you son of a bitch! How could you leave me like this?" Gracie cried into her handkerchief, which by now was a wet ball. She held it to her nose, her eyes. She pulled it out by the corners and smashed it up again in her fist. She poked at the corners of her eyes with it.

"Let's get out of here. It's time to go to Anona's," Mary said and Helen nodded.

Chapter Thirty-two

They came to Anona's to escape the neighborhood, the commotion, the excitement around Frankie's tragic death. The drama on Spring Street could go on without Gracie for now, Mary said. For now, they should all stay close.

Mary filled the coffeepot while Helen took down the cups and saucers from the china cabinet they shared with statues of the saints who had fallen out of favor with Anona for one reason or another.

Gracie was quiet. The widow of the moment, Anona called her behind her back. Helen came over, lit one of her French cigarettes and handed it to her. Gracie shook her head but Helen insisted. "Take a break," she said, "and besides, it's black."

"I can't believe he's . . . just . . . gone," Gracie said. "He said such nice things just this past weekend . . ." She stopped, overcome, to cry softly. "He said he was gonna take me and Charlie for

Chinks. 'One Saturday,' he said, 'we're all gonna go down to Mott Street and eat Chinks.'"

She started to seriously cry. Anona came by and gave her a clean handkerchief. "Chinks," she said. "They catch the pigeons in the park and call it chicken."

Someone pounded on the door. "It's open," Anona said and Signora Merelli opened it. Helen didn't recognize her until she called out for help. Her face was a blur of features under the thick black veil that reached almost to her waist. They helped her inside. She began trembling and Helen shoved a chair under her. She fell into in it like dead weight, legs splayed, eyes rolling. She fanned herself with her handkerchief. Helen was surprised to see it was white. Mary brought a glass of water.

Signora Merelli sat up in the chair. She pushed Mary and the glass of water away and lifted the veil. She flung it back over her hat. She pointed a finger at Gracie. "Where were you?" she said. "You left me on the floor like a dog." She pointed around the room. "All of you!" Signora Merelli screamed. "One worse than the other, and here I am, alone with this knife through my heart. My only son, dead in the river like a . . . like a . . ."

"Fish?" Helen said.

Signora Merelli started coughing. She covered her mouth with her handkerchief and Helen patted her back. Mary held out the glass of water again.

"*Grazie,*" Signora Merelli said, handing Mary the empty glass. She sat up straight, pulled at the hem of her dress, covering the black lace of her slip. "Now," she said, "we have to talk about the wake." Gracie opened her mouth but Mary came behind her and put her hands on her shoulders. "I spoke to Nucciarone," Signora Merelli said. "The old man, not the son. The son is a moron. I told him if he didn't handle it himself, we were going to Perazzo even though they're Genovese and always look down on us. He said fine, whatever I . . . we . . . want, but he needs the body." She turned to Gracie and sniffed. "You have to do that. In this country, a mother counts for nothing."

"The police have the body," Mary said.

"The police?"

"Well, the coroner's office, somebody like that. There could be an investigation. We don't know."

"But Nucciarone can't do nothing. He needs the body!"

Anona went into the cupboard and took out four candles. She struck a kitchen match against the wall and lit them one by one. Signora Merelli looked over at the sound of the match. "It's nothing," Helen said. "Anona lighting candles."

"For Frankie," Mary said in a low voice. "But go on. Make believe Nucciarone has the body."

Signora Merelli folded her hands in her lap. "We'll wake him the three days. We'll need cars for the funeral. Frankie had so many friends. And I said we need the front room. That's the big one. And I have the plot. Frankie's father's already in there but there's room for three. I know that sounds like you're out in the cold, Gracie, but you're gonna live a long time. No use worrying now about where you're gonna go. We have to think of Frankie . . . and it's easy to get to Second Calvary. We take the train. We can go every Sunday." Signora Merelli started to cry. "To have outlived my son! Who threw this curse on me?"

Anona was chanting in front of St. Rita. "Pay no attention," Mary said, when Signora Merelli swung around to glare at her. "She's an old woman."

Helen shook her head in agreement while Mary's fingers dug into Gracie's shoulders. She could feel Gracie's muscles knotting under her hands.

"That's it?" Gracie said.

Signora Merelli closed her eyes, nodded her head yes, sighed with great effort and then looked around. "Where's Charlie? What have you done with Charlie?"

"He's with Nick," Gracie said.

Signora Merelli moaned. "At least you have your son." Her eyes filled up with tears. "Me, I've lost everything."

Helen took her hand. "At least you had a son. God never blessed me with children."

Anona snorted. She had taught them all about children, about having them and not having them, and no one had learned the lessons better than Helen.

"You all right, Anona?" Helen called over to her.

"Is she?" Signora Merelli asked.

"Oh, she's fine," Mary said. "She's just tired."

"I should go back to Spring Street."

"I'll put you in a cab," Mary said.

They helped her up, flipped her veil back over her face and led her out the door. She whimpered all the way down the stairs.

"Sometimes I could just kill her," Gracie said. "Who does she think she is?"

"She's a *buttinski,*" Anona said. "Her nose is up everybody's behind."

"Anona, the woman lost her son," Mary said.

"So, who said life's a sandwich?"

"What are we doing about the wake?" Mary said. "I can go see about Houlihan's. You don't want to wake Frankie on Sullivan Street, do you? Cry yourself blind for three days?" She went to the refrigerator and took out a beer, prying off the cap with the opener that was tied by a string to the refrigerator door.

"No veils. Veils are for Arabs," Helen said.

"And Sicilians," Mary said.

"Same thing," Anona said.

"Maybe little veils," Helen said. "If Gracie wants veils, little ones, on top of our hats, or maybe just enough netting to flip down."

Gracie was crying again. Her sisters came to either side of her and held her hands in theirs. She looked at them both, turning her head from side to side to face first Mary and then Helen. "There's only one thing I want," she told them. "Frankie has to look good, really really good. It would kill him to look like crap his last time out. He always hated those guys lying in the coffin with a shirt didn't fit right around the neck."

"We'll take care of it, Gracie," Mary said. "I promise you that. They'll think Rockefeller's in the coffin, down to his socks."

Gracie wiped her eyes with the handkerchief Helen handed her. "It's the least I can do for Charlie. Let him remember Frankie at his best."

"You're a good wife," Mary said.

"And a wonderful mother," Helen added.

"And Frankie's going to Nucciarone's," Gracie said. "Frankie came into the world down there; he's gonna leave from the same place."

Anona agreed. "*Appunto!* People should stay where they belong. Gracie shoulda stayed here; he shoulda stayed there."

"Enough," Mary told her.

"And what about the veils?" Helen said.

"I'm gonna wear a veil. I'm a widow. Widows should wear veils."

Helen nodded. "Actually," she said, "the right veil can be very attractive."

It was showtime at the Copa. The lights dimmed. Miranda met Doris in the locker room. She took off her tray. "Well? Now what? I don't understand. Not a friggin' word all night."

"Miranda . . ." Doris's mouth twisted with sympathy.

"What could have happened to him? He was telling the truth, I know it. I know Frankie. He was getting the money this afternoon. Monday. He told me he was getting it first thing. So where the frig is he?"

"It's early yet, honey. Give him a chance." Doris went into her locker and took out a little box with a mother-of-pearl top. She snapped open the hinge and held it out to Miranda. "Take one," she said. "In fact, you know what? Take two."

"He's not coming, is he, Doris?" Miranda's baby blues started filling up with big tears.

"Oh, honey, it's not the end of the world. Don't cry, sweetheart. You're breakin' my heart. He's not worth it, believe me. So maybe you got burnt. That's how you learn." Doris put her arms around Miranda. "Everything's gonna be all right." She rubbed her hands up and down Miranda's bare back, moved them around to Miranda's satin-covered breasts. One hand moved down to her waist, her hips, fingers working their way under the edge of her costume and up.

"Oh, baby . . . oh, baby . . ." she whispered in Miranda's ear. "Doris will make you forget all about him. Doris'll take care of you. Wait and see. You won't even remember his name."

Chapter Thirty-three

The morning of the funeral dawned a beautiful day. Signora Merelli, a black cloud of crepe and net and satin, was with Gracie and Charlie, waiting for the limousine Nucciarone would send to take them for one last viewing. Last night after the rosary, Signora Merelli had broken down, screamed for the wake to continue, to go on and on, for the lid never to close on Frankie's coffin. But the black was creeping in around Frankie's hairline and the tips of his ears and Old Man Nucciarone had sent his son to take Gracie aside and tell her that they could not go on even one more night.

Signora Merelli had wailed but agreed. Gracie knew how to talk to her, what to tell her. Her Frankie? Black? And on this morning, she sat at Gracie's table, stirring sugar into the cup of espresso Charlie had brought to her, and she sighed. "Look at this day," she told Charlie, pointing to the kitchen window. With one hand she circled his arm, the black satin of her glove stark against his white shirt. "You can't see from here, this miserable back apartment, but I could see from my apartment, from the front. "It's sunny—*una bella giornata*—a day to be born, not to be buried. Frankie always did things ass-backwards. He was born upside down. I almost died, you know. It was a miracle." She pulled Charlie close, her lips at his ear. "The midwife threw up her hands. She walked out. Your grandfather carried me into the street. They took me to the hospital and I lay there for five days . . . Gesù . . . your father was upside down. He almost killed me. He's killing me now." She sniffled, held her handkerchief to her nose with both hands, a window of opportunity for Charlie to slip to the other side of the table. He looked at his mother, eyes wide. Gracie waved away his concern. She came behind Signora

Merelli and put a hand on her shoulder. Signora Merelli reached up and covered Gracie's hand with hers. "On his wedding day, it rained cats and dogs . . . and today? Nothing but sun. His father always said he didn't know his ass from his elbow."

Jeannie Popeye from across the hall knocked on the open door. "The car's downstairs, Gracie. You need help?"

"No, we've got her," Gracie said, and she motioned to Charlie to put on his jacket and take one of his grandmother's arms.

There were people downstairs. They pressed the Merellis' hands as they came off the stoop and got into the limousine. Everyone rode like a rich man once in his life, that very last ride in the coveted Cadillac that until then he had only watched drive by or maybe touched the shiny surface with his fingertips when one was parked on the street.

The limo went the two blocks up Sullivan Street to Nucciarone's funeral parlor, Charlie sitting between his mother and his grandmother. Signora Merelli clutched his hand so tightly it was numb and asleep before the car passed Prince Street. He leaned over to complain to his mother but Gracie was staring straight ahead, lost in her memories, and more important, in her future. She wasn't the same woman who had come to this neighborhood as a bride. She was on her own now. She was terrified, and to tell the truth, strangely thrilled.

"Ma . . . Ma . . ." Charlie shook her arm with his free hand. "This car is bigger and better than Uncle Nick's!"

"I know, Charlie. Daddy would have really liked that." The limo pulled up to the curb in front of the funeral parlor and the driver got out and opened the door. Signora Merelli tentatively put out a black oxford-shod foot. The driver took her hand, but she swooned back onto the seat and in the more than two yanks it took to get her out the door, any elegance she might have hoped for was lost.

Helen and Mary were waiting on the sidewalk. Anona was already inside, sitting in the upholstered chair. Helen and Mary came forward and pulled Signora Merelli inside. She looked up at them. "If this doesn't put me in my grave," she told Mary, whom she had always preferred to Helen, "I'll live forever."

They walked her down the aisle to say her last goodbye in front of the open coffin. They stood beside her as she bent at the velvet kneeler. Mary leaned down. "Doesn't he look handsome?" she whispered into Signora Merelli's ear. "I think Frankie would have died just to wear that suit."

Signora Merelli nodded. She reached out and touched Frankie's crossed hands. She stood up and leaned over and laid her head on his chest. Her tears wet the front of his shirt. She threw back her head and howled like a wolf. The coffin was shifting with her weight; her little black feet were off the floor. Old Man Nucciarone was ready to step in but Helen and Mary took Signora Merelli's arms and led her to a seat in the front row of empty chairs to rest a moment before they had to leave for the Mass.

"This is so goddamn morbid," Helen whispered. "How many goodbyes can we say? Why don't they just throw acid in everyone's eyes?"

"Shhh," Mary said. "This is how they do it. It makes them happy."

Helen shook her head, turning to watch Signora Merelli rummage in her big black pocketbook until she came up with a pair of black rosary beads. "I want these in Frankie's hands," she told Mary. "His father gave them to him for his First Holy Communion."

Mary took the beads. "Of course," she said, but Helen told her to forget it. There were rosary beads in Frankie's hands already and who felt like moving things around now? Helen said she'd just slip them in the coffin, the way the Irish put in bottles of whiskey and pairs of dice.

Gracie eased down onto the kneeler. She pulled Charlie down beside her and put an arm around his waist. She looked at Frankie's face, at his beautiful hands that death, not even the inky river, had changed. She wished she could see into his eyes. She wished she could tell him how she felt, how she was sad and how she loved him, but how she was excited, too. She thought that he would understand. They had fallen for each other, she thought now, because both of them had wanted more than was possible, more than was available to people like them. But they had slipped into the life everyone expected.

Except now Gracie had a chance. The neighborhood didn't know it. Signora Merelli would not have believed it. Teresa Gigante and the St. Ann Society of Mothers would be shocked. Even Helen and Mary would be surprised. But Anona, Gracie thought, would understand. Anona would know.

Gracie put out her hand and touched Frankie's face. "Thank you, *caro*," she said, and just to keep the peace, she leaned over and kissed his cold dark lips. She could feel Charlie shiver next to her and she moved her arm to his shoulder. "Just lean over and say goodbye," she told her son. "No one can see. You don't have to touch him." And Charlie did just what his mother said.

They caught up with Signora Merelli, who was stumbling out

to the limo between Mary and Helen. The sisters held her on the side to let Gracie and Charlie get in first so she wouldn't have to climb over the seat. "The veil," Helen was saying to Signora Merelli. "It's dangerous. You can't see."

"What's left to see? My son is dead. *Povera me!*" Helen nodded in sympathy and with an easy shove, pushed Signora Merelli into the limo and closed the door.

The funeral procession drove up Sullivan Street and down Thompson, around Prince and back up Sullivan and minutes later was at the steps of St. Anthony's Church. When the family walked into the church, on the arms of the pallbearers, the organ swelled. When they were all seated, when the neighborhood friends and acquaintances and some who came to Mass every morning even if it was a funeral Mass, lined the pews, you could tell who was family. They were all beautifully dressed. Nick and Charlie wore starched white shirts and black ties and suits, boutonnieres in their lapels. Signora Merelli, Anona, and the sisters glittered like ravens. The others hung farther back in the church. It wasn't their day. They knew they would all get their turn to sit in front. They would all get the chance to weep while Father Demo, in his purple robes, raised his arms and eyes to heaven to implore God for mercy for the lamb who was on the way home.

Frankie's friends from the pier were his pallbearers since he had no brothers or grown sons. They carried Frankie's coffin, draped in purple cloth with a cross embroidered in gold by the women of the St. Ann Society of Mothers, up the long aisle. The school kids sang the "Ave Maria" and the two altar boys, with scuffed shoes under their cassocks, carried the long white candles in their solid gold holders to place at either end of the casket.

When the Mass was over, the procession filed out and Gracie and Charlie and Signora Merelli and Helen and Mary stood at the bottom of the steps, waiting for the coffin to be loaded into the hearse, waiting to get back into the limo for the ride to Calvary.

Gracie felt a tap on her shoulder and turned to see Dibby, her downstairs neighbor who worked with Tony down the docks. He hugged her and pressed something into her hand. "I was there when they pulled Frankie out," he told her. "This was in his pocket."

Dibby stepped back into the crowd. No one saw.

Chapter Thirty-four

Gracie climbed into the limousine waiting outside the church. Signora Merelli was already inside, cleaved to the far door, her arm linked tightly with Charlie's. She had pulled him in after her and held him so tightly that he could not lean back, but sat at the edge of the seat, resisting her other hand that she kept using to push against his head, to force it down onto her bosom, where she felt it should be if she was going to comfort him. Gracie sat upright beside them, her hand on Charlie's knee, despite the glare of disapproval from Signora Merelli. The hearse pulled away from the curb, headlights lit, the crowd breaking up around it. As the other cars followed at a snail's pace, Gracie thought about all the men outside the church who would see the funeral procession pass by and pause to scratch their balls, to keep the *malocchio* at bay. She could hear them on the corners, in the cafés, in the storefront clubs where they sold liquor without a license and played cards for money.

"He's dead."

"Holy shit! What happened?"

"An accident down the docks. They found him floating in the East River."

"Ugh, the river . . . I hate that river, full of them goddamn eels. Even when I was a kid, I hated it. Everybody jumping in off the piers. Not me. I always said you gotta be nuts to swim in that river. I always said it. Gee, that's too bad. I feel bad. He was a good guy."

"Yeah, well, these things happen."

"What a shame."

"Yeah, a crying shame."

The funeral cortege made a right on Bleecker Street and again on Thompson Street, circling around into Spring Street so Frankie could pass his earthly home one last time before taking the Delancey Street bridge to Calvary cemetery. The limo with Gracie and Charlie and Signora Merelli followed behind and behind them was Nick in the Cadillac with Helen and Mary and Anona.

"No point in getting another car," Signora Merelli advised Gracie. "You'll need every penny you can get your hands on now that you're a widow. Believe me, I know. It's no picnic being left young."

They were burying Frankie in Calvary in the Merelli plot with his father. It was the least they could do for Signora Merelli, Mary convinced Gracie. Gracie was not easily convinced. "It's a grave for three people. The old man's on the bottom. If Frankie goes next, there's only room for one more . . . on top . . . Signora Merelli—just where she likes to be. Perfect. If not in life, then in death. And me? Frankie's wife, his son's mother, where do I go? Potter's Field?"

Anona clucked her tongue. "Never mind," she said. "A grave costs money. You need the money for yourself now, and the boy. I got room in my grave. You can come with me."

"Besides," Mary said, "you're gonna live a long time. Signora Merelli said it herself. You could end up with a second husband in a marble mausoleum, with a bottle of brandy behind the altar, never mind some crummy old grave in Calvary. Why worry now?"

At the graveside, Father Demo said the prayer for the dead. "As I walk through the valley of death . . ." he droned. Gracie held Charlie in front of her, her arms around his neck, choking him until it was time to say the very last goodbye. She threw a red rose onto the closed coffin as it was lowered by ropes into the grave. She blew a kiss. She held Charlie tightly against her and moved to the side as Signora Merelli came to the edge. *"Mio figlio! Non lasciarme qui!"* she shouted. "My son! Don't leave me here!"

Two burly undertakers Old Man Nucciarone hired for just this reason stood on either side of Signora Merelli, holding her back as she threw her weight against them. She leaned far over the grave, her tears falling into the freshly dug hole.

"For all the trying," Anona whispered to Helen, "at all the funerals I been to, I never saw not one live person fall in the grave."

They filed back to the waiting cars, the women's heels sinking into the soft grass between the neat rows of gravestones. Gracie took one last look around. Within one week, her life was forever changed. She marveled at the lines and lines of gray stones, so many stones, lined up beneath the highway underpass. The sky above Calvary was always gray, the trucks were always rumbling past.

"Frankie hated Calvary," Gracie said to Anona. "He always told me he wanted to be buried someplace else, someplace pretty."

Anona took her arm and turned her around. "Too late now," she said. "And just like him: always wanting, never doing."

"You're not supposed to talk bad about the dead," Gracie said.

"Ha," Anona answered her. "I'm not afraid of the dead. It's the living that get you every time."

Back on Spring Street, Napoli had closed the restaurant and set up long tables. Gracie had invited everyone from the church and the graveside against the objections of Signora Merelli, who kept cautioning her about money. "I have nothing," she told Gracie. "I can't help you. You have a son to raise." But Gracie wouldn't listen. She wouldn't even let her side of the family put in a word. She had gone to Napoli and told them to close the restaurant, and to open the doors to whoever wanted to say goodbye to Frankie. She wasn't going to let him go out like a creep. He would be a big shot for once in his life. Gracie gave them carte blanche to show everyone a good time.

The mourners came in from the outside, the men stopping to have a drink at the long bar before taking a place at one of the tables piled high with plates of hot and cold antipasti. Gracie, elegant in her black crepe suit, her veil raised to sit on the brim of her hat, her hands gloved, stood at the door, Charlie beside her, greeting everyone who came in.

Signora Merelli was seated at the head of the table where she told everyone who passed by that her tears were not water but blood. Anona told the story of the Widow Francese, back in Bocca al Lupo, who lost both her sons down a well, and had really cried tears of blood that the priest gathered in a glass vial to put in front of the Madonna. Then she grabbed Charlie as he passed by and sent him to the bar for a Seagrams and soda.

Vincent Violotti, the lawyer with the office on Bedford Street, arrived and stopped in the doorway of Napoli's. He stood on the side and waited until Gracie was alone. He came up to her, his hat in his hands in front of him. "Signora," he said and extended his hand. Gracie took it and felt the pressure of his fingers. They were manicured fingers, a *padrone*'s fingers. She thought he held her hand a little too long but she didn't object. "I'm sorry for your trouble," he said. "It's a terrible thing that's happened. What will you do?"

"I'm not the first," Gracie told him.

"If I can help you in any way . . ."

"You mean that, signore? You would help me?"

"You know where my office is. Come and see me." He handed her a small white card, nodded to her and moved into the room. He had probably stood with her too long, she thought. She'd have to watch herself, so suddenly single. She was still young enough for scandal. She scanned the room for Teresa Gigante.

But then she didn't care, wasn't concerned that she hadn't lowered her eyes or acted coy. Vincent Violotti was immediately swept into the room, to a position of honor, next to the banker, the district leader and the Cardinali brothers, who had a grocery store but were very active in the church. She watched him until Lena Santulli touched her elbow and she turned to accept her kisses.

Chapter Thirty-five

It was a Tuesday, one week and a day since Frankie Merelli had drowned in the East River. Gracie left Charlie sitting on the couch with six comic books and three Baby Ruth candy bars. She told him she was going to see a man about a horse and would be back in no time at all.

It was nine o'clock that same morning when Helen said she hadn't been up so early since her days in the candy factory. Mary said she couldn't remember back that far. They were on their way to Spring Street to get Gracie, to get her out of there for good. They had plans. They had surprises.

They walked quietly past Signora Merelli's door even though it was closed tight, and up the stairs to Gracie's apartment. The door was open, held ajar by the string that went from the doorknob to a nail in the wall. Helen went first; Mary followed behind. They saw Charlie on the couch starting his second comic and third candy bar. He didn't hear them come in.

Helen plopped down next to him on the couch. "Hey," she said, "where's that old lady of yours?"

He raised his shoulders. "She went to see a man about a horse." Mary raised an eyebrow. Helen shrugged. They heard heavy footsteps in the hall outside. Someone knocked on the open door. "Come in," Helen said.

It was Jimmy "The Dick" Cuciaro and Matt "The Pepper" Rizzo.

"Excuse us, We're looking for Gracie Merelli."

"Yeah?" Mary said, moving into the kitchen.

"She's not here," Charlie called out from the living room. "She went to—" Helen poked him in the ribs hard. He scowled at her but shut his mouth.

"Why don't you go downstairs?" she told Charlie. "Uncle Nick's down there. Make him teach you how to drive."

"My mother told me . . ."

"It's okay," Helen said, pushing Charlie off the couch and following him into the kitchen. "Let me worry about your mother."

"But . . ."

"Here," Helen said, handing him a dollar. "Buy some more comic books on me." Charlie took the money and Mary shepherded him out the door and closed it.

"It's okay," Mary told the men. "We're her sisters. I'm Mary and this here's Helen." The two men nodded. They held their hats in their hands. Rizzo wiped his forehead.

"What is it?" Mary said. "Frankie didn't owe no money, did he? Because . . ."

"Oh no," Rizzo said, waving his hand, his hat flapping. "Nothing like that." He stole a look at Helen. She stared straight at him.

"You fellows want coffee?" Mary said.

"No, no, we just came to . . . The boss feels bad about Frankie, him getting killed like that. He wants to do a little something extra, you know, besides the union." Jimmy "The Dick" Cuciaro held out an envelope.

Mary took the envelope. She smiled and put it on the table under the sugar bowl. "You tell Vito that the family appreciates it. You tell him thank you from all of us," she said.

"You sure you don't want something to drink?" Helen asked them as they turned to leave. The two men shook their heads. They put their hats on and backed out the door.

"What was that all about?" Mary said.

Helen made sure the door was shut before she took Vito's envelope from under the sugar bowl. "I don't really know. I did mention something to Joe Black but I didn't expect this kind of action." She was counting. "Look at this." She fanned the money in her fingers. "I love men, especially wiseguys, don't you?" she said. "Insurance companies are such a pain in the ass. By the time they come across, you're half-starved." She paced the kitchen floor. "Now, where the hell is Gracie?"

Where was Gracie?

She had gotten up very early that morning. She had stopped for a coffee at Dante's, where she had taken out that small blue leather case with the snap that Dibby had given her the day of Frankie's funeral. Inside was an odd-shaped key and it had a number printed across it. She had thought about showing it to Helen and Mary—they knew so much more than she knew—but she wanted to figure it out for herself and when the big clock over the espresso machine showed nine o'clock, she paid her check and left. She walked to Bedford Street, to the law office of Vincent Violotti. The front desk was empty but a bell rang when she opened the door and he came out from the back.

"Signora Merelli. How nice to see you. Come in," and he led her into his office, to the chair across from his desk.

Gracie sat down and leaned over the desk toward him. She opened her hand and showed him the key, hoping she wasn't being a fool, an idiot, hoping this key was important, that it meant something, and that he would know.

He took it from her hand and held it up. "A safe deposit box key," he said.

"It was in my husband's pocket when they pulled him out of the river."

"How did you get it?"

"One of the men Frankie worked with. He lives in our building. Dibby Santulli. He went through Frankie's pockets before
the cops came."

"And this is all he found?"

"That's all he gave me."

"Well, Signora, I would think that your deceased husband has
a box in the bank in his name. He must have owned something
valuable to have kept a safe deposit box."

"What could Frankie have had that was valuable? We had
nothing."

Vincent Violotti smiled with only half his mouth. "Nothing
that you know of."

Gracie sat. She knew the value of silence. She had always been
the quiet one. It was going to pay off. She could tell. She sat with
her pocketbook in her lap and she crossed her ankles carefully.
She leaned back and waited.

"Let's assume your husband had a safe deposit box," Vincent
Violotti said. "Let's assume it was in the Emigrant Savings Bank
on Varick Street where everyone in the neighborhood keeps their
money. The thing about a safe deposit box is that you have to sign
to get into it. Your name has to be on file. And when you die, the
box is sealed. So," he said, and here Vincent Violotti leaned over
the desk and tented his fingers, "let's assume that no one knows
that your husband has passed away and you can get into the box
even if your name isn't on it." He stood up from behind the desk.
"Signora Merelli, shall we go to the bank and find out if we can
assume all these things?"

Gracie stood up and took his arm. His secretary had arrived
and was sitting at the desk in the front room. Her name was
Josephine and she was ugly with very black hair. He said good
morning to her and told her that he would be back in a little while

and would bring her coffee and a cake from Dante's. He didn't say where he was going.

Gracie came into the building at 196 Spring Street and when she reached the fourth floor, Jeannie Popeye opened her door and called her into her apartment. She made Gracie sit down and pushed a dish of crullers, fresh out of Canapa's oven, across the table. Her Gerry got Dibby Santulli a job with him as a night watchman at the Kinney parking lot, Jeannie Popeye told Gracie. "After Frankie, he said he couldn't work the piers anymore. He's the one found him, you know."

"I know," Gracie said. "Poor Dibby . . . what a thing . . ."

"You don't have to talk low," Jeannie Popeye said. "Nothing bothers my Gerry."

"Everything bothered Frankie," Gracie said. Her pocketbook was heavy on her lap and she moved it to the floor.

Jeannie Popeye nodded. "Poor Frankie," she said. "He wasn't such a bad guy. He was nervous. Look at his mother. You ever see such a nervous wreck?"

Gracie nodded back.

"It was a good day when he found you," Jeannie said. "Me and Gerry always said it. 'When Frankie found Gracie, he found gold.' C'mon, have a cruller. Don't make me eat them all."

"Thanks, Jeannie, but I've got to go. I left Charlie alone," Gracie said, getting up to leave. She picked up the bag and held it to her chest.

Jeannie Popeye nodded. "Sure," she said. "Oh, and don't worry about Charlie. I could swear I heard your sisters in there."

Chapter Thirty-six

"Where were you?" Mary and Helen said together when Gracie opened the apartment door.

"I've been taking care of things, thinking about what to do next for me and Charlie." Gracie looked around. "Where is Charlie?"

"We sent him with Nick," Mary said. She came up to Gracie, smoothed back her hair from her face. "And don't you bother thinking. We're taking care of everything."

"You don't have to worry about nothing, not for a while anyway," Helen said. "Look at this." She took out the envelope that Jimmy "The Dick" and Matt "The Pepper" had left and opened the flap so Gracie could see inside.

"What's that?"

"Poor Frankie gave the Standard Fruit Company his life, didn't he? Vito Genovese knows that. He sent a couple of goons to drop it off," Helen said.

"And there's still the insurance from the union. You and Charlie are gonna be all right," Mary added. "It's hard to lose a husband," and she looked over at Helen. "We both know what it's like, but you'll be fine. You can stay here or move in with Anona, whatever you want to do. We'll look after you. And Frankie, he's up there looking after you, too."

Mary and Helen touched hands behind Gracie's back. "I'm sure's he's looking down right now," Mary said.

Gracie stepped into the kitchen, put her pocketbook on the table. She opened the gold clasp and took out a brown paper bag. She emptied it onto the table. There were ten packets of bills, each packet banded with a white strip of paper that had "$5G" written across it.

She looked at her sisters. "If Frankie's looking down, just what do you think he's saying right about now?"

"Mercy!" Helen said. "Where did that come from?" Mary's tongue tied. She'd seen that kind of money before but never sitting on Gracie's kitchen table.

"I don't know. Frankie had a key in his pocket when he fell in the drink. Dibby gave it to me outside the church the day of the funeral. Seems my Frankie had a safe deposit box and this was in it."

"Jesus Christ," Mary said, sitting down. "Maybe you should make a pot of coffee. Maybe you should crack open that sambuca you been saving for the second coming of Christ."

The money sat in the middle of the table, all of it, while they drank cups of espresso filled to the brim with the homemade sambuca Signora Merelli had given Gracie when Charlie was born and told her to guard with her life. "What are you gonna do?" Mary said.

"You mean what does she wanna do?" Helen corrected. "Just sitting on this table . . . Fifty large, legit . . . It's unbelievable."

"Wait a minute. We don't know for sure if it's legitimate."

"Sure it's legitimate. Gracie didn't steal it."

"True. So, Gracie, what *are* you gonna do?"

"I'm gonna fix the apartment. Put a bathroom in." Gracie counted off on the fingers of one hand. "No, no, forget it! I'm gonna move. Near the park. Fourth Street Park. I'm gonna look at the arch from my window. Yeah, I'm gonna move to Fourth Street Park and Charlie's gonna go to St. Joseph's Academy where all the money kids go."

"The wiseguys' kids, you mean," Mary said.

"Why? Wiseguys don't have money?" Helen said.

"Shut up," Gracie said. "You want to hear the rest or what?"

"Of course, sweetheart," Mary said. "Tell us more."

Charlie called up the stairs and they scrambled to hide the money. Gracie swept it into the big black pocketbook and Mary held the chair while Helen reached up to the top shelf in the bedroom closet to shove it behind the box of Christmas decorations. Charlie came in, out of breath from the four flights. "I don't know, Aunt Helen," he said. "I'd think about trading in that Lincoln for a Cadillac."

"Don't tell me," Helen said. "Tell your mother." Gracie hit her shoulder. Mary gathered their coats from off the bed. There were kisses and hugs all around. Gracie and Charlie stood in the hallway to listen to the clatter of Mary's and Helen's high heels and the last shouts of goodbye from downstairs before the outside door slammed. Gracie took Charlie by the sink to wash his face and neck and ears before she made him go to bed.

"You sad, baby?" she said, caressing him.

Charlie shrugged. "I got you, and Aunt Helen and Aunt Mary."

"Don't forget Uncle Nick."

". . . and Uncle Nick."

"So you'll be okay?"

He put his arms around her waist, rubbed his face against her. His whole life he had been loved and fed and petted and pampered by women. He had loved his father but Frankie had come and gone. It was Uncle Nick who took him to ball games and bought him those wing-tipped shoes.

"Yeah," Charlie told her. "As long as I got you."

• • •

At Anona's, there were candles covering St. Rita's shelf and on tiered iron stands in front of the cupboard that made it impossible to open the cupboard doors. Mary worried the oilcloth would catch on fire. Nick said if the building burned down, Anona would finally have to move. They were drinking wine and soda. They were laughing, all except Anona, who was mumbling about what a burden they had always been. How they had always done whatever they wanted and she had always had to make it up somehow. It would take her at least another twenty years of burning candles to catch up with all their sins. Anona hoped St. Rita was listening with both ears and would keep the evil eye away as long as she could. Anona hoped to convince St. Rita that she really needed extra time on earth to set things straight. She couldn't even think of dying. Emma had found her peace early. It was up to Anona to stay on earth and suffer for all of them.

"I'll miss Frankie," Helen said. "Never a dull moment when Frankie was in action."

"Speak for yourself," Anona said. "That . . ."

"Stop right there," Mary told her. "Nick, tell her to stop. You're gonna go right to hell you keep saying things like that."

"What? What am I saying? That *moltedevane*, how did he fall off a pier like that? What a fool."

"You know what happened?" Nick said.

Anona looked at him. "Me?" she said. "How could I know?"

"The last anyone remembered was Frankie smoking a cigarette near the gangplank," Nick told Anona. "He was standing near the edge of the water. The only strange thing were these two little guys. They had shaped up that morning. No one had ever seen them before. They were wearing red handkerchiefs around their necks. And when the drizzle started they kept going out to the ship; everyone else was waiting out the rain."

"So why didn't they question them later, after they fished Frankie outta the river?" Mary said.

"What a good question, babe. They couldn't find them. They'd vanished. The boss thought they might show up the next day but no one ever saw them again. They never even got paid."

Helen tipped her glass and jiggled the ice. "Maybe they were demons," she said.

Anona got up to sit in her rocking chair. She looked over at her saint, bathed in the light of a hundred candles. "Maybe," she said, "they were angels."

"Oh," Mary said. "I've heard enough. It's over and done with."

Nick came and stood behind her chair. "You think so, huh? Well, the word on the street is they're looking for those two little guys."

"Who's looking?" It was Helen asking the questions now, tapping her box of black French cigarettes against her palm, taking one out, feeling the smooth gold paper filter on her lips.

Nick rubbed the white stubble on his chin. He didn't shave every day anymore. "The cops are looking, and I hear there's a few guys tied up with Genovese who are looking, too. They like to take care of their own business. Those guys don't like that the police are poking around the docks. They don't need that kind of attention. None of them guys do, you know? I hope for their own sake, those little guys are far away by now."

"Yeah?" Mary said. "How far away?"

"Europe."

"That far?"

"At least that far."

Mary tipped back her glass. "I always wanted to go to Europe."

Helen narrowed her eyes, took the cigarette out of her mouth and looked at it. "Me too," she said. "Paris, where these cigarettes come from. I'd like to see where these cigarettes come from." She clicked her lighter, put the cigarette back in her mouth and held the end to the high blue flame. She blew out a long stream of smoke. "Or we could take Anona back to the old country, back to Bocca al Lupo. Whatta you say, Anona?"

"I say no." She spat in her handkerchief and put it back in her front pocket. "I went through all hell to get out of there. Why should I wanna go back? Months in the black hole of a ship. Everybody throwing up. Forget it. I'm leaving here feet first. How many times I gotta tell you?"

"It wouldn't be like that."

"No. No. No. How many times I gotta say the same things? Why all the time I gotta repeat? I got no interest. Leave me be. Never . . . but maybe . . ." Anona sighed. Her chest heaved. She tilted her head like a coquette. "Maybe I'd give Paris a flop."

Acknowledgments

Grazie infinite to Marysue Rucci.

And much gratitude to Binnie Kirshenbaum, Ira Wood, Elaine Markson, Sara Nelson, Kate Walbert, Madelaine Jaynes, Patrick Moffitt, and the Ucross Foundation.

About the Author

Louisa Ermelino is Chief of Reporters at *InStyle* magazine and the author of the novels *Joey Dee Gets Wise* and *The Black Madonna*. She lives in New York City with her husband, Carlo Cutolo, and daughters Ruby, Lucy and Ariane.

A READING GROUP GUIDE

THE SISTERS MALLONE

Louisa Ermelino

ABOUT THIS GUIDE

The suggested questions are included to enhance your group's
reading of Louisa Ermelino's *The Sisters Mallone.*

1. As in her previous novel, *The Black Madonna,* the author emphasizes the importance of women's relationships, in both families and friendships. What are some of the ways she conveys the significance of women in each other's lives?

2. Why does the author skip around in time to tell her story? How does this device prove useful to the unfolding of the narrative and your impressions of the characters?

3. At the beginning of *The Sisters Mallone,* Gracie decides not to escort her son, Charlie, and her mother-in-law to the funeral parlor, saying, "I needed my sisters . . . I needed my family." What meaning does "family" hold for her? Is she right not to escort her own son to the funeral parlor?

4. Gracie says that she did not expect Signora Merelli "to understand what it had been like to grow up Italian in Hell's Kitchen, three girls and an old woman, with no men to protect them, to support them, or as Anona said when they were sad, to tell them what to do." Do you think that because she was raised in a protective, female-centered household, Gracie would never be able to fully trust or depend upon men? Did she become more self-sufficient because of the way she was raised?

5. Anona tells Gracie at one point, "If you can't find a good man, you're better off without one." She also believes that "all men are bad until you teach them different." Is it true that Anona hates men, as Mary claims, or is she just overly protective of the girls? What effect does Anona have on the girls' relationships with men and their notions of men? Does she have a positive influence?

6. Is Frankie in any way a sympathetic character, or is he, as Mary puts it, simply a "rat bastard"? Does he think of himself as a responsible husband and father? How does he justify his shortcomings?

7. How does the author convey the tensions and differences between two immigrant groups in New York City—the Irish and the Italians—during the early twentieth century? What does Joey Gigliano mean when he says derisively of the Mallone sisters, "You live with [the Irish], you act like them." In what way is he expressing what it means to be an "authentic" Italian-American? Why does he judge the Mallone sisters for living among the Irish?

8. When Frankie first finds out that Gracie is from the Hell's Kitchen neighborhood, "he got a little nervous." Why would that make him hesitant about dating her?

9. How does having a seemingly Irish name harm the reputation of the Mallones among Italians in the neighborhood? How important is "community" to the characters in this novel?

10. The three Mallone sisters—Helen, Mary, and Gracie—all have strong, distinctive personalities. What characteristics define each sister?

11. Did Helen and Mary do any better than Gracie in their relationships with men? Why or why not?

12. Helen says that she "never wanted children, never felt any pull to be a mother, to swell, to nurse, to nurture. She was content to be the eternal aunt." How does *not* having had children affect the way Helen relates to her sisters? Does she seem to have more freedom than they do, and does her in-

dependence seem to bring her happiness? How does Mary's experience of having lost a son affect her relationships with her sisters? Why might she have decided never to have another child?

13. What are some moments in the novel when the author employs humor during a particularly tense scene? (For example, when Helen slugs Signora Merelli after they get the news that Frankie has died.)

14. Why does Gracie stay with Frankie as long as she does and tolerate his infidelities? One day Gracie decides, "Things were going to change . . . She didn't know when, or how, but she wasn't going to twiddle her thumbs waiting for him to get old and fat." What is the breaking point for Gracie?

15. Are there any similarities between Frankie's mother, Signora Merelli, and Anona?

16. Can you explain the significance of food in this novel? How does it convey family connection and comfort?

17. How does New York City figure in the novel as a kind of character? How does the weaving in of actual historical events (such as the stock market crash of 1929) make the story and the characters seem more realistic or vivid?

18. What role does religion (and prayer) play in the lives of the Italian-Americans portrayed in this novel?

A conversation with Louisa Ermelino, author of *The Sisters Mallone*

What inspired *The Sisters Mallone*?

I'm always interested in the interaction of different cultures. When I was growing up on Prince Street, the "others" were the Irish. . . . their grandparents didn't speak a foreign tongue, they didn't eat our food, they didn't look anything like us, but their neighborhood bordered ours, their nuns were teaching us in school, and we interacted with them more than any other group. We repelled and attracted each other. It was intense and I wanted to capture it as another aspect of "the neighborhood."

You've said that your books celebrate the power of women. Are the Sisters Mallone your most powerful women to date?

Absolutely. I expect my female characters to be in charge regardless of their circumstances but with *The Sisters Mallone* I could be more playful, (and they could be more overtly "tough in controlling their destiny") because they were not subject to the caveats of the Old World. They have the advantage of coming of age in the liberal 1920s and living in a house of only women in a neighborhood that let them be part of the outside world.

Who are the Sisters Mallone? And why Hell's Kitchen?

My novels usually begin with a story that I've heard and that resonates and won't go away. *The Sisters Mallone* is based on a series of stories, or rather many afternoons sitting at the kitchen table gossiping with my mother-in-law who grew up in Hell's Kitchen with her two sisters. They are the Sisters Mallone. I was surrounded by women all my life, but they were so traditional, nothing like my mother-in-law's family. So my interst was sparked, and after I did some reading about life in "the Kitchen," I was hooked. The neighborhood has an incredible history. It's one of the most colorful New York City neighborhoods. Also, I seem to have an organic connection with transformed New York City neighborhoods. I don't think there's anything left of the old Hell's Kitchen anymore.

You incorporate historical events into the novel. Is there a particular reason for doing this?

There are several reasons. One is simply that I love history, especially the history of New York City. I collect and read anything I can find about New York City. But aside from that, many of the real life characters that appear in the novel were actually part of the gossip, for example, Owney Madden. Somewhere there's a letter his wife wrote to my mother-in-law's sister from Arkansas (that's where Owney Madden retired to and married the postmaster's daughter. He was one of the few racketeers who actually managed to retire and to die in his bed). And then, I like anchoring the story in history to flesh out the time period, to make the characters and plot come alive. I also have an excuse for doing research, a legitimate reason for working but still not getting down to business.

The sisterhood bond is central to the novel. Why did you choose this relationship for the characters?

I have no sisters, but I became fascinated with the relationship from watching my daughters. And it got bigger from there: My mother had three sisters, my mother-in-law was one of three sisters, my girlfriends have sisters, there were three sisters in the neighborhood who went everywhere together, and they all had their hair dyed the exact same shade of red. I started thinking about these relationships playing out under my nose and what it means to have a sister. You have the bond of being female, you have the bond of common experience, you have the bond of blood . . . what could possibly be tighter? The Sisters Mallone are a prime example of this bond. I could only create them, watch them from the outside.

Do you plan to continue writing about "the neighborhood"?

Well, Faulkner had Yoknapatawpha county and Nabokov said a writer could have no experience but his childhood and never want for material. I have three novels set in "the neighborhood" but with each one the landscape gets bigger, moves further out. I don't know if I could ever leave completely (I'm even still here physically) because it is so vivid in my mind, and it's influence colors everything about me. I went so far away but it was always right there with me, and I'm happy to chronicle it, to save it, if only on the page.

Do you think the experiences and the values of the neighborhood are disappearing forever?

Probably . . . and I don't necessarily think it's a bad thing. I have conflicting emotions on the subject. On the one hand, I can mourn for what's gone and on the other I can take a very buddhist approach that everything is transitory. I'll always have the

neighborhood, and I'm saving it for everyone else. I think all im-
migrants to this country have similar experiences, and my novels
speak to everyone. The language and the customs and the food
might be different, but we all pull closer to the familiar and also
struggle to leave it behind. I still can feel like the outsider, but I'm
eternally grateful that my grandparents got on that boat. I'm also
glad they came to Thompson Street. Both my parents were born
on Thompson Street. There was always a certain stigma to
Thompson Street. It was block after block of charmless tenements. I love that it's so *de rigueur* now.

What is your next book?

A woman from the bassi of Naples and a younger man from New
York . . . mothers and daughters, the New World and the Old . . .
obligations and passion . . . and ill-fated love.

Please turn the page for
an exciting sneak peek of
Louisa Ermelino's
next novel,
JOEY DEE GETS WISE,
coming from Kensington in June 2004!

CHAPTER ONE

Sonny Magro's body was in the street when the ladies went to church. The ladies had on big hats and wore them tilted to one side. Sonny Magro's blood made a pool in the gutter along the curb. It was August and hot.

Joey Dee, Mikey Bats and Carmine stood on the corner in their best clothes. They went into the church late, after the Mass had started, and they stood in the back.

In the church the ladies put their heads together behind their prayer books. They whispered to one another underneath the big hats.

It wasn't the blood in the street. It wasn't that Sonny Magro had been killed in a way they had never seen a man killed before, but that Sonny Magro was a working guy, a pants presser, Joey Dee would say, and today was Sunday.

When Father Giannini let out the Mass, everyone crowded onto the church steps, wanting to stay near the top, wanting to see better into the street where Sonny Magro's body had been.

Joey Dee stood off to the side, leaning against the railing that the ladies would hold on to when the church steps were wet. He was standing alone when Vito Santero came next to him and pulled on his arm.

Vito Santero was crying with his mouth wide open and no sound coming out. He wiped his nose with the sleeve of his coat, and when he looked at Joey Dee, his bad eye rolled in his head.

Vito Santero was slow. He was born that way, the ladies said, but Joey Dee knew the truth.

Standing on the church steps now with Vito Santero made Joey Dee think about Sister Agnes, but then he put an arm around Vito and thought about getting snot on his suit. Joey Dee hoped he wouldn't.

"C'mon, Vito," he said. "What's the matter with you? Why you crying?"

Vito Santero opened his eyes wide. "I seen," he said. "I seen what happened to Sonny Magro."

Joey Dee pushed him when he said this. Vito Santero slipped off the step onto the one below. "What are you talking about?" Joey Dee said. "What the hell are you saying? You didn't see nothing."

"I did. I seen what happened." Vito Santero grabbed Joey Dee's arm. He put his mouth up close to Joey Dee's ear. "They killed Sonny Magro last night. It was late. He gets home late. They threw him off the roof. They killed him and threw him off the roof." Vito Santero pointed across the street, at Sammy One-eye's building, the building Vito lived in, the building Sonny Magro lived in before he was killed. "I seen them," Vito said.

Joey Dee and Vito Santero were alone on the church steps. There were footprints down below on the sidewalk made in Sonny Magro's blood. The ladies had moved across the street into Canapa's to buy rolls and crumb cake cut into squares. Joey Dee didn't want to hear what Vito Santero was saying.

Joey Dee thought about being too grown a man to be in church anymore, even in the back. He made the others go, Mikey

Bats and Carmine. They would be glad if he told them they could stop. He looked for them. They usually waited for him after church, but today they were gone.

Vito Santero pulled on Joey Dee's arm. "I was going to put out the ashcans," Vito was saying. "My mother got mad, me putting them out so late, having to go down so late. 'Shit him,' my mother said. 'Shit Sammy One-eye and his lousy couple of bucks. He stinks on ice,' my mother said. So I didn't. I didn't put them out."

"So how the hell did you end up on the roof?"

"I went to see the birds, to stay with the birds," Vito said.

"I told you to leave the birds alone at night. I told you, Vito, once they're inside you gotta leave them alone. You don't do like I tell you, I'm not gonna let you clean out the boxes no more. I'm not gonna let you take care of them."

"I love the birds, Joey. You know that. I don't do nothing to bother the birds. I like to go up there and see them. I like that sound they make. I like how warm it gets in there."

"Jesus, Vito, it's August. It's dying out and you gotta go sit in a pigeon coop to get warm?"

"I open the little windows like you showed me, so it stays nice in there. I take care of the birds, Joey. You got some nice birds."

Joe Funz had given Joey Dee the birds when his wife died and he went to Staten Island to live with his daughter. Joe Funz's daughter told him to leave his dirty habits in New York. She meant his birds, and Joe Funz knew this, so he gave everything to Joey Dee: the birds, the coops, the feed that was left. It was all up on Sammy One-eye's roof. Joe Funz had some of the best birds around. He had some that had carried messages in the war.

"You don't have to be up there at night," Joey Dee told Vito. "How many times do I have to say it?"

"But that's how come I seen what happened. They came up the roof. Three of them, with Sonny Magro. Nicky Mole, he was there. I could see them good."

Joey Dee looked down at the tips of his Siegel Brothers shoes. Vito Santero stood in front of him on the step below, bobbing up and down, waving his hands.

"And you know what they did?" Vito said.

"Listen, Vito. I don't want to hear it. . . . I gotta go."

Vito Santero held on to Joey Dee's arm. "They killed him," Vito said. He twisted up his face and shook his hands in front of him. He put one hand around his neck and choked himself. He opened his eyes wide. The bad eye, the left one, rolled in his head. "They put the rope around his neck, Joey. His tongue was hanging out. Then they took off his pants and they cut him, they cut off his . . ." Vito Santero lowered his voice. "You know what I mean," he said, moving closer to Joey Dee, stretching up, his mouth at Joey Dee's ear. "They cut it off and they put it . . ." Vito squeezed his eyes shut. "They put it in his mouth."

Joey Dee thought that he would throw up on the church steps and that the ladies would step in it and make footprints on the sidewalk down below. Joey Dee thought about Vegas, in the desert. It was a place he wanted to go.

"You should see the blood, Joey. The street's nothing. It's all up the roof. You wanna go see?" Vito Santero was excited telling this to Joey Dee, Joey Dee listening. "All that blood," Vito was saying, "because they cut it off. The rope don't make you bleed. I know that." What he was saying didn't mean anything to Vito Santero. It was that he was saying it, all of it, to Joey Dee, telling his secret to Joey Dee, standing with him alone on the church steps, just him and Joey Dee.

It was hot standing on the church steps. The sun was on the

side of the street where the church was and Joey Dee took off his tie and folded it twice so it wouldn't wrinkle when he put it in his pocket.

"Why don't you shut up, Vito?" Joey Dee said. "You're supposed to be stupid, remember? How come you know so much?"

"I'm not stupid, Joey," Vito said. "They didn't see me, did they? Everybody thinks those guys know everything, but they ain't so smart. Nicky Mole ain't so smart." Vito Santero twisted up his face. He could do that, twist up his face so that his mouth and nose and one eye, the bad one, came together. "Sister Agnes used to call me stupid. You remember Sister Agnes, Joey? You remember her?

When Vito said this, he opened his mouth wide and cried with no sound coming out. Vito always cried with no sound. His mother said it was enough to drive her crazy, that and the bad eye that rolled in his head.

Joey Dee took Vito Santero's arm and squeezed it hard. "Listen," he said. "How do you know they didn't see you?"

"I was with the birds, Joey. I told you. You don't listen. I heard somebody coming and I got inside. I closed the door and stayed inside with the birds. I stayed still. I didn't come down for a long time. My mother, she didn't know where to look."

Joey Dee let go of Vito Santero's arm. "You listen to me," he said. "You go home and you forget what you saw and forget you told me anything. Sonny Magro's dead. It don't matter what you saw unless you want to be next."

Joey Dee went down the church steps two at a time. He didn't hold on to the railing.

Vito started after him. "Where you going, Joey? Where you going?"

Joey Dee stopped. "I'm going home," he said, "and lie to my

mother. I'm gonna tell her I took communion and sat in the front of the church. She's gonna be so happy she's gonna kiss me on the mouth and feed me crumb cake from her fingers."

"Yeah, Joey, yeah?" Vito said. He followed Joey Dee down the street and Joey Dee let him, but when they passed the cafe where Nicky Mole stood outside and Vito Santero started pulling on Joey Dee's arm and whispering in his ear, Joey Dee pushed him into the next doorway and held him against the wall.

"This time I mean it, Vito," Joey Dee said. "Go home and keep your mouth shut like I told you."

Joey Dee didn't go down that Sunday afternoon to look for Mikey Bats and Carmine, and he didn't go up the roof to fly the pigeons. He believed Vito Santero. He believed what Vito had told him about the blood up the roof.

It rained that night and for days afterward. It rained as though it were part of a plan to wash the blood from the roof. It rained for all the days of Sonny Magro's wake.